By Amy Lane

Published by DREAMSPINNER PRESS
www.dreamspinnerpress.com

By Amy Lane (cont.)

FISH OUT OF WATER
Fish Out of Water
Red Fish, Dead Fish
A Few Good Fish

KEEPING PROMISE ROCK
Keeping Promise Rock
Making Promises
Living Promises
Forever Promised

JOHNNIES
Chase in Shadow • Dex in Blue
Ethan in Gold • Black John
Bobby Green
Super Sock Man

GRANBY KNITTING
The Winter Courtship Rituals of
Fur-Bearing Critters
How to Raise an Honest Rabbit
Knitter in His Natural Habitat
Blackbird Knitting in a Bunny's Lair
The Granby Knitting Menagerie
Anthology

TALKER
Talker • Talker's Redemption
Talker's Graduation
The Talker Collection Anthology

WINTER BALL
Winter Ball • Summer Lessons

Published by Harmony Ink Press
BITTER MOON SAGA
Triane's Son Rising
Triane's Son Learning
Triane's Son Fighting
Triane's Son Reigning

Published by DREAMSPINNER PRESS
www.dreamspinnerpress.com

Choose your Lane to love!

A Fool and His Manny

"I loved every sentence from beginning to end. I got sucked into the story right away, and it held my attention until it was over."

—Joyfully Jay

"Reading this novel is like being enveloped in large, welcoming mommy arms or walking in the door home and getting the welcome you always dreamed about from the family you always wanted."

—Scattered Thoughts and Rogue Words

Stand by Your Manny

"…it is an amazing ride. This is a wonderful addition to a heartwarming series."

—Paranormal Romance Guild

"If you're looking for a nice, sweet romance that has some real obstacles to overcome before a happily ever after, you will definitely enjoy *Stand by Your Manny*."

—Top 2 Bottom Reviews

More praise for
AMY LANE

Crocus

"It's everything I expect and want from an Amy Lane novel, plus the chance to revisit a favorite couple and their family. Very much recommended."

—Jessie G Books

"*Crocus* is a story of family and love and acceptance. It's about overcoming obstacles and keeping what's important at the forefront. It's about love. So, so much love."

—Diverse Reader

Regret Me Not

"It's what I come to expect from this author when she's not trying to rip my heart out. A little fluff, a little drama, a little sex, and a lot of romance!"

—Love Bytes

"*Regret Me Not* by Amy Lane is just the right blend of sweet and romantic—a lovely Christmas story you won't want to miss."

—The Novel Approach

Christmas Kitsch

Amy Lane

Published by

DREAMSPINNER PRESS

5032 Capital Circle SW, Suite 2, PMB# 279, Tallahassee, FL 32305-7886 USA
www.dreamspinnerpress.com

This is a work of fiction. Names, characters, places, and incidents either are the product of author imagination or are used fictitiously, and any resemblance to actual persons, living or dead, business establishments, events, or locales is entirely coincidental.

Christmas Kitsch
© 2018 Amy Lane.

Cover Art
© 2018 Alexandria Corza.
http://www.seeingstatic.com
Cover content is for illustrative purposes only and any person depicted on the cover is a model.

Trade Paperback ISBN: 978-1-64080-898-0
Digital ISBN: 978-1-64080-503-3
Library of Congress Control Number: 2018907621
Trade Paperback published December 2018
v. 2.0
First Edition published by Riptide Publishing, December 2013.

Printed in the United States of America
∞
This paper meets the requirements of
ANSI/NISO Z39.48-1992 (Permanence of Paper).

To Mate. This is our 31st Christmas together,
and we have so many more plans to go.
This story has been Mary's from the very first.

Acknowledgments

Thank you Elizabeth and Lynn for always having my bacon.

THE HOME POND

IT WAS sort of a shock. I mean, I was *supposed* to be coming home for Thanksgiving, not getting kicked out of the house a month before Christmas. If I'd been mean about it, I would have blamed Oliver, but I couldn't. I mean… you can't *really* blame Oliver for anything. He's just too damned nice.

In fact, that was why we hung out together all through our senior year. I mean, I'd been hanging with all those other jokers for my entire life. Kindergarten, grade school, middle school—you could have thrown our jock genes in a blender and pretty much swapped all our parts. We were interchangeable. White boys, blue/green eyes, sandy blond/sandy brown hair, good bones, good nutrition, some sort of Teutonic conspiracy to produce a football team in the nouveau riche suburbs of the foothills— that was us. I mean, I had *brown* eyes and blond hair, and I was the closest thing to an ethnic minority our high school had ever seen.

Until Oliver.

Oliver showed up in early September of my senior year, slender, brown on brown on brown. Dark brown hair cut with long bangs around his narrow face, dark brown eyes with thick, thick lashes, and light brown skin. He slouched quietly in the back of Mr. Rochester's English Literature class and eyed the rest of us with sort of a gentle amusement.

"Yo, Rusty," Clayton called to me as I took my seat by the new boy. "What's the new guy?"

I looked at Clayton blankly. He was one of those big white-blond kids with a face that ran to red whenever he exerted himself. He was a defensive lineman on the football team, and his father sold insurance. He was also a sadistic fuck who liked to haze freshmen by slamming them against lockers and calling them names until they cried. That shit had been sort of funny when we were sophomores, but my little sister told me the last kid he'd done that to had needed to change schools and see a shrink, and that's sort of a horrible thing to do to a kid.

It suddenly occurred to me that the dark kid slouching in the corner of the room was a prime target for Clayton, but he was looking at us all amused, like he didn't give a crap, and that might have offered him a little protection right there.

I liked that. He didn't give a crap. The last girl I'd dated had been so excited about dating a football player, she'd literally gone down on me before dinner, and, well, I'd liked her, but I hadn't been sure I wanted to know her that well. I'd also been hungry. I'd sort of pulled her away from my crotch and asked her if we could go eat steak. I think I hurt her feelings—she didn't say much during dinner, and she'd taken my kiss on the cheek like it was some sort of insult or something.

So this kid, smiling at us friendly but not slobbering all over us or being afraid of us—that was sort of nice.

I didn't like Clayton saying "What" in conjunction with those laughing brown eyes.

"What do you mean 'what'?" I'm not that smart, but I knew I probably wasn't going to like that answer either.

"I mean Indian, Mex, darky, what?"

That snapped my head back. My mother wasn't the warmest person on the planet, but she was *not* pro on us being rude like that.

"Where the hell were you raised?" I snapped, appalled. "Jesus, he's a kid. Leave him the hell alone!"

Clayton rolled his eyes at me. "Oh my God, Baker, could you *be* any more of a fairy princess?" That was fine, though. He was so miffed at me, he'd forgotten about the kid, who was watching our byplay like he was watching a tennis match.

"Do you see me in a dress blowing you?" I asked, and the rest of the class chortled. Clayton turned red(der) and glared at me as the teacher walked in. I leaned back in my seat and gave the kid a reassuring grin.

"He should leave you alone now," I said quietly as Mr. Rochester pointed to the warm-up on the board. "See that? That's the page number. There's a quick assignment we do in our grammar books, and then we correct it."

"Thanks," the kid said. "But you know, I'm gay. I'm not really big on the princess dress, but if he wasn't an asshole, I wouldn't mind blowing him." And that was Oliver.

I sat there, my mouth open, while the class got out their books and started the assignment. After about a minute, the kid looked at me sideways, and *finally* I saw a waver of uncertainty in him.

"You never met a fag before?" he asked, and again, those painful manners that had been beaten into my and my little sister's hard heads— pretty much from the cradle—asserted themselves.

"Nope," I said honestly, "but my mother wouldn't let me use that word." I wasn't sure she'd let a homosexual sit at our dinner table either, but then, that was my mother.

The kid looked at me for a minute, considering. "Okay, if we keep that word off the table, could you make sure I don't get stuffed in a trash can during lunch?"

I grinned at him. "I can do that. Can I copy what you got on the grammar warm-up? You scrambled my tiny brain with the big, scary word."

The boy laughed and handed me his paper so I could copy superquick before Mr. Rochester could call on me. That's when I saw his name: Oliver Campbell, which wasn't Hispanic or Indian, but he didn't look African American either.

I sat with him at lunch that day, and a few of my friends sat with us. (Not Clayton—he had his own squad of goons, and that was a relief.) My buddies harassed Oliver, don't get me wrong. Brian Halliday asked him if he got a thrill out of sitting with all us football players, 'cause we were all buff. All Oliver had to do was look him up and down once and say, "I may be gay, but I got better standards than that," and Brian was smirking and talking about cheerleaders. They kept at it, but Oliver was great at rolling his eyes or saying something just as good, and my buddies would start giving each *other* shit and leave him alone.

It's kind of sad when I think about it now. At the time I thought I hung out with a bunch of okay kids. I figured we were spoiled and sheltered, but that wasn't our fault, really. I mean, I was proud because we sat down with someone new and different and didn't beat him into the ground. Pathetic, really—that's what I had to be proud of, right? That my peer group didn't bully people *too* badly? But it was something to hold on to, even if it was something small. I needed any pride I could find, because I knew college was coming along like a big steamroller to cream me into the fucking pavement.

NOW SEE, I know I'm not that bright. I mean, give me time, and some hints, and an example, and directions carved in rock, and I can power through almost anything.

Not like Oliver. There's a quickness to him.

When he walks, his elbows come out from his sides in fluid, graceful little motions, and when he talks, his hands dart around his face and shoulders like fish. He can tell jokes, stupid ones but really funny, and rattle off the joke and then the punch line, and before I have a chance to laugh, surprised because he's always surprising, he's on to the next joke.

"Hey, Rusty, why did the chicken cross the road slllooooowwwlllly?"

"Why?"

"Because he doesn't believe in cars. Why did the squirrel haul ass across the road?"

"Heh-heh… doesn't believe in… wait—why?"

"Because he *does* believe in the ghost of chickens past."

"Wait, is that because the damned things are always getting killed on the—"

"What did the werewolf say to the vampire on the night of the full moon?"

"I have no idea."

"Things are about to get hairy. What did the vampire say when he got the power vac?"

"Hairy! Hah! Uhm, I dunno—"

"I vant to suck your mud."

And so on. We could spend an entire lunch, and Oliver would be dropping one-liners like firecrackers behind him, and the rest of us would be dancing in his wake. Most times he knew what the class assignment was going to be before Mr. Rochester finished his usual joke about his own name. "We're going to find the allegory in *Jane Eyre*, right?"

"Very good, Oliver. How'd you guess?"

"'Cause no one names a guy St. John unless they're making a point about saints—*especially* if he's the guy who gets *dumped* for some guy whose name sounds like a rock."

The whole class laughed at that, me included, but I'd had to spend some time in the bathroom the next morning, contemplating God, before I finished, flushed, and said, "Wait. That St. John guy wasn't real warm, and Mr. Rochester was really solid and good… Is *that* what Oliver meant?"

So Oliver—hellsa quick. Me—hellsa slow. He should have laughed at me, right? Written me off as a dumb jock and gone and huddled with the coven of übergeeks who watched anime, or the girls who read yaoi. But he didn't. I guess because I'd been nice to him when I hadn't needed to be, he'd spent our entire senior year returning the favor.

By the end of senior year, after he'd helped me study for the SATs when my football friends were out getting drunk, I was really fucking grateful.

I also felt bad, because I sucked *ass* on the SATs. My scores were (and Oliver said this, and I'd had to spend another morning in the bathroom to get it) *toiletastic*! I'd applied to Stanford and Berkeley, because my grades were pretty good and my old man made me, but it wasn't until I saw the second round of SAT scores that I realized just what a meatloaf I really was. I was so embarrassed, I couldn't look Oliver in the face for an entire day. I bailed on him during lunch, and most other guys, they would have been hurt and bitchy and whined to their friends about what a conceited asshole I was, but not Oliver.

"What the fuck is up with you?"

He cornered me in the locker room, of all places, because I was taking PE sixth period for elective credit like the dumb jock I was.

"What do you mean?" I knew exactly what he meant, but I didn't know what to say.

"You don't email me this weekend, you don't talk to me today— c'mon, Rusty—I thought we were friends." His black eyebrows were drawn together over his eyes, and his mouth was all pursed and pillowy. He looked cute, like a little kid, and I wanted to hug him and tell him it was okay and make the tantrum go away.

I looked down at my toes instead and clutched my towel tighter around my waist. I wasn't afraid of him checking me out—I'd been naked in front of girls before, and, well, I'd stopped caring—but I felt naked inside too, and that was new.

"Nothing, I... you know. You...." I had a lightbulb then—a *truth* I could tell him that would mean he didn't have to waste his time with me. "You have smart people to sit with." I looked up and met his eyes then and smiled, because I was proud of that—it made me sound like an asshole, but it meant he didn't have to waste his time with me either.

Something funny happened to his face then. He squinched one eye and wrinkled his lip and sucked air through his teeth. His front teeth were a little big, and his canines a little crowded back—like he *maybe* could have had braces, but it wasn't so bad that he *had* to, so he didn't. He opened his mouth to say something, and then closed it, and then opened it again, and *then* he narrowed his eyes suspiciously.

"Didn't you get your SATs back?"

Oh God. It was like he'd read my mind. I looked at my toes again—I had *really long* toes, to match, well, you know.

Not to brag. "Uhm…."

"How bad?" he asked, and his voice was absurdly gentle.

"I don't wanna talk about it," I said, crossing my big toe over my middle toe. I could wiggle them from that position too.

"That's pretty bad. What'd your dad say?" Because we both knew my dad had this vision: me in some big college with a letterman's jacket or something.

And this was the part that *really* made my toes curl on the wet concrete. "He said he could pull strings. Get me into Stanford anyway. Told me I'd have to *really* study when I got there, because this slacking shit wasn't going to cut it."

I was surprised when his combat boots snuck into my field of vision and a hand came out and touched me awkwardly on the shoulder.

"I'm sorry, Rusty."

I shrugged away, feeling *worse* than shit now, and ignored the shiver down my arm where Oliver had touched me. "I don't know why *you're* sorry. You're not the idiot who sucked up all your time trying to learn to fuckin' read and write. You're the kid who *should* be going to Stanford, but you gotta go to junior college instead." I turned to my open locker and tucked my towel tight around my waist and started to rip out my cargo shorts and tennis shoes and tank top so I could get dressed and give him a ride home. He lived sort of far from my neighborhood—in fact, I'm pretty sure he'd transferred to my school for the AP classes only—but the house itself was cherry. It was small but painted white, with red and pink flowers growing up the white fence that surrounded the yard. From where I usually sat in the car when I dropped him off, I could see four tiny dogs, who always about lost their minds with pure joy that Oliver was home, and it was getting so I could relate. Anyways, our pattern was for me to let Oliver off outside the gate of his little house, and since I had the car, and it meant *he* didn't have to take the bus, I didn't have a problem with that.

"Yeah," Oliver agreed, back there in the locker room. "Stanford would be great. Ain't gonna lie. But a JC will give me a chance to get my skills up and running, and I'm damned grateful. Rusty, you're gonna get *killed* if you go there and you're not ready. Can't they see that?"

I leaned my forehead against my locker and swallowed, trying to breathe past the panic. "I'll be fine," I lied. "You know me. Time and an instruction book, and I can conquer the frickin' world."

"Yeah," he said, but he didn't sound optimistic.

The week after that, he asked me if I wanted to work for his dad that summer, part-time or full-time, my choice. His dad was a contractor, and I'd get to do real simple stuff—carry boards, push brooms, run water to the guys with nail guns and screwdrivers who were framing houses or sanding drywall. It wasn't a lot, but, well, my other job prospect was pushing papers for my old man or someone else's old man ('cause we were swapped around like action figures) in an office.

Guess which one sounded better, right?

Not that the old man saw it that way.

"Rusty, this job could get you valuable contacts in whatever field you pursue—" Dad's hair had gone brown and gray, but I've seen pictures. It used to be blond like mine, streaked by the sun, with undertones of red-brown. His cheeks used to be wreathed with smiles too, but his mouth was a lot thinner now. I couldn't remember seeing his smile for a while.

"But Dad, this job doesn't need a suit."

"Well, maybe you're old enough to actually think about your future instead of the next girl or the next sunny day. Have you thought of that?"

I hadn't had a girlfriend since the girl who'd rather have had dick than dinner. It just didn't seem worth the trouble, really, explaining to them that they didn't need to put out. And getting some wasn't as much fun as it used to be—but then, having a friend at the movies had always seemed to be the best part of girlfriends anyway. But, well, Dad had this vision of me, and football-jock-superbanger seemed to be it.

"Dad," I said, trying to sound grown-up. "You know, maybe this… this thing you've got set up for me in the future, maybe it's not really a good fit. You ever think of that? I mean, a college education, I get that, but maybe not Stanford and the whole nine yards—maybe a JC and some life experience, you think?"

"Russell, we're not screwing around here—this is your life. You go to a good college, you network, you move on to graduate work. Why would you think that's changed?"

I opened my mouth, a lot like Oliver had, and closed it, and opened it again. "I… I mean, I'm not great at school—you know, there's tech schools and vocational schools all over the place for guys who don't, you know—"

"You are *not* graduating from Western Career College," my dad snapped, and I grinned and tried to get the smile from him that I vaguely remembered from when I was a kid.

"You can *do it!*" I sang to the commercial, and apparently that was exactly the *wrong* thing to sing, because Dad rolled his eyes and walked away.

So I tried Mom.

Now in some houses, Mom would be the guaranteed win, right? "Oh, honey, of course. I understand that you're feeling out of your depth and you'd like to see if maybe something a little less cerebral might be a better match for your much vaunted future." Or, you know, at least "Yeah, go out and sweat in the sun, you're eighteen, who gives a shit?" right? But that wasn't the way it was in my house. It wasn't like Mom was the guaranteed win; it was more like she was better at calculating what was in it for her.

"What will you be spending your money on?" she asked, narrowing her brown eyes at me as though trying to figure the angle. I'd gotten her eyes, but there was something wrong with mine. They were wider, and nothing about me looked like I had anything to do with angles. I was all about the curved muscle and brick walls.

I blinked. "I don't know. Clothes, the car—I mean, you guys pay for everything else. Maybe I'll put it in savings and see what I need."

She nodded consideringly. She worked part-time from home. She had a degree in finance, and she did business for a day-trading firm. "That sounds prudent," she said. "And I think once you spend some time doing manual labor, it might lose its charm." As. If.

Best summer of my life. Oh my God, give me simple tasks and a logical progression and I am a happy boy. And you know what I figured out after, like, the first month? I figured out that once I understood where I was and what I was doing, once I was comfortable with things, *I could think for myself.*

On my third day, if someone left a bucket of nails in the middle of the path I was walking, I walked around it. On the sixth, I picked the bucket up and moved it out of the way. The second week I was there, I found the guy with the nail gun and set it next to him. During the third week, I checked to see if the bucket was full enough, and if it wasn't, I filled it. Then I asked the guy with the nail gun if he could show me how to use it, and by the second month, I could spell the guy with the nail gun, and then, when he came back to do his thing, I went and asked the guy sanding the drywall exactly what the hell *he* was doing.

They thought I was a frickin' *genius*. It was *awesome*. After the first week, I was totally full-time.

And Oliver's dad couldn't get enough of me. I loved that guy! When I moved the nail bucket, he told me good job. By the time I was using the gun, he was telling me I was a natural and asking my opinion and showing me how to use the equipment and shit. He was great. I mean, my dad probably wouldn't have thought much of him. He was a short Latino guy, his black hair going iron gray, with beefy forearms and a thick middle. He had a bushy mustache and faded tattoos on his sunburned brown skin, but not a day went by without him asking me how I was doing and telling me—hell, telling everyone on the site—what a good job we were doing, or asking our opinion, or letting us know if we needed to hustle and why.

Oliver would come by the site on his lunch hour—he was working at the library, and he seemed to love the hell out of that—and brought us sandwiches and told us funny stories and made sure we drank lots of water. I wanted soda, but Oliver, he told me that shit was bad for me.

"Man, I know it, but I've been drinking water all my life; I want something *bad* for me that doesn't give me a headache." My mom didn't let Estrella pack the good juice in our lunches. It was all this high-end shit that tasted like crap but was good for us.

Oliver studied me over his turkey on dry wheat toast. "Well, if it doesn't give you a headache, and it makes you feel good, it's good for you, right?"

I had a sudden thought about his little oval face and how just looking at it, with the bright and shiny black eyes staring out at me—*that* was good for me.

"Yeah," I said, forgetting about food. "Yeah. Good for me."

I don't recall what he said after that. I *do* remember talking him into going swimming at my house after work, *that's* what I remember doing, and after he laughed and agreed, and then left for his job, his dad looked at me, head tilted to the side.

"I thought Oliver said you weren't that kind of friend," he said quietly.

I looked at him blankly. "What kind of friend?"

Arturo Campbell, whose dad was white and whose mom was Venezuelan (I know this because he told me the first day I met him, which was funny because I really wasn't curious), shook his head. "Kid, I think that's gonna be the sixty-four-thousand-dollar question for you, you know that?" And then, before I could embarrass us both by trying to figure that out when we both knew I wasn't capable of that shit, he took my napkin and my water bottle from me. "Tomorrow I'll bring you a soda. Just one. I think you've earned one lousy fucking soda."

So Oliver came over to my house that afternoon and swam, wet and agile as an otter, moving with the same quick little motions with which he walked and spoke. My mom saw him and smiled in greeting and then walked away. My father walked in and out of the house without acknowledging he was there. My sister was a freshman—she knew all about Oliver. As we were swimming in the cool water under the oppressive heat layer, she came out and asked him if he liked to shop. When he said no, he liked to read, she blew a raspberry at him.

"What was that for?" he asked, smiling that innocent white smile up at her. She was on the deck and he was in the pool. I was in the deep end, treading water, hoping my little sister wouldn't be shitty to him so I wouldn't have to act like a three-year-old and call Mom to make her go away.

"*That* was for being the wrong kind of gay. *Jesus*, what are stereotypes for?"

I snickered, because she was sharp, and Oliver cracked up so hard he splashed water when his otter-swift hands moved. "Well, mostly they're to throw back in people's faces," he said. "But I'll go shopping in a bookstore, if that counts."

Nicole stripped out of her T-shirt and dropped it on the patio, wearing a plain old blue one-piece because she was a little curvy and Mom said it was tasteful. Suddenly I sort of yearned to see her in a paisley bikini; not because I'm a sick perv or anything, but because Nicole was a lot more interesting than that plain blue bathing suit and the plain white T-shirts she always wore.

"Hmm…," she said, thinking hard as she walked gingerly down the pool steps. It was hot enough outside to make the cool sort of a shock.

"Would it be the kind of place that served cappuccino and had poetry readings and music nights?"

Oliver's grin grew a little dreamy. If you went up toward Placerville, there were arty little places like that, but here? Nope. Everything was the big bland Costco of its stock. Pottery Barn was considered unique and one of a kind, because God forbid anything stand out or anything. I always figured that's why people liked the football team and the basketball team and the marching band so much: put everyone in a uniform, and they all looked the same. I think in our community that was reassuring.

So it didn't take a genius to figure that small, brown Oliver would be excited about a place not populated by big hunks of clone meat like myself.

"If we get a place like that up here, you let me know, okay?"

My sister laughed and then dove into the water with a little shriek. When she surfaced, a few feet from me, she said, "I think we're going to have to build one, sweetheart—and that means we'll have to shop together after all."

Oliver laughed and conceded that maybe they *would* have to bond via retail. Whether she knew it or not, my little sister—who had been a giant ugly bug crawling up my ass when I had my football buddies over—was suddenly on our side.

Estrella came out then with sandwiches and snacks, and I was surprised. She'd never done that when I'd had my other friends over, although there had always been potato chips we could serve.

I climbed out of the pool and toweled my hair before coming over to check out the spread. "This is awesome," I told her, meaning it. She'd always been really nice to Nicole and me, cooking our favorite stuff, smiling at us when we were eating dinner in the kitchen, or asking us about our day. When we'd been younger, she'd been the nanny, but as we'd gotten past needing one, Mom had kept her on as the housekeeper/cook. I always thought it was because Mom loved her too, but that was something else I think I got wrong. For Mom, she was just super competent help. It was only to Nicole and me that Estrella meant something special.

"Well, I like this friend," Estrella said, smiling. She had little teeth, with a gap in the front, and a round face and body. She was probably my mom's age, but she seemed older somehow—maybe it was the softness. I knew she'd listened to Oliver and me talk in the kitchen when we were studying for the SATs, and she and Oliver had sometimes had snow-flurry conversations in Spanish that had felt intimate and real. She'd never spoken Spanish to me and Nicole. I felt like I knew her better after she'd made us sandwiches and hot chocolate—and the snacks, by the way, were pretty much one of the best things about the SATs, period.

"I know. I like him too. His dad is pretty awesome. I wish I could work for him forever."

Estrella looked at me thoughtfully. "I don't think your father would like that very much," she said kindly, and I shrugged.

"Yeah, well, he might change his mind when I flunk out of Stanford."

She sighed and patted my hand, which was still wet from the pool. "Maybe you should think of a way to avoid that?"

I winked at her to make her smile. "You know me—anything to get out of hard work."

Estrella shook her head. "You're a good boy, Rusty. Keep bringing Oliver by. He's a good boy too."

Nicole and Estrella were smart—they saw the lines being drawn. But not my parents.

They treated Oliver like they treated all my other friends, and didn't, not once, notice that the enemy, the secret marauder who would topple all their hopes and their plans for their baby boy, was in their swimming pool, smiling up at me with bright brown eyes, wearing a pair of plaid shorts that weren't made for swimming at all.

HE CAME over to swim a lot that summer. I remember little photo shoots in my head, his thin, brown limbs shiny and wet as he stood on our white concrete patio. I liked the way he flipped his hair out of his eyes, and the way he'd swim with his arms at his sides, rippling his long, skinny body. In the water, standing on the bottom step of the pool, he looked exotic, like a merman or something.

I started to think about him, *dream* about him, in his plaid not-swimming shorts, standing mostly naked on my parents' patio.

At first the dreams weren't anything remarkable. He'd just be smiling at me, like I'd done something great. I mean, I'm not a *complete* asshole, but great? I have never, ever been accused of greatness. As a football player, I was good enough to play, but that was when I was pushing myself into the ground. As a student, I was in the honors classes because I had *outstanding* tutors, but that was their smarts, even if it was my sweat that made it stick. But at least in my dreams, Oliver was staring up at me like I had just won the Super Bowl and solved world hunger during the commercial break.

The first time I dreamed that, I woke up almost in tears. I wanted to be back asleep, having that dream, so bad.

I didn't think about it then, and when I *did* think about it, I tried to focus on the fact that maybe I should stop being a pussy about how bad I *didn't* want to go to Stanford. That if I wanted people to look up to me like that, maybe I should try to be someone worth looking up to.

When I wasn't working, or at the pool, I was reading. I figured if I could read some of the books Oliver read, I'd maybe get some of his quickness. I read *A Separate Peace* and *The Chocolate War*, but all I really got out of them was that big clots of peer pressure really fucked a kid up. I figured I didn't have to worry about that shit anymore. My friends had all taken off.

I mean, we still texted and saw movies together sometimes, but they were all working the same internships and jobs my dad had wanted *me* to work. Between the working, the reading, and the swimming, more and more and more, my world revolved around Oliver.

I was okay not having that crowd of friends anymore. With all the reading Oliver and I were doing, we were starting to get the same jokes. Like, when him, me, and Brian Halliday saw that new Bourne movie. We were sitting there, watching guys kick ass on screen, when suddenly it hit me. These movies were about spies who didn't want to spy anymore. They were getting *reborn* as someone else. And then, *bing-bang-boom*, I was back with that *Crime and Punishment* book Oliver had given me, and then holy shit and hallelujah, I remembered Mr. Rochester and St. John and *Jane Eyre*.

"Omigod omigod omigod!" I hissed at Oliver. "*Bourne!* Get it? It's like he's been re*born*!"

Oliver jerked, like I'd given him a wedgie or something, and then he turned to me with a smile so big, I swear it made the theater brighter. "God, Rusty, you totally nailed that one."

I grinned and then turned to Brian, and he was shoving popcorn in his face. "Get it?" I whispered. "It's his name, but it *means* something. It's like… like *allegory*."

Brian squinted at me. "Shut up and watch the movie," he muttered. "People are looking at us funny."

For a minute I was real disappointed. I felt like I was seeing the sun for the first time, but Oliver elbowed me and grinned and gave me the thumbs-up. For an irrational, terrifying moment, I thought about grabbing his hand and kissing it, because I was that fucking grateful, right?

But I didn't. I turned my attention back to the movie. Afterward, Oliver and I asked Brian if he wanted to go out to ice cream with us, but he said no.

"I gotta be up early in the morning," he said, sounding like my dad. "If I'm not there on time, your dad gets on my case. Jesus, Rusty, I can't believe you *came* from that guy."

Yeah. Brian had taken the internship in *my* dad's office, and I guess I was supposed to have taken the one offered by *his* dad. Nice. Swapping us like the little game pieces we were supposed to be seemed more and more cold-blooded.

"Don't look at me." I shrugged. "I'm working construction. I get there at nine, I leave at five, and my boss buys me soda when his son's not looking. I got it good."

"He does not." Oliver looked properly horrified. I smiled back at him. I loved grinning at him. I wanted to wrap my arm around his neck and ruffle his hair, but that had never been us.

"He does too," I told him, figuring Mr. Campbell wouldn't mind too much if I gave this away. "But only once a week. The rest of the time it's horchata." Which I didn't particularly like, but he meant well, so I drank it anyway.

Oliver smiled, very proud of himself. "Yeah. My dad, he listens to me if he knows what's good for him."

I looked at Brian to try to share the awesome that was Oliver's dad. "He does too," I told him seriously. "I mean, I never in a million years thought anyone could actually… you know… *listen* like this guy. He's awesome to work for. I wish I lived with him."

Brian sneered. "Yeah, well, you and Oliver get any cozier, maybe you can."

I recoiled. "Man, what crawled up your ass?"

"Not the same thing that's about to climb up yours."

I looked at him, floundering. "That's so ugly," I said at last, my voice low. "How come you gotta be like that? You weren't like that in school. You guys were always really nice to Oliver in school."

"Yeah, well, that's when we thought he was your friend. It's a little different when he's your *boy*friend. You know that, Rusty. It's like… like we can let them hang around us, but there's got to be a line."

"Besides," Oliver said quietly at my side. "They *were* like this in school. You were just too sweet to take it that way."

"Is that how you like 'em? Sweet?" Brian's voice was nasty, and something in his face was hurt too. It hit me that he felt like he was losing me. And he was mad at Oliver because Oliver was the one who would get me in the end.

"I…." I shut my mouth and opened it again, and I wished suddenly that I was a kid again, in grade school, where all you had to do was go out and catch the ball, and that made kids your friends. "I'm sorry," I said, turning to Oliver. "I'm sorry I was too stupid to know they were being mean. You've been a real good friend to me. I wouldn't have let anyone be mean."

Brian scoffed—and I never knew what that word meant until I heard that sound come out of his mouth.

"God, Rusty. Have a nice life. Give your mom my apologies for your going-away party. I'm not going to make it."

"You're having a going-away party?" Oliver asked, brightening, and I wanted to sit down and cry on my knees.

"I guess it was a surprise," I said.

"And I guess you weren't invited," Brian said to Oliver. "Which is great. It'll just be Rusty and his family staring at each other. I'm pretty sure after tonight, nobody else is going to want to have a damned thing to do with you either."

And he turned and walked off to his car. I watched him go, feeling empty and dumb.

"You know," I said into the warm night, "you're really the only person I would want to come."

Oliver reached up and patted my shoulder. "That's okay. I'll show up anyway. You tell me where and when, and I'll be at your party."

I was planning to tell my mom, but she brought it up first. She's like a ninja. I was walking out of my room after my post-work shower, going to hunt up some more food in the kitchen. I swear that woman heard the floorboard creak as I passed her office, because her voice shot out like an arrow and stopped me in my tracks.

"Rusty, have you had a falling-out with your friends?"

I turned around and looked into her office and saw the back of her head. Mom had blonde hair. I think it was dyed, though, because if she missed her stylist appointment, her roots were brownish-gray. But I rarely got to see that; it was almost always perfect. Some guys had moms who went running in public or sometimes wore sweats or went camping and didn't wash their hair for a week. My mom only sweated at the gym, and since she went to one of those women-only gyms, we had to take her word for it. Every day: slacks, a twinset, and pearls. I don't think I remember her wearing jeans.

Right now she turned the chair away from the dark wood desk to face me and brushed her blonde hair from her eyes in a way that looked like ballet.

"Yeah, Mom," I said, because apparently being not bright meant I couldn't lie either. "They were being mean to Oliver."

Mom blinked and adjusted her summer cardigan. This one was pink. "The little dark-haired boy?"

He wasn't *that* little. Five six? Five feet seven? Sure, *I* was almost six feet tall, but Oliver wasn't child-sized.

"Yeah, that's the one."

"What would they have against him? I mean, I know his father's in construction, but I don't think any of your friends are that poorly mannered—"

"He's gay, Mom—"

Mom jerked her head back. "I did not know that," she said. Her voice didn't really rise, but she gave the impression of a big ocean wave: same thing on the surface, but a vast swell of power underneath. "Why is he here so often?"

I swallowed. I reminded myself I'd suspected this. I'd thought my friends were decent, and I'd been wrong, but I'd always known my parents were dicks, and I'd been right about that.

"He's my friend. He helped me study for the SATs. And his father gave me my job."

"Oh," she said, and her eyes were narrowed. She was doing some sort of calculation, I could tell. "You owe a debt. I understand. Well, then…." Her voice trailed off, and I could see she was struggling with the sham of the "surprise party." And then an odd look crossed her face. Her eyes got big and shiny, and for a moment her chin wrinkled. She took a deep breath, and everything smoothed out. "You should invite him to your going-away dinner," she said simply, as though this was something I'd always known about. "It's Tuesday, in two weeks. We'll be going out. Make sure he dresses appropriately."

I heard her later, canceling caterers and fighting for her deposit back, and I felt bad. Maybe *that* had been what the shiny eyes were all about. She was going to lose money on this deal. That sucked, but I wasn't going to go make up to all my shitty friends and drop Oliver. For one thing, I was almost done with that *Crime and Punishment* book, and I needed to talk to Oliver and find out if that really scummy guy was a bad guy or just doing that stuff because he felt like he was supposed to.

So Oliver came with us. He was wearing an old suit jacket and jeans, with a white shirt underneath, and he looked good.

His wrists stuck out of the sleeves, though, like he'd grown since he got it, and the color was blue. I don't think the fabric was that good. But that was okay. We sat through dinner while Nicole teased me about how I was supposed to send her all the skinny on the professors and the quad and the good places to hang out. I rolled my eyes and asked her how I'd know these things anyway.

"You've always been better at knowing the cool stuff," I told her, and it was true. Nicole *did* like to shop, but she liked to shop vintage music stores and antique shops and stuff. She went to poetry readings in her spare time and could tell you who on the bookstore shelf had actually grown up in our little spot in the foothills. Before our town exploded into feeder suburbs to Intel, it used to be a little artsy place with windy roads and lots of trees and big stretches of nothing. A lot of our local authors wrote about the evil of industry and the soullessness of the suburbs, which did absolutely nothing for me. At least Raskolnikov *killed* people, right?

Nicole sighed and rolled her eyes. "At least look for the places that *Oliver* would like to hang out, okay?"

I grinned at Oliver. "That's easy. The library."

Oliver grinned back. "I even think that's on the campus map," he conceded.

I was suddenly struck by a thought. (Which, you know, gets me into trouble.) "Wait, Oliver. Where *do* you like to hang out?" I couldn't remember him ever being anywhere besides my house except for his house or the library.

Oliver's face did a weird thing then, and in a way, it reminded me of my mom's face when she'd had to cancel my party. "With you, dumbass." He said it with a smile, and for a moment I thought he was going to zing me, but he pulled back somehow. *Dumbass* didn't sound like an insult when he said it. It sounded like *sweetheart* or *baby* or one of those other gross words girls liked us to call them.

But because it was *dumbass*, it didn't make me gag.

"Oh my God!" Nicole rolled her eyes. "That's gross. Men should never talk to each other that way. Ever. I don't care *who* they sleep with!"

"Ni*cole!*" my mother snapped, and my sister turned to her chicken and asparagus with a meekness I did *not* believe. Sure enough, she looked up at me under her lowered brows, and I stuck my tongue out at her. Her shoulders shook and her look shifted to a glare, and then she looked next to me, to where Oliver was sitting (he got the end on account of being left-handed), and I saw him sticking out his tongue *and* crossing his eyes.

Nicole burst into giggles, and Oliver and I joined her. My parents glared at the three of us, but they weren't going to start shrieking about manners in the middle of the restaurant—that would be rude.

So it was a good dinner. I thought I might miss Nicole when I was gone. When we were little, she used to sneak into my room at night and sing silly kids' songs to me. I don't know where she heard them— kindergarten, maybe? Preschool? Our mom wasn't one for singing nonsense songs, but Nicole remembered every one she heard. Probably why she loved vintage vinyl records so much. Anyway, as we all walked through the balmy air to the parking lot, I remembered that.

We'd driven in two separate cars so I could pick Oliver up, and my Prius with the moonroof had a decent back seat. I thought maybe some company would be nice.

"Nicole, you want to ride with us?" I asked all of a sudden. "We can go for ice cream and then get home."

Nicole looked up at me with a smile on her round face while she pushed brown hair out of her eyes, and for a moment it looked like she was going to say yes. Then she grew thoughtful, and she said, "No, Rusty. You go ahead. We've got tomorrow before you leave, but you've only got Oliver for tonight."

I shrugged and got into the car, but, as dumb as I am, there were a few things I didn't miss.

I didn't miss the way my parents glared at Nicole, and I didn't miss the way she looked at them, innocent as pie, which is how she usually looked when she'd been robbing my drawers for those awful white T-shirts.

And I didn't miss the way Oliver beamed like a dark sun either. It made me feel good, right? Because he was my friend.

I MEANT to take us to ice cream, but as I neared the turnoff for the strip mall that had the Ben & Jerry's in it, Oliver made a *no* sound.

"Just keep driving," he murmured, and so we did.

We rolled down the windows, and the wind was perfect. It smelled like cut brown grasses, because the hills were scorched, and we drove the long straight highways through Amador, listening to music and talking about what we *thought* college was going to be like.

I said, "You know, it's probably going to look like the inside of my dorm room. I'm never going to cut it."

Oliver sighed, and then I sighed too. It would have been nice if he could have lied to me, just once, but that wasn't him.

"Rusty?"

"Yeah?"

"You know, you can email me when you're gone, right? Text, Skype, all of that."

I brightened a little. All that shit. I'd forget. Oh crap, I should tell him that. "You're going to have to poke me a little, okay? You know, like now? I forget."

Oliver shook his head. "You don't, really," he said with an apologetic smile. "You just don't like calling people out of the blue. Once I text you or something, you're all okay." His teeth glinted a little in one of the rare streetlamps, and he shook his bangs out of his eyes. "Actually, Rusty, you're sort of a little bit shy."

My face heated in the confines of the car, and I wished I could have stuck my head out the window like a big yellow dog.

"You say that, and now I'm all embarrassed," I told him, and his laugh was a soft sound blown away by the wind.

After about an hour of driving out in the mostly rural country off Jackson Highway, I stopped at a gas station to fill up. Oliver trotted inside and came out with two frosties in cups, mine with lots of caramel and nuts.

He waited until I was done pumping gas and said, "Pull over to the back of the station. You can savor it then."

I looked at him quick and saw he was laughing a little at the idea of savoring gas station ice cream, and I laughed too. But behind the gas station, there was miles and miles of nothing. Far off in the distance, you could see the lights that meant the urban sprawl of Sacramento was starting, but there wasn't even one light behind the store.

Oliver and I both leaned against the Toyota and "savored" our sweating ice cream. A breeze blew across all that dried nothing and I found I was scooting up against Oliver a little for warmth. He didn't seem to mind.

For a few moments, we didn't say a word, and the world was perfect.

Then, into the quiet, Oliver said, "Rusty, if I try something, do you promise to still call me if it doesn't work?"

God, I'm dumb.

"Try something like what? That thing with the computer so we can see each other? Because I can do that already."

Oliver laughed into his empty ice cream cup and talked about something else. "Rusty, who was the last girl you dated?"

"Jennifer Brukholtz—you remember, I told you about her?"

"No dick before dinner," Oliver said dryly. "Yeah. Not easy to forget."

I sulked and scooped out the last of the ice cream with my spoon and then sucked the spoon upside down on my tongue, creating a perfect seal. Oliver turned toward me, looking up at me with those eyes that said I was all that. My tongue got sucked in around the spoon, and for a minute I was stuck, Oliver laughing at me, my tongue glued to the roof of my mouth like every bad dream I'd ever had about public speaking, except I wasn't naked.

I had a sudden thought then, of me naked, and Oliver in front of me the same way.

I stopped breathing, and the spoon loosened from the top of my mouth and started to slide out. Oliver caught it before it could stop dangling off my lips and put it in his ice cream cup. Very deliberately he took the cup from me, put it in his own, and set them both on top of the car behind me.

"You just thought about it, didn't you?" he asked quietly.

I'm dumb, remember? No lying. I nodded my head and swallowed. "Yeah."

There was just enough light from behind us to see it dancing in the brown of his eyes.

"I've thought about it a lot," he said quietly. "And you're leaving tomorrow. Which means if this doesn't work out, it'll be okay. We'll be friends and we'll text and—"

"If what doesn't work out?" I asked, and his lips quirked upward, leaving perfect apostrophes on either side of his brown mouth.

"Just close your eyes," he said softly, and I did.

He moved slowly, reaching behind my head and pulling it down, and when I was right where he needed to be, he raised up a little. I could feel puffs of breath against my mouth, and then a tickle against my lips. And another, harder. And one more, warmer.

I gasped, opening my mouth, and his tongue swept in, teasing a little, until I teased back.

He sighed into my mouth, and for a moment it felt like he was going to pull away, but I wasn't ready. I reached behind him and pulled him closer to me, and his tongue went deeper. Ohhh... *this* was kissing. I sighed back at him, and he pulled away, leaving me to suck on his tongue until the last minute, because I wanted him some more.

And then it hit me.

Oliver had kissed me, and I'd kissed him back.

I dropped my arms and jerked back, cracking my elbow on the side of the car. Oliver took a hurried step backward himself and gave a startled laugh, clapping his hand over his mouth.

"Oh my God, Rusty, are you okay?" His words came out muffled from behind his fingers. He was still laughing.

I rubbed my elbow and tried to breathe through that funny-bone pain that is almost as not funny as getting kissed by your best male friend when you thought you were straight.

"I'm a little confused," I told him honestly. "And my elbow hurts."

He ventured closer and hesitantly put his hands on my shoulders. I wanted to shrug them off and remind him that I wasn't gay, but I didn't. They felt good there, soothing, and I lowered my head and let him touch me.

"You don't have to do anything," he said quietly. "You don't have to kiss me back or worry that I'll do that again. Just… think about it, okay? Just think about it, and we'll be friends like we always have been."

I nodded, but I didn't move. I must have at some point, I know, because we eventually got back into the car and drove home, but I don't remember that moment when we stepped away from each other. In fact, for a long time, my head was still there, listening to cicadas and feeling the touch of his hands and the tender wind of his breath on my face.

I DROPPED him off at his house, like usual, except, well, it wasn't usually one in the morning. He hopped out of the car and stood for a moment, in front of that wildly overgrown fence of jasmine, morning glories, and tiny roses, and looked at me, his mouth pulled down with worry.

"Call me," he said. "Text me. Email me. IM me. Anything—just don't think you're down there alone."

I smiled at him, relieved and more than relieved. He was still my friend. That hidden moment behind the gas station hadn't changed the one important thing.

"I promise," I said, and he nodded soberly.

"That's something you're good at," he reminded me, and I smiled. That look was back in his eyes. The one that said I could do anything. Keeping a promise—that was a good thing. I could do that.

I got home and walked quietly into the house. No one was waiting up for me—I thought. But then I found my little sister asleep in my bed, wearing one of my T-shirts and a pair of my basketball shorts.

I stripped to my sleep shorts while she was still out and kept on my tank top. Then I shook her carefully.

"Nic—Nic, you gotta get up. I'm home."

She looked at me groggily. "Where'dyougo?"

"Just around. Get up."

"No. There's room. Go on my other side."

I was tired. I'd worked that day for half the day, and Mr. Campbell had bought me lunch as a send-off. He'd told me I was welcome to come work for him anytime, and I was grateful. Those checks had really added up in my savings account, and I'd earned that money, fair and square.

"Fine." I scrambled over her and tucked into the covers. She was on the outside, and I reached down and grabbed an old afghan that Estrella had made me and pulled it up so she could tuck it under her chin.

"Why do you want to sleep here?" I asked, my eyes closing too.

"You're the only one in the house who likes me," she said, and it sounded like *she* at least was waking up.

"Estrella likes you," I said, and it was true. Estrella always saved the best cakes in the kitchen for Nic. Of course, it probably didn't help her waist size, but if someone offers you love, you don't really count calories. I knew she'd been baking cookies for me all week so I could take them to Stanford with me. I wasn't going to argue.

"Estrella does, but she doesn't live here." She was wide-awake now. I could tell by the peevish little lilt in her voice.

"Are you trying to say you'll miss me?" I asked. It had just occurred to me, like *that night*, that I would miss her.

"Yeah, dorkfish, I'll miss you."

I opened my eyes and grinned at her, then made the fishhook gesture. "I'm a dorkfish!" I said it with the Bill Engvall inflection and everything, because it had been making her laugh since she was nine years old and I'd first learned how to surf YouTube.

She laughed softly, and then she looked sober. "Rusty, if I ask you something, do you promise not to get mad?"

My smile faded. I knew what she was going to ask before she said it. "Do we have to—?"

"Are you gay?" Her eyes were big and brown, like Oliver's, but not quite as dark.

That morning I would have thought I knew the answer to that question.

"I don't know," I whispered, and she blinked those big brown eyes slowly.

"I know Mom and Dad would freak if you were," she said, and her eyes got shiny. "But I wouldn't. You'd still be my hero."

My eyes burned, and I remembered the way Oliver had looked at me—like I was great. Nicole was looking at me the same way. "When have I ever been your hero?" As far as I knew, I was just her way station for free shirts and a place to sleep that wasn't alone in the big quiet house.

"Always," she said, smiling a little. "Your girlfriends always used to try to chase me away, you remember that?"

I did remember. I'd never been as interested in being alone as they had. "Yeah. You just wanted to… I don't know, be in the same room as us. Read, watch TV—it's not like you were talking or butting in. You were great."

She nodded. "You never let anyone pick on me. Not even your friends when they came over to swim. But until you brought Oliver home, I worried, you know?"

"About what?"

"That you'd… I don't know. Turn into them. Turn into *Dad*. Just… suddenly wake up and assume you were captain of the universe and that I had to listen to what you said because you were a boy and my brother."

I laughed a little. "Lucky you, Nic, you got the dumb big brother. Captain of the Universe has to be smart enough to go to Stanford."

She bit her lower lip to keep it from trembling. "Email me, okay? And Oliver. And remember that if you have to come home, we'll both be here. You're smarter than you think you are."

I had a sudden thought. "You'll look after Oliver, right? He doesn't have any brothers and sisters." His mom had passed away when he was a little kid—he'd told me that. It was just him and his dad, and aunts and uncles that I could never keep straight.

Nicole nodded. "If you're gay, you and Oliver could live together and make a home. What kind of home would you have?"

I was falling asleep and confused and sad, so I didn't even ask myself the big question, the hard question. I remembered Oliver with his back to the jasmine and the morning glories and the loud pink flowers whose names I didn't know, and thought about how bright he'd looked for a little brown person. It was like he and the flowers went together.

"Someplace with flowers," I mumbled. And that was all I remembered before I fell asleep.

Big Fish, No Water

My roommate was a big, beefy guy named Rex.

Seriously. Rex. Who names their kid that if there's not a tyrannosaurus in front of it? Anyway, he met me with a handshake as we both set up our room and promptly ate about half of Estrella's cookies. During the next six hours, several things became apparent. He was taller than me, wider than me, smarter than me, would bang anything that moved, and had a smaller cock.

The first two were pretty obvious, and the third one became obvious as he was fixing up his computer and talking some foreign language about comp sci and astrophysics and how he was really starting as a sophomore because he'd nailed all his AP exams and early entrance classes, but he was going to use his freshman year to take all the humanities stuff he would miss out on as he became some sort of scientist I couldn't even pronounce.

The last two became obvious after we were all moved in, and I had my gift poster from Oliver of Patrick Dempsey in *Crime and Punishment* put up, and my new sheets in the prerequisite navy blue. I was stripping down to my underwear, only to be whirled around by a hand on my shoulder.

"Holy *fuck*!" He shoved my shorts down around my thighs. "That thing is *huge*! I mean, I thought *I* was gifted. Girls must *love* that. Can you get it hard for me?"

I smacked his hand. Seriously, like he was a little kid. "That's *mine*!" I grabbed my shorts and yanked them up over my hips. "Seriously! I mean, I've been in locker rooms before, but no one's *ever* made a grab for that thing." I did not mention Oliver, who hadn't grabbed for that thing at all, but who had only stood on his tiptoes, closed his eyes, and offered up a kiss.

Rex stood back, looking a little depressed. "Really?"

"You expected something else?"

Rex shrugged. "I saw you checking out my ass when I was bent over my desk. You went to half-mast. I thought, you know, since we don't have any girls right now, you wouldn't mind some...." He made the time-honored open-fist jerk-off motion, and my face heated.

So I'd been checking out his ass? I guess I had been. I remember thinking that Oliver's was smaller, with less muscle, but Rex's wasn't bad. He must work out like a madman.

"I'm, uhm...." My face was still hot, and I shoved at his chest a little—not mad or mean, just to get some space. I came up with the word then and was proud of it. "It's like being a freshman," I said with some dignity, although I'd already told him I was pre-law. "I'm undeclared."

Rex raised his brown eyebrows over his bright green eyes. "Undeclared?"

I couldn't look him in the face anymore. He was like... like the me I should have been. He was brilliant, and he was here partially on a wrestling scholarship, and he obviously loved sex and didn't care who it was with.

"Undeclared," I said to my toes. I used to think it would take a lot to make me feel small. Apparently it only took Rex. His hand on my shoulder was powerful, and he squeezed, making me look up.

"Well, 'Undeclared,' let's see if we can't help you find your major, okay?"

I smiled a little, not really sure what he meant. "If you're talking academically, I already told you it's pre-law, but I'm pretty sure I'm going to wash out by the end of the semester."

Rex laughed and shook his head. "Well, in that case, we've only got a couple of months to go."

Well, yeah, I figured. It was the only reason I'd been able to throw my shit in my car and drive away from the hills.

THAT NIGHT, I lay in bed and set my phone next to my pillow, where it could charge *and* wake me up. I checked for messages and saw one from Oliver.

Hey—you forgotten me yet?

No. I sort of wish you were here. My roommate has NO respect for personal space.

Yeah? He make a pass at you?

I had to think about that one for a minute. Then:

No, but he seems to want me to figure out my major.

I thought you were pre-law.

Not that major.

LOL—yeah, well, I wouldn't mind either if you figured that one out.

Trust me, O—you'll be the first to know.

There was a long pause after that, and then he told me that my sister had called him up and was forcing him to come get her after school next week so they could go shopping. It took me a long time—long after Stanford and Thanksgiving and Christmas were over—before I figured out that maybe he already *was* the first to know. I'm pretty sure it wasn't *me*.

WHAT DIDN'T take me long to figure out was what "finding my major" meant to Rex. But it wasn't until every sock—and I mean *every fucking sock*—had disappeared from our dorm room that I began to have a suspicion.

My first class was Monday/Wednesday/Friday at ten o'clock sharp—Early American History with Pritchard, and I swear, I was more confused after our orientation than I had been before I walked in. Oliver and I had both read the online syllabus, and he'd helped me through the reading, but that guy walked in and started lecturing and writing on the board before I even had my shit out to take notes.

I had a two-hour break before my next class, and I walked back to my dorm with my reading list addendum in my hand, hoping to buy and download my books before it started.

So I was distracted and sort of pissed off when I threw my dorm room door open to see Rex, naked, bent over the bed, licking between a naked blonde girl's thighs, while *another* girl, this one with big tits and curly black hair *everywhere,* wearing a dildo strapped around her hips, gave it to him up the ass. I stopped there with my book list in my hand, the door open behind me, and my mouth open in shock.

Rex sucked two fingers into his mouth, then thrust them delicately into the girl's glistening vulva, grinning at me over her shiny, juice-slickened thigh.

"Close the door, brother," he said cheerfully. "And by all means, join in." The girl behind him groaned and gave a particularly hard thrust. She must have had something going on inside her too, because she shuddered like she was about to come.

"You're fucking two women," I said, because stating the obvious, that was so me. "I don't even know anyone's *name*."

Rex wiggled his fingers and stuck out his tongue. The perky blonde girl thrashed on the bed for a moment, obviously close, and then she groaned when he stopped.

"What's your name, darlin'?"

"Chlo…. Chlo…. Chloeeeeeeeeeee!" And he was back in business.

Behind him, the brunette thrust *hard* into him, and his own groan was muffled in Chloe's lady parts. "I'm Vanessa," she panted, looking me over. "I'd take it up the ass for *you* any day."

I shook myself all over and walked to get my computer and my charger. "That's a nice offer," I said sincerely, "but I'm going to go to the library."

No, OF course I couldn't study. I mean, I *tried*, but, like in high school, I found my fingers going to my phone. There were only two numbers there that I'd text now, and I *wasn't* telling this story to my little sister.

Guess what?

What?

My roommate's fucking two women in our dorm.

Well, now you know what team he plays for.

One of them's giving it to him up the ass with a strap-on.

Maybe the vote's still out.

I still would rather not walk in on that again.

I was actually sort of proud of how I typed that. It sounded like I was holding it together.

Make him put a sock on the doorknob.

A sock?

Yeah—it's like a signal. It would tell you when he's having sex, and you don't have to see.

Okay, a sock. He can use one of mine. I'll consider it a brain condom.

Heh heh heh… who says you're stupid.

I do. What in the holy fuck is the New Historical school of thought?

Oh. Oh shit.

What? What's "Oh shit"?

Oh shit is that we can't do this over text. Get out your computer and scan your assignment.

I CAN'T. My roommate is fucking people where my printer is, remember?

Oh. Okay. Well, how about I email you some links?

I felt like crying. Oh thank you, Oliver. Thank you thank you thank you. Two plans of action in the same day. Best. Friend. Ever.

Thank you. That would so help.
Hey, Rusty, what do you say when a dinosaur crashes his car?
What?
Tyrannosaurus Wrecks
Tyrannosaurus Rex Wrecks Sex
Ha! Good one. Why shouldn't you write with a broken pencil?
And so on.

One bad joke at a time, he talked me through a miserable hour in the library. When I finally decided to go back to the dorm, after my next two classes and some dinner, Rex was asleep—alone, thank God—and the place reeked of air freshener and randy butt sex.

I texted good night to my sister, and she said good night back, and I counted the hours until I could text Oliver again.

THE NEXT morning Rex was completely unrepentant.

"So, what'd you think?" he asked after he'd woken up, yawned, and stretched. I was sitting at my desk, weeping over my trig homework, so it took me a minute to figure out what he was talking about.

"Think?"

"Yeah. About our guests yesterday?"

I squinted at him. "Uhm, yeah. Next time you have guests, maybe you can put a sock on the door. You know. As a signal?"

Rex squinted back at me. "As a signal?"

"Yeah. You know. So I don't walk in on you again."

Rex squeezed his eyes shut. "You're not that bright, are you?"

I looked at the trigonometry figures in front of me and prayed that everywhere, all over the world, this textbook would disintegrate into ashes and all the electronic copies would magnetically wipe themselves, proving, once and for all, that math was the devil's handiwork, and nice dumb jocks should have nothing to do with it.

"No," I said, meaning it. "I never have been."

WE LEFT that morning to two completely different departments, and I reminded him, "A sock, okay? If you're there and doing the thing?"

Rex smirked. "I can promise you that there will *never* be a time when I feel the need to put a sock on that doorknob." Oh, okay. So this had been a one-time thing—sort of a loosening up before the big academic charge. I *got* that. I did. Some of the few times I'd had sex with girls had been for that very reason. Football season had been starting and I'd needed to let off steam, and, well, the girls had been willing.

"I'm so relieved to hear that," I said sincerely, and Rex laughed and walked away, that happy, from-the-gut chortle ringing up between the buildings in the quad. And I thought that was the end of it.

I WALKED in three days later, and he was tied to the bed while a girl was tickling him with a feather. *And* sucking his cock.

"But...," I sputtered, after closing the door behind me. "You said you wouldn't need the sock!"

"No," he panted—I think he was close. The sight of him, head thrown back, erection rampant and purple, *was* actually doing something for me, but the girl's lips around his crown were big and red, sort of like two painted slugs stretched out on a pane of glass, and that made my stiffy shrivel damned quick.

"You *did*—"

"I *promised* I wouldn't need to put a sock on the door."

"But you *do*—you're getting a blowjob *right now*!"

Rex let out air through his teeth, and I watched as the girl used the feather on his inner thigh while she dropped her head and sucked one of his hairless balls. His breaths came slow with an obvious effort, and I was sort of impressed that he managed to talk.

"Rusty, do you want to help her, or do her, or not?"

"English," I said unhappily, because the teacher had told us to read a novel by Thursday. I'd double-checked the syllabus too, and that shit was *not* in there. "I want to do my English."

He let out a moan, and I looked up to see the girl pinching his nipple.

"Okay then," he managed. "Grab your porta-scanner this time, and give Oliver my best."

"Do you want me to bring food?" I asked, and Rex's eyes popped open.

"Yeah, sure—pizza! Two hours. I'm good for it. Courtney, you want some?"

Courtney pulled off Rex's cock long enough to wipe her mouth and think about it. "Naw," she said, and looked at me apologetically. "It gives me gas, and I was sorta hoping for…."

And then the naked girl in the middle of a blowjob actually blushed, her pale pink cheeks going one of those deep red colors I don't even have a name for.

"You know," she said, and then she batted her eyes at Rex, who smiled. It was a hooded-eyed, sexy smile, and looking at it made my cock think about getting hard again.

"Oh, honey, I do. I've got the lube, I've got the condoms….I'm your backdoor man."

And there went my stiffy again.

"I'll be back at six," I said, and grabbed my porta-scanner and my computer and boogied.

HEY, O—how you doing?

I'm bored. My homework's all done, your sister can't come play today, and I don't have work. How about you?

My roommate's having sex again.

How many?

One. But she's got handcuffs.

Nice. Did you tell him about the sock?

I think he forgot. I'll remind him when I bring home pizza.

You're bringing this douche-pickle pizza?

It's better than eating alone.

How's class?

What's the difference between exposition and narrative?

Okay, get off the phone and open your computer. I am no longer bored.

Hey, Oliver—

Yeah?

Did you ever need handcuffs and dildos and all that shit to have sex?

Wouldn't know. Never had it.

Don't worry. It's not all it's cracked up to be.

Maybe you were having it with the wrong person, you think?

Too close for missiles, switching to guns.

You're going to have to answer that question sometime, even if it's only to yourself.

I'd rather answer it to you. Email. Now.

Sigh.

I BROUGHT Rex pizza—two of them, in fact. Enough pizza that we'd be dining on takeout for days. I brought his date rice cakes and hummus, and she kissed my cheek in thanks. When Courtney was dressed (or, well, wearing one of Rex's T-shirts, sans underwear) she was actually a very pretty girl. She had brownish hair and freckles and those plump lips and sort of a wide face. Well, maybe *pretty* wasn't the word—but she smiled at me, and made me feel welcome, and sort of laughed away the awkwardness of eating dinner with a girl I'd just watched fucking my roommate, so she *felt* pretty to me.

"So," she asked, crunching delicately on a rice cake, "who's Oliver?"

"My friend from home," I said. I was eating a big slice of combo pizza; I'd discovered the campus gymnasium and had started working out again. I missed the days in construction where my body was always active.

"What kind of friend?" she asked, all curiosity.

What kind of friend? "The kind that helps you study for your SATs and doesn't mind when you text him at four in the morning begging for help on your trig."

Courtney gave Rex a sardonic sideways look. "You told me you wanted to have sex to help out your roommate!" she accused, and Rex gestured to himself, all innocence.

"I did. It was all an attempt to help him, you know, decide what he likes."

"He already knows what he likes. He's gay."

I almost choked on my pizza. We were all sitting on the indoor/outdoor carpeting, and I bent double over my crossed legs so I could cough out that last freakin' piece of pepperoni.

Courtney waited patiently until I was done and had cleaned up my mouth and set the pizza down with a depressed look at it. I'd totally lost my appetite.

"You didn't know you were gay?" she asked, like it wasn't the sort of thing that got kids beaten up and written out of wills and completely demoralized all the fucking time.

"I'm undeclared," I said stubbornly, and Courtney's look at Rex was softer this time.

"Oh," she said, nodding. "I see. Rex, honey, I think you're going to have to try a different direction."

"The only thing I wish he'd try is a sock on the frickin' door!" I protested, not wanting to think about how many directions I could see Rex fucking around.

Rex snorted. "I'm sorry, my man. We're out of socks. Now eat your pizza."

I thought he was kidding too, until I had to get dressed the next day. I opened my sock drawer, and there was nothing in there but a check for seventy-five dollars.

"Rex?" And how did he end up with all the classes that started at noon? Seriously. "Rex, wake up. Where in the hell are my socks?"

"Threw 'em away," he muttered, and my jaw dropped.

"You *what*?"

"Threw 'em away." He woke up a little more, sat up in bed, and rubbed his eyes.

"Well, can I borrow some of yours?"

"No," he said, smirking. "I don't have any either."

"What am I supposed to wear on my feet?" My brain was starting to hurt. And, yes, my feet were cold.

"You can buy footies. That's why I left you the check."

"But footies won't fit on…." Oh yeah. "The door. You bastard. Do you get off knowing I'm going to walk in here while you're living *Boogie Nights* in our dorm room?"

He actually had to think about it. "I can't lie," he said, stretching his arms above his head. He had a truly magnificent chest and armpit hair that was oddly red in color. I swallowed, feeling an unwelcome punch of desire in my stomach. "I *do* like it when you walk in on me. But part of that is I want to see you whack off—man, even if you're not into guys, that thing… I mean, it doesn't get any smaller, does it?"

"I don't know, I think I can feel it shrinking every time you bring another girl in here."

Rex's smirk went nuclear. "Well then, I'll stop bringing girls in." He sighed. "Except maybe Courtney. I *like* her."

"Awesome. Do you think you could give *her* the check, and have *her* go get footies? Today's a three-class day."

Rex's grin relaxed, and he nodded. "No worries. I'll get them. We wear the same size. God, if only our *dicks* were the same—"

"I'll wear flip-flops," I said, to cut off that sentence. "You lay back and enjoy that thought."

He was ahead of me, actually, and I watched with a combination of revulsion and arousal as his hand moved under the covers. With a sigh I turned around and left, adjusting myself uncomfortably as I went.

Oliver, can I ask you a personal question?

Yes, I do floss regularly, why?

It's about sex.

Ooh—I'm suddenly interested.

What do you think about when you jerk off?

You.

I'm serious.

You really aren't a quick study, are you? Who do you *think about?*

I swallowed. I hadn't jerked off in almost a year, and for once I was smart enough about myself to know why.

I'll let you know the next time I jerk off.

Excellent! Can I watch?

You'll have to get in line. Rex made it his life's mission.

Rex can kiss my skinny brown ass. You were my friend first.

I'll tell him that.

But you'll let me know if you do, won't you?

Jerk off and think of you?

Yes. Please.

I was alone here, and I missed him. Who would know but us?

Yeah. I promise.

Good.

I WAS up late studying that night so I could go to bed after Rex did. I fell asleep thinking about Oliver, about his smile, about the funny, quick way he moved, and how he always let his bowl-cut bangs grow into his eyes before he trimmed them, so those darting hands were always pushing it out of the way. I remembered his kiss, and the heat of his body, and the way his mouth had felt under mine, and just when my groin started to ache and tingle a little, I fell asleep.

I woke up the next morning *literally* with my dick in my hand, and Oliver still in my head from my dreams. It took one, two, three strokes, and I was coming, biting my other hand to keep Rex from hearing, the orgasm boiling up from my balls with so much heat and pain that tears slid through the creases of my eyes. *Oliver.* Oh God. My body wanted him so bad, my skin ached because he wasn't there to touch me, or, hell, even talk to me. My breathing was fierce, and I spurted hard, hot, spattering into my underwear again and again until I could only roll over to my side and groan softly. "*Oliver.*"

OLIVER?
> *Yes?*
> *I did it.*
> *And?*
> *I miss you so bad I can't talk about it.*
> *I miss you too.*

FOR A couple of weeks, Rex took it easy on me. I was wearing the damned footies, so the anticipation was something—I *still* never knew what I was going to see when I opened the door to our room. Sometimes it was Rex beating off, in which case I could usually come back later. But still, I lived on a sort of sexual edge, not sure what Rex was going to do next.

In a way it was the perfect distraction, because as much as I'd known I wasn't ready for college, tanking hard and spinning out in flames was not as easy as it sounds. For one thing, I couldn't tank. I was *at college.* If nothing else, Oliver had shown me that not everybody *had* the opportunities I did. Yeah, maybe I would fail, but that didn't mean I was going to give up.

Unfortunately.

Because that meant I was grinding away every day, working my ass off on papers, on assignments, using my Kindle dictionary until my battery died, *praying* that at some point some of this shit would all get easier. It didn't. I'd go to the library and text Oliver for help, hoping his patience would sustain us both, but even Oliver had limits.

Oliver, you got a sec?

Sorry, Rusty, man, I really don't.

What's doing?

Fighting with my dad.

Really? Oliver's dad was the nicest person on the planet. And he obviously *adored* his tiny gay son. I couldn't imagine them fighting about *anything*.

About what?

I don't want to talk about it.

Okay. Sorry. Tag me later.

Love you.

What?

Oh shit. Forget I said it. Slipped out. Gottagobye.

And I was left trying to struggle through my history paper on my own.

REX REALLY *was* taking it easy on me. All I had to worry about was walking by a sex-mussed person—male or female—coming out of his room right when I was due back, or, more often, walking in on him when he was waxing his own knob. When that happened, he wasn't even awful or crude about it. Just smiled at me and asked me if I wanted to join in. The horrible part was that the answer was starting to be *Yes! Yes, I want to join in! I'm lonely, and I miss my best friend, and I'm starting to realize this* isn't *going away, and I just want to be touched.* But it would have been all wrong—even I knew that. Rex was like... like a bastion of raging sexuality, all on his own. I was clingy and needy and...

And I didn't want to be alone. In the past I'd had sex just to get my knob polished, and I don't know how Rex and all these other people could do that all the time. Now, when I thought about having stupid nameless sex, I thought about Oliver, and about confessing to him because I told him *everything*, and, well, I couldn't.

But I did start waking up more and more often, early in the morning when Rex was fast asleep, thinking about Oliver.

It started to be my favorite thing. Sometimes the only thing that got me out of bed was the fact that my come got clammy and sticky when I stayed curled under the sheets too long.

But not even *that* could take away my pathological dread of History 101. I didn't understand it. I mean, I could memorize the dates, but I absolutely did *not* get things like how they could know Franklin Pierce was a bad president because all the literature about him said he was a good one.

So I plodded through, and Oliver tried to help me, but he had his own life and his own family, and I figured I'd stop asking.

RUSTY?

Yeah?

Haven't heard from you for a day—what's wrong?

Nothing. Didn't want to bother you.

The radio silence is bothering me. What's up?

The question made my eyes burn, and I started to tear up in the damned library.

Nothing. Same old bullshit.

Rex giving you any more grief?

No. He's been good about getting off without me.

Ha ha ha!

Wait—that's not the way I meant it!

I know—I'm sorry. What else is going on?

I'm stupid and I shouldn't be here.

Please stop saying that.

Why not? You know it, I know it, the professors know it.

Well, maybe you can ask your parents to change schools at the end of the semester.

But first I'll get myself kicked out of Stanford so I can hear them telling me I'm a failure. I can hardly wait.

You're not a failure, Rusty.

You could have fooled me.

You're in over your head—it happens to everyone.

Not you. You know exactly who you are and exactly what you want from life. I'm like a big sea creature, and no place is the sea.

There was a big long pause then, and I surreptitiously wiped my eyes before going back to my homework. After a few minutes, I looked at the phone, but Oliver had apparently lost patience with me, because he hadn't answered.

I'm sorry.

You should be. You're breaking my heart there. Come home.

You mean for Thanksgiving?

I mean for me.

I'll try to come home at Thanksgiving.

That'll be a start.

BUT THE conversations and the steadily building certainty that I was *never* going to want to bring a girl back to my dorm room or home to my parents weren't enough. I was still lost, and Professor Pritchard seemed to hate me with a vengeance.

I actually made an appointment to see him. We'd just gotten our second papers back. My first one had gotten a resounding C, so I'd talked to Oliver and he'd helped me with my thesis and everything for the second paper. I got the paper back, and it said, *I don't know whose work this is, but it's not yours! F.*

I knocked on his door, a plain wooden door in a plain white corridor, and when he boomed "Come in!" I went through.

He was, what? Fifty? Early sixties? But he liked to wear Hawaiian shirts and jeans, and his long, curly, thinning hair was gray and bushy at his shoulders. He might have been a redhead when he was younger, because he had the sort of skin that once went with freckles, and he *looked* like one of the übercool teachers you'd see in an after-school special.

So far, though, he'd been nothing but a rank bastard who liked to scream at all of us about how useless it was to be rich when we couldn't think for ourselves. He loved the scholarship kids—praised them to the skies—and I was pretty sure he'd enjoy the hell out of Rex, because Rex just smiled at people and admitted he was a spoiled horndog, and people ate that shit up.

But me? I was a spoiled rich boy. I mean, I was, but I wasn't. I was starting to realize that I would rather have grown up with Oliver's family than mine, even if that meant no car and no letterman's jacket and no motherfucking Stanford.

"Professor?"

"Mr. Baker?"

"I, uh, this *is* my work." I held out the paper with the big fat F in stark red pen. I hated that. Even the color was incriminating. "I… my friend helped me with my thesis, but… I mean, I'm not a cheater. I cited all my sources and everything."

The professor gave me a hard look from top to bottom. "Baker, you can't even put two sentences together and make sense. How in the hell am I supposed to believe you came up with the idea that Nathaniel Hawthorne was the reason Franklin Pierce got elected?"

I swallowed. "You only said it about six thousand times. I'm not stupid. I mean, I *am* stupid, but I'm trying. I listened. I took notes. My friend, the one who helped me with the research, he sent me all these books to look up. I *worked* for this, professor! I mean, it's not genius stuff, I get that, but I earned more than an F."

"You haven't earned anything in your life," he sneered. "There are kids all over the country *killing* themselves to get here, and I have *you* in my class? Jesus, kid, did you think your daddy's money was going to buy your grade as well as your ticket in?"

And suddenly all this misery I'd been tamping down on exploded out of me. "Do you think I don't know that? Do you think I don't *know* it's unfair? Oliver should be here! He's hella fucking smart, and if I could have sent him here in my place, I would have. I didn't want to be here—I *saw* it coming. It was gonna be a clusterfuck from beginning to end, but I had to, right? Just like I had to play football, and I have to be straight? And I hate it! *I hate it!* I miss Oliver so fucking bad, and I don't give a fuck about my dad and his money, but *I want to go home*!"

I stopped, breathing hard, and realized what I'd said, all of it, and I swallowed. I didn't know what to say or how to salvage this. I wasn't straight, and I wasn't cut out for Stanford, and Oliver was my home.

And I'd just screamed all that in my professor's face.

I couldn't look at him. I held up the paper, curling the edges in sweaty fingers. "I'm sorry, professor," I mumbled. "I deserve a better grade." And then I let the paper float to the ground and turned around and walked back to my dorm.

Rex was in there, fucking a boy this time. A slightly built, dark-haired Hispanic boy, and for a moment my heart jumped with joy, because I didn't give a damn *what* Rex was doing, I thought it was Oliver.

It wasn't. His face was wider and his chin was more square, and his nose was flatter. I didn't see his eyes. I walked to my bed and crawled in without even taking off my shoes. I listened to their sex noises and felt a disturbing mixture of despair and arousal, and I hadn't even sorted out which was which before I went to sleep.

I WENT to bed on Friday, and I must have gotten up sometime to go pee and take off my shoes and my jeans. I don't remember when, but I must have, because I wasn't wearing them when I heard Oliver's voice shrieking in a tinny echo over a computer speaker. The phone by my pillow said Monday, November 3, which meant I'd gone to sleep on Halloween and missed it.

It also said I had something like forty messages on my phone, voicemail and text. I checked the register—Oliver, Oliver, Oliver, Oliver, Oliver, Oliver, Nicole, Oliver, Oliver, Nicole, Oliver's *dad*, Oliver, and so on. My message box was full, and I blinked blearily, wondering when I'd turned the phone down.

"Oliver?" I mumbled. "Oliver, keep it down. I'm trying to sleep."

"Oh, for fuck's sake," Rex said, his voice alive and loud, right by my bed. "I've been trying to wake you up for two days!"

"Go away. I don't want to whack off. I just want to sleep."

"Man, your class starts in ten minutes—that history one you've slaved over—can you at least get up for that?"

I pulled the covers over my head. "Fuck no!"

"Is that him?" Oliver's voice again. "Is that him? You put your damned computer next to him and let me yell at him—"

"I've been trying to get him up for days, man." Rex protested. "I don't know if he's going to—"

"You shut up, Mr. Naked Sexy Man! You're half his problem—you and your 'declaring a major.' He'll declare a major when he's good and ready, and it's not going to be pre-law, and it's not going to be sex ed, so just leave him the fuck alone!" There was a pause, and I actually pulled the covers down because I'd *never* heard Oliver yell like this, not even when my supposed friends were giving him shit at school.

"Oliver? You're mad? You never get mad." Suddenly my phone was moved and Rex's computer *thunk*ed down by my head. I had a sideways vision of Oliver, looking furious and worried through a phone lens. His hair was longer, no longer bowl-cut, and the bangs had grown past his eyes so they were pushed back on the side. He'd let his sideburns and mustache grow, but they were sparse and wispy, and basically he looked sort of like a beatnik—all he needed were glasses.

He was beautiful.

And I was pretty sure I smelled bad.

"Rusty, get the fuck out of bed," he said, and his voice sounded clogged and snotty.

"Whose phone are you on? Your computer doesn't Skype."

"Nicki's—she was freaking out over you, I was freaking out over you, my *dad* is freaking out over you. Finally I remembered your damned roommate's on your list of people you send stupid rabbit videos to, and we contacted *him*."

"Jeez, Oliver, that's a lot of trouble. I just wanted some sleep."

"You've been in bed for three days, asshole. Get your lazy ass out of bed and shower. I can smell you from here!"

I wrinkled my nose. "That's untrue," I said with dignity. "I got up to pee. I think."

Oliver sighed, and his voice was getting thicker. "Rusty, baby. What happened? You were going to talk to your professor and then you… you just disappeared. Talk to me, man. What did he say?"

"He said I was worthless," I mumbled, although the professor hadn't used those words. "He said I was worthless, and I was spoiled, and I didn't deserve to be here."

"Did he really say that?" Rex asked, and I nodded even though I couldn't see him.

"Yeah." It came out as a whisper. I barely heard Rex moving across the room, and then our door slammed, and I didn't care.

"Well, he was wrong!" Oliver snapped. He was openly crying now, and even though it was stupid, I reached out and touched the screen.

"Don't cry, baby. He was right. I'm spoiled and dumb, and we both know you should be here. I… I mean, I was trying, right? I didn't just give up? I mean"—because it couldn't be argued—"I gave up *now*, but, well, no big loss."

"That's what *you* think, you clueless motherfucker!"

"Oliver, you *never* swear!"

"Well, look what you made me do. You've got one hour to get up, get showered, and get to class to try again, do you hear me?"

"And then what happens?" Because my parents hadn't called me once, and we both knew it. No calls, no texts, just a receipt from the bank when they put their money in my checking account. I was pretty sure they'd cut me off if I didn't get out of bed. That would be fine. Some janitor at Stanford would pick up my bed and haul me out and leave me on the side of the road, and I could rot in peace.

"You listen to me, Rusty," Oliver said, his voice low and serious. "If you do not get out of bed right the fuck now, me and my dad are going to go down there and get you. We will pick you up and throw you in the car and abduct you and throw you in the shower until you come to your senses. So you get up now, or we'll do it for you!"

I straightened up a little and frowned at him. "But Oliver, I don't want you to see me like this."

Oliver's face wrinkled, like a napkin. "Baby, when was the last time you ate?"

"I don't care."

"Well, I do! You must have lost thirty pounds in the last two months. Could you, please, for me, just get up, take a shower, and eat some fucking pancakes or something?"

"You've got to stop swearing. Man, you're freaking me out."

"*Get the fuck up, you dumb motherfucker, you are hurting me by lying there!*" He yelled so loud his voice blacked out in the high parts, and the speakers squealed. I managed to push myself up so I was looking down at the screen, and my bladder gave a big, fat, thump in my abdomen.

"Sorry, Oliver. I don't ever want to hurt you, you know that. Jesus, I've got to pee."

Oliver nodded, then wiped his eyes with his palms. "You do that, okay? You go take the world's longest piss. Then you come back. But—hey, you got your phone?" I reached behind the computer and held it up. "Good. Now set the alarm. You've got an hour, Rusty. You text me or talk to me, or get on Skype with your sister on your own computer, and you show me that you've showered, you've shaved, and you've changed. And I wouldn't object to you shoving some food in your mouth while you're on the phone. And if I don't hear from you *in an hour*, my dad and I are coming to get you. He's been trying to talk me into doing that since the end of September."

"I looked this bad a month ago?"

"You sounded this bad," he conceded. "Now you look fucked-up too."

Shit. All my fucking self-pity, and I'd pulled him into it. Now I *felt* bad. "I'm sorry. How'd he talk you out of it?"

Oliver shook his head. "I talked him. I wasn't sure you'd want me to come. You weren't even thinking about me the same way I was thinking about you."

I remembered shouting into Pritchard's face, and I thought I should probably tell him this. "Oliver?"

"Yeah?"

"I'm pretty sure I'm gay."

"Me too, *pendejo*."

"And even if I'm not gay, you know what?"

"What?"

"I'm pretty sure I'm Oliver-sexual." I nodded, smiling, proud of this, and the smile he gave me back was like a solar flare.

"Then go clean up and eat something. Can you do that?"

"Yeah. Sure."

"And don't forget to text me."

"Yeah, okay."

"Love you, Rusty. Don't let that freak you out none."

"Love you too."

I signed out of Rex's Skype then and swung my legs around my bed and tried to stand up. My knees wobbled, and I sat down on my ass again and wondered if Oliver was going to have to come get me because I hadn't eaten since… when? Thursday? And I was too weak to actually do all that showering stuff, but I still needed to pee.

I'd managed a wobbly-legged trip to the bathroom to pee and had just sat back down on the bed, dizzy and frustrated, when the door was thrown open. Rex marched in, dragging Professor Pritchard by the arm. I tried to use the blankets to cover up my knees.

"Rex? What in the fuck did you do?"

"Mr. Baker?"

Reluctantly I looked up and met the professor's eyes.

"Sorry I missed your class today," I apologized, but it was sort of insincere. The pull to go back to bed was so strong, I felt my shoulders hunching.

"Yeah, so am I." He sat down next to me, and I flinched back.

He looked up at Rex and said, "Can I get a chair, since you dragged me up here?"

Rex *thunk*ed the roller chair from my desk down in front of Professor Pritchard. He was *scowling*, which I'd never seen him do.

"Be. Nice."

Pritchard grimaced as he moved to the chair. "Yes, I hear you."

Rex scowled back, and Pritchard turned his attention to me.

"You forget," he said, looking suddenly old. "You forget how fragile young people are sometimes. We think they're all grown-up because they're here, but they're not always. It's your first time away from home, and it's not always easy." He grimaced again. "*Especially* if the people at home aren't exactly warm. And you're having a hard time."

"I don't belong here," I said miserably, pulling my knees up to my chest, and his hand on my shoulder was a surprise.

"No," he told me honestly. "But not because you're stupid. I reread your paper. It was really very good."

I perked up. "Really?"

"Yes, I made some assumptions about you. I shouldn't have. I'm sorry."

I shrugged. "I am spoiled."

"Maybe. But I think you're spoiled for the wrong things. Do you really have a boyfriend back at home?"

That made me lift my head. A boyfriend? Oliver was my boyfriend? For some reason that was *so* much less scary than saying I was gay.

"Yeah," I said, and I arched my back, suddenly needing to stretch. "I need to call him in a bit, after I shower; he's worried about me."

"You do that. I will go," and here he glared at Rex, "*finish teaching my class*, and Rex will get you some food, okay? We'll meet back in an hour. How's that sound?"

"I have other classes," I told him, thinking about it, and he nodded, but then surprised me.

"No, no, I don't think you do. I think what you have is a long conversation with a guidance counselor, and a walk around the campus, and at least two good meals. Today you become a big exception to everything we ever tell you about college, how's that?"

I smiled a little. The conversation with the guidance counselor sounded boring, but the rest of it? I was *really* starting to get hungry.

I CAME back from my shower with a growling stomach and the dizzy vision I used to get after a football game if I forgot to have my banana and milk beforehand. When I got to my room, Rex was there with a *stack* of peanut butter and jelly on wheat, as well as a half gallon of milk and a bunch of bananas.

My eyes got big when I saw that plate of sandwiches on his desk, and I'd shoved half the first one in my mouth before I remembered to talk. "Mmmf omf fa frrrkn mnnds."

"Milk," Rex said with a tired smile. "Here."

I wiped out a quarter of the bottle, and after I swallowed, he handed me another sandwich. This one I took actual bites from, and on my second bite, he said, "So, what did you say?"

I grinned through the PB&J on my teeth. "Food of the fuckin' gods."

He laughed then, and I thought he looked like he'd gotten a little older too.

"What's the matter, Rex? You look *exhausted*."

Rex gestured to the chair Professor Pritchard had vacated and sat down on his own bed, pulling one knee up under his chin. "Did it really bother you? That whole 'declaring your major' thing?"

I took another bite of my sandwich. "You weren't trying to be mean," I said, thinking. "I mean, you gave a shit, and that was nice."

"But it bothered you," he stated, and I shrugged.

"You know… I guess I just wasn't ready to be pushed. I'm not smart—"

"Rusty!"

"Okay, I'm not *quick*. But I get to most stuff on my own. I just… I needed some quiet, I guess, you know, in my head? To think about Oliver and me."

Rex laughed a little and nodded. "But you know, you've hardly talked in the last couple of weeks. How much more quiet did it need to be?"

I shrugged and set my sandwich down. It was my third—I figured I'd done enough damage. "It wasn't quiet," I said, feeling empty after the storm that had blown through me. "It was all messy and loud."

Rex nodded like he understood. "What'd'ya have to do to quiet it down?"

I thought about it for a moment. "I had to decide who I was."

A slow grin bloomed on Rex's uncharacteristically thoughtful face. "Who are you?"

"I'm not a Stanford man," I said, and for the first time, this didn't make me want to cry. "And I'm not going to be my dad's little clone. And women *don't* turn me on. And Oliver is my home."

Rex put both feet on the floor and hopped up. "Well boo-fuckin'-yah!" he whooped and then picked me up in a colossal bear hug and whirled me around the room. Two months ago I would have batted him off and called him a fucking moron, but not now. Now I laughed, and let him hug me, and tried to remember, *really* remember, the last time I'd been touched.

He set me down, and I was standing there in his arms, my head on his chest, when he gave me a friend-to-friend kiss on the top of the head.

"Nicole," I said out loud, and he jerked back.

"Rex. And I thought we were celebrating your coming out?"

I looked up at him, because he *was* six five, and shook my head. "No. It's my little sister. She's the last person who hugged me."

So that's what was happening when Professor Pritchard came in with my guidance counselor. We were standing in the middle of the room and Rex was hugging me, and *he* was crying. I couldn't ever get him to say why.

THE PROFESSOR brought us pie. I don't know why I remember that, but I do. Banana cream pie from the grocery store. Oh man—it was, like, the *best* pie. We sat around the dorm and ate pie for no reason at all, and the guidance counselor—a short, round Asian woman with a mouth that formed a flat line when she was thinking—made polite talk. She sort of looked scary, but she was very nice, showed me pictures of her grandkids, who she said were all going to be doctors. For a minute I felt bad—they were going to be doctors and I was going to be no one—but she didn't come across like that. It was more like, they could be doctors because they could be *anything*.

That was nice. I told her that sincerely. That permission to be *anything*, that was a big deal.

"So," she said innocently, taking a *very* large bite of pie, "what do you want permission to be?"

I didn't even have to think about it. "I want to work construction," I said. "I want to be a contractor, like Oliver's dad. I want…." My face got hot, and I took a bite of pie to hide.

"You want what?" she insisted, and I sucked every last calorie of happy out of that pie before I answered, and when I *did* answer, I was pretty much studying my pants across my legs. There were wrinkles across my thighs when there didn't used to be. I guess I *had* lost weight.

"I want to kiss Oliver some more," I mumbled, and Rex heard me from across the room and guffawed.

Professor Pritchard smiled and then took that as his cue. He stood up and started gathering plates and said, "Rex and I are going to leave, because Rex is going to try to make it to class. And Rusty?"

"Yes, sir?"

"I'll see you Wednesday, okay?"

I nodded. "Yes, sir. Thank you for the pie, and for… you know. Coming to see me."

Pritchard's look was… well, I guess it was uncomfortable, really. "Thanks for not screaming obscenities in my face," he said after a moment. "And thanks for writing me a really good paper."

I smiled. "It *was* good, right?"

"Yeah. Whatever you decide, you may want to make sure you write more of those, okay? A college education—that doesn't come to everyone. Whatever happens, tell me you won't just throw it away."

I nodded. "Thanks, professor. I won't."

They left, and I don't even want to know what Rex was saying to Professor Pritchard, but they were sort of laughing like equals. I guess Rex did that to people—lucky him. Some of the rest of us had to earn that feeling some other way than just by being awesome.

Squat little Mrs. Li waved goodbye while she was eating another piece of crust, and then she said, "So, Oliver. Tell me about him."

And that was when the hard shit started, you feel me?

'Cause I for damned sure started feeling it myself.

SURFACING

THE NEXT three weeks weren't easy, but they weren't the cesspool of misery I'd been in either. I talked to Mrs. Li a *lot*, and I realized somewhere in there that Rex, being the Superman he was, had completely bypassed about six dozen people in his quest to get me help. Apparently I *should* have seen my RA first, and then the school shrink, and *then* gone up and talked to actual professors and counselors and stuff—but not with Rex. With Rex you got your professor dragged out of a lecture and hand-delivered to you on a platter with pie. Just as well; our RA was a weaselly little guy with a chia beard who smelled—you know the aroma where you can't decide if it's pot or body odor? In his case I think it was both.

And in the end, after all that talking and stating the obvious—my parents were sort of cold, Stanford was sort of hard, and Rusty was sort of gay—we came to the same conclusions I'd known when I'd graduated from high school: I shouldn't be here.

But, on the side of progress, I guess now I knew where I *should* be.

OLIVER, YOU there?

Define "there," Rusty. I'm at the other end of the phone.

I don't know if you're being a smartass or what. You just had to say yes.

Sorry. Fighting with my dad again.

About what?

Nothing important. It's just irritating when he's right.

You were right the last time. I DID need to figure stuff out.

Yeah? What'd you figure out?

I want to kiss you again. And feel you up this time—I totally missed my chance.

Nope. I'm pretty sure you'll get a few more chances over Thanksgiving break.

Awesome! What about Christmas?

That depends.

On? 'Cause I have the feeling I'm going to want more.

That depends on what you're doing after *Christmas?*

Well, according to my guidance counselor, I'll be signing up for classes at Folsom Junior College.

Excellent! In that case you can feel me up a LOT *over Christmas. What are you going to tell your parents?*

I sighed. The guidance counselor and I had gone over this too. She seemed to think my folks would be all right about it, but if Professor Pritchard had taught me *anything*, it was never to underestimate the stupidity of people in power.

I'm going to tell them I'm in love.

Because that was the truth. But when he texted back, I realized I hadn't said it out loud since the day I'd gotten out of bed.

With me, right?

Yeah. Is that okay?

Can't text now. Crying like a girl.

I've never seen Nicole cry.

That's because you didn't see her freak out over you.

I'm sorry.

I'd actually texted Nicole a lot, and she seemed all happy and shit. I had no idea she'd been losing her mind. Well, maybe I wasn't the only one who was repressed.

You should be. You stupid white people. Man, my family, we'd never let that shit happen.

I'd never thought of it before.

Why? What would your family do instead?

I told you. My dad was going to drive down there and get you. And I don't mean talk you out of bed. He would have put you in the shower in your clothes and thrown you in the truck all naked and not stopped until he got you food.

Well, yeah. But that's your dad. He likes me.

My Aunt Gloria would have been in the back seat. She'd be looking up directions to the health food store, and we would have fed you the good stuff. Your peanut butter would have been organic and your bread whole grain.

Your aunt knows about me?

My mom had an obnoxious older brother who had two obnoxious daughters and a trophy wife. They would probably *love* to hear that I was a big fat failure. And my parents hadn't known the names of the *girls* I was dating.

Yeah. Whole family knows about you. Man, they got me through some rough moments this summer. There I was, eating my heart out, and they were telling me to give you time.

Wait. How did they know I was gay?

There was silence.

Silence.

Silence.

Oliver?

My dad told them.

How did HE *know?*

He said it was the way you looked at me. It was like how my mom used to look at him.

That's... that's sweet, I texted. *But I'm sorry I made you wait so long. You could have dated too, you know.*

He sent me an emoji with its tongue sticking out. *I got asked out on a date when I was at the library. My dad said that was fine, just don't do anything I couldn't tell you.*

That was so close to the reason I'd never taken Rex up on his offer that I got the chills.

Your dad is scary awesome, you know that? Stop fighting with him.

Explain that.

I can't. I've got to write this paper so I can go have Thanksgiving break and not work the whole time.

Look at you, being a good student.

Yeah, well, we finally figured out what my major should be. It's not pre-law.

What is it?

Liberal studies.

I don't know if your folks will like a degree that starts with liberal ANYTHING.

Well, if they want to dictate my life, they actually have to be in it, ya think?

OMG. You're like a whole new Rusty. I hope you still look the same.

I took a picture of myself there in the library. I'd meant it as a joke, and I was going to smile all cheesy and shit, but at the last moment my eyes veered off, and I remembered the last time Oliver had seen me, I hadn't been out of bed in three days, and my teeth had been *gross* and my hair had been falling in my eyes. It was longer now, like his, and my teeth were clean, and my complexion had cleared up (because it does that when you wash your face), but I was still thin, and I was still pale. I'd woken up three days earlier with Rex smashed up against my back, just holding me. When I asked him what the hell he was doing there, he'd mumbled something about me making noises.

My head had been achy, and it hadn't taken a genius to figure out I'd been crying in my sleep.

But I didn't tell Oliver that. I just took the picture, and my smile was shy and my eyes were far away, and I sent it anyway, because I figured he wouldn't care.

You need to come home.

Well, duh! That's what break is for.

That's not what I meant. And you know what?

What?

You were right. My father is seven kinds of scary freaking awesome.

It was funny, though. I was sad, and sometimes every step out of my dorm felt like a baby's first step into the world, but I was still better than I had been when I'd crawled into my bed with the intention of never getting out.

AND WITH that "better" came being better with school in general. I guess I figured that if my paper had been good enough for Pritchard, then I *was* capable of doing the work. That didn't make it any easier, it just made it less hopeless. And the idea that I was going somewhere else—somewhere where the kids weren't all freakin' geniuses—made it easier for me to face the fact that I might fail.

And the fact that Oliver would love me even if I did—*that* made all the difference in the world.

So by the time Thanksgiving rolled around, I was excited.

Rex grew up in Seattle, so he was saving all his traveling time for Christmas. He said his moms were both climbing the walls to see him, and it had *still* taken me almost two months to figure out why he was okay with the gay thing and the bi thing. He said they weren't exactly excited about the "fuck everything that moves" thing, but still, I was highly aware I wasn't the brightest bulb in the socket.

I confessed this to Rex, and he'd laughed but looked troubled too. "What?"

He shook his head. "I'm just sorry we're not going to be roommates next semester, that's all."

Shock to me. "Are you kidding? This semester? I'm pretty sure you could have had a garden slug as a roommate, and he would have been more interesting than me."

Rex was sitting on his bed, watching me pack. His moms had sent him a homemade quilt when they'd realized Thanksgiving was probably right out, and it was there, in blue and brown, and it reminded me of sea and sand.

"You're funny," he said seriously. "And you're kind. And I've never seen someone try so hard to get things right. Don't sell yourself short, Rusty. I'm looking forward to the whole three weeks after Thanksgiving so I can take you out after finals. Do you realize you've never been to the beach? Or even downtown? Your entire impression of Stanford is the dorm room and the lecture halls. It's like flying to Paris and never seeing the Eiffel Tower."

I felt a sudden pang. He was right. This was my big college experience for the moment, and it was over.

I winked at him, though. "Well, yeah, that would suck. But not if you were flying to London right afterward, and you got to spend the evening having tea with the queen."

He laughed then and hugged me, and I had a worry about this larger-than-life, beautiful guy who fucked everything that moved because he *loved* everything in the world.

"I don't want to leave you here," I said. "Promise me you'll call on Thanksgiving, okay?"

He grinned. "I promise."

"And when you're lonely, call your moms and tell them they did a good job for me, okay? You turned out *really* well."

THE ONLY reason I didn't go eighty all the way home is that it was wall-to-wall Thanksgiving holiday traffic. I went thirty most places, and what was normally a three-hour drive on the outside was suddenly a five-hour drive, and I was almost crying with the itch between my shoulder blades pushing me to get home.

Oliver was on the other side of all these cars. He was waiting for me.

I made a pit stop, though, right after I pulled off on Iron Point Road. There were a bunch of outlet stores there, a nice bathroom, and a McDonald's, and I was *starving* beyond all reason, and I had to pee, and I felt mussed and like my breath smelled from all the coffee I'd been drinking to keep me sharp.

So I stopped to pee and brushed my teeth in the bathroom sink and combed my hair and splashed some water on my face when I was done. I tentatively looked in the mirror, remembering that a year ago I'd looked dumb and happy. And healthier. I mean, I'd been a *jock*—girls had wanted me, that was for damned sure!

Now? In the washed-out lights of the gas station, with pale skin and bags under my eyes and my arms thinner and a little blue because I'd come in without a sweater and it was *cold* in the foothills?

I looked… faded. Would Oliver want me faded? Had he fallen in love with the jock? Silly, right? Because I'd looked *way* worse after he'd kicked me out of bed that day—I'd avoided mirrors for the last three weeks. But still, the idea took some of the hurry out of me when I got back to the car, and I drove up the highway with a little more patience for the now-thinning traffic.

But I didn't turn around and go back, and after getting off at El Dorado Hills and taking the long series of winding turns that got me to our exclusive little suburb, I was relieved to see my house, white stucco peeking out through the old trees that had grown even taller since I was a kid.

Parked on the road at the start of our driveway, out of sight from the house itself, sat Oliver in his dad's truck. He was watching the road avidly, and even from a distance I could see his eyes widen and his face light up as I pulled into the mouth of our driveway.

I parked on the side, so someone could get by. The driveway itself was about half the length of a football field, and our front lawn was a big expanse of green in front of the two-story white house. If someone was watching for me, yeah, they'd see my car there—but I wasn't worried, really.

Seeing Oliver again—*touching* Oliver again—that was the only thing on my mind.

I threw open my door and tried to launch myself out of the car, but my seat belt brought me back with a jerk, and then I *felt* like a jerk, because, really, who does that? I unhooked my seat belt so quickly it snapped up *hard*, and the belt buckle caught my chin, and my elbow got tangled in it as I was trying to get out of the door and get out all at the same time, and….

I sat back in my seat and took a deep breath, then looked at Oliver sheepishly through the open door. He was trying manfully not to roll on the ground in laughter. I could tell. I held up one finger, took another deep breath, and exited the car with slow, methodical movements before I hurt myself. As soon as I shut my car door, I turned around and was assaulted by a full-court press of Oliver.

I wrapped my arms around his body and held him tight and steady, like you would a wriggling puppy, and he threw his arms around my neck and plastered himself to me, a whole new second skin. I burrowed my face in his neck and breathed him. He smelled like beans and rice and chili powder and, incongruously, turkey and gravy—which made me wonder what *his* family was eating for dinner tomorrow night. Underneath the food was the smell of his skin, and I breathed it deeper, rubbing the side of his neck with my nose until he made a little noise— not protest, really, but more of a wanting sigh. He lowered his head then, keeping his chin pointed up, and I bumped my nose and my lips along his jaw and up until I came to his chin, which I kissed delicately while looking into his eyes.

"I missed you," I said unnecessarily.

"I missed you too." His voice was soft, and his breath was on my face. All my nervousness melted into a warm, buttery need in my stomach. It was the most natural thing in the world to brush my lips against his, trace them with my tongue, taste. Chili spice, horchata, and Oliver, who tasted so good I started to like horchata. Mmm… taste again. Groan, open my mouth, feel his open against mine and take everything inside.

He threaded his fingers through my hair and let me take over, and I reached down and grabbed his tiny, bony ass in two hands. He gave a hard moan, and suddenly I was pushed back against the car as he hopped up and wrapped his legs around my hips.

Oh... oh... oh God, I'm home....

The kiss went on. The only sounds were the starlings under the black-gray sky and our ragged breathing as we pulled back and then melded mouths again. We were both wearing hoodies and jeans, and the cold was starting to seep through our clothes, but I didn't want to let go. Oliver would keep me warm. Oliver *was* keeping me warm, and I *almost* wished he'd let me put him down so I could shove my hands under his sweatshirt and stroke the heated silk of his back.

I'd just had this thought when I heard two things, one of them welcome, and the other?

"*Russell Calvin Baker!*"

"Jesus, Mom! I told you they were talking."

"You *knew* about this?"

Oliver dropped his feet down and turned, his back up against my chest, his head tucking right under my chin.

"Sorry, Nicki," he said, grimacing, and my sister ignored him and came running at me. Oliver dodged out of the way so I got to hold my sister, and for the first time since I'd arrived, I felt weepy. She was still here, still in this house. How could I have left her, defenseless and all alone?

"We were so worried," she said, and then she was literally jerked out of my arms.

"*Russell!*" Mom was wearing a twinset, this one Christmas red to match her cheeks. "We've been waiting for you—I had no idea you were.... *Oh my God!*"

I tried a smile and wiped self-consciously at my face. Oliver had a sparse mustache, and my mouth felt a little razor burned.

"Uhm, we're sort of in love," I said, with a half smile.

"You most certainly are not."

I squinted a little and looked at Oliver. "We are," I reassured him. "I don't know what she's talking about."

Oliver grabbed my hand and sent my mother a stony look. "I do," he said. "You can't be mean to him." His voice was edged hard, and my mother eyed him distastefully—but also like an equal.

"I have no idea what you're talking about," she said, eyes narrowed. "Just because he chose to—"

"There is no choice," Oliver snapped. "If it wasn't with me, it would have been with another boy. If it had never been another boy, it would have been a gun to the temple. There is no choice. I didn't choose to have brown hair and brown eyes, and I didn't choose to be gay. But I *did* choose Rusty. And he chose me."

Wasn't he awesome? Looking at him, it was like the whole world stopped, and it was Oliver telling my mother all the stuff my guidance counselor and I had talked about, and he hadn't even been there.

My mother rolled her eyes. "That's very sweet, but I think that, in the end, Rusty will choose the things his family can give him over anything *you* have to offer."

I thought about it. "Well," I said, trying to figure out what she was saying, "I'd keep Nicole—but really, I think that's all."

Nicole gave a little squeal and clapped, and it looked so childish my brain slipped, and she was six again, and Estrella was taking us to the zoo.

"Really, Russell? Your sister? What about your education? Your future? The clothes you seem to love, and that car?" I looked behind me at the brown Toyota Prius, which I really did sort of love, because I didn't ever have to worry about it starting.

"I thought the car was a birthday present?"

"We're still making payments. We can stop doing that." She looked really smug, her arms crossed, her eyebrows arching, and it suddenly occurred to me what she was really offering me.

"So you're saying that if I want to live here and have you guys pay for school and everything, I *can't* have Oliver?"

She nodded like she knew what I was going to choose.

"And if I choose Oliver, I never have to go back to Stanford?"

Next to me I heard Oliver snicker, and my mother's expression shifted, like there was something she hadn't thought of.

I thought of all the work I'd done, and of the solid C+ average I'd been earning, which, although it wasn't going to set the world on fire, was something I'd been proud of.

"That's a shame," I muttered. "I was *finally* getting the hang of that place."

Oliver patted my hand, and I looked up to see him smiling kindly but also like he could hardly contain his happy dance.

"You'll do better in junior college," Oliver said, and I nodded before turning to my mother.

"Wow, Mom, that's really sort of a no-brainer. Which way did you think I was going to choose?"

"Rusty, don't be stupid."

I wasn't sure what noise was coming out of my mouth then; it was almost a laugh, but it was too shocked, and almost a sob, but too sane.

"Stupid…." Oh my God. Of all things. "Stupid?"

Oliver's arm was tight around my waist. "Rusty, don't."

"Did you hear that? She wants me not to be stupid?" In that word I went from sort of removed from this whole idea to right there *in* the moment.

"Russell?" She sounded uncertain. Oh thank God—uncertainty. It would be nice to think she wasn't doing all this *knowing* it was the right thing.

"You know what's stupid?" I asked, my voice pitching hysterically. "I mean, *really* stupid? I actually thought you'd be happy to see me. *That's* what's stupid." I looked at Nicole, with her round face and her freckled nose and her sober brown eyes. "I don't want to leave you here," I said, and my eyes were hot and my face was hot, and she kissed my cheek and wiped my face with her thumbs.

"Don't worry. I won't be here for long. Keep texting, okay?" She stepped out of my arms, and I nodded, thinking I was going to have to buy another phone, one of my own, and my own data plan and—

"Rusty, how are you going to live? Your checking account is in our name."

Oh God. Every argument she was making to keep me here just made me glad I never had to set foot through the door again.

"But my savings isn't," I said, swallowing. "And I've got birthday money and Christmas money and four months working at a decent wage." I guess I wasn't stupid after all, if I could claim that. I opened the back seat of the car and started pulling out my clothes, and my brain, which had seemed to be a big, unholy void at Stanford, was suddenly moving the nail bucket and figuring out where it went and then jumping to the nail gun and how to use it as a craft.

"Here, Oliver, can we put this in your car? I'll find a hotel."

"Bullshit," he said, taking the stuff from me. "You'll come sleep on our couch. My dad loves you. You'll hurt his feelings if you don't."

I smiled at him, and even though his face was all blurry, I could still see his supernova grin back.

"I told you, man. Your dad is full-on superheavyweight awesome."
I popped the trunk and grabbed my winter coat and the scarf and gloves
I kept in there, but I left the blankets that smelled like motor oil.

My mother was watching us the whole time, and I didn't know
what to say to her. I saw my dad walking out of the house, probably
wondering what was keeping us, and I decided I wasn't going to do that
shit, not right now.

"I'm sorry you couldn't love me," I said simply. "I'm *really* sorry
you couldn't love Oliver. He saved my life when I was gone, but you
probably don't give a shit about that either, so I'll see you around."

"I'll pack your stuff for you," Nicole said, and Mother glared at
her, probably because she was speaking for herself.

"The hell you will, Nicole—"

"Oh, please. Stop me, go ahead. I dare you. I'll tell the whole world
you were too cheap to let Rusty have his own clothes." Nicole's voice
broke, but she waved us away. Dad was getting closer, and I grimaced.

"When I get settled, you can come visit," I promised Nicole, and
she beamed.

"Happy Thanksgiving, big brother. I'm thankful you're gonna
be okay."

I hopped up into the cab of Oliver's dad's big half-ton company
truck and wondered where she got that idea. I kept wiping my cheeks
with my sleeve for a really long time, and even when I stopped having
to do that, Oliver was kind enough not to say anything for a while after
that. I felt as clean and as cold and as empty as the wind in the gray sky,
and I didn't know if the shivers were ever going to stop.

HIS FATHER'S house looked familiar and alien at once. It was November,
so most of the flowers were dormant, but in the foothills everything was
mostly green too. Oliver pulled the car into the driveway on the side of
the house, which is somewhere I'd never been.

It was pleasant. The driveway was weeded, and the jasmine and
stuff was still grown over the fence. It seemed like someplace exotic, like
England or Ireland, which, considering the fact that Europe was where
my people came from and not Oliver's, was probably a little funny.

Of course, I'd have to think something a whole lot funnier than that
before I laughed.

"Well, *that* sucked," I said as Oliver and I both grabbed some of my luggage. My mom was right about my clothes. I *did* like the high-end mall stuff, but thinking about it? I could probably live in Walmart jeans without too much trouble. Besides—I had a *whole* lot of clothes at home and back at campus and—

"Shit," I muttered. "I'm going to need to drive back to Stanford and drop out officially."

Oliver made a noise, sort of a hurt one. "After all the work you did… I mean, Rusty, you only have three weeks."

I hefted my duffel over my shoulder and my suitcase in one hand, and Oliver struggled with my winter coat. It could get cold enough to snow up here in the foothills—not often, but sometimes. The coat was big, my size, and slippery, and Oliver was fighting it like a third grader fighting a giant octopus.

"My parents won't let me stay," I said with certainty. I knew them. If my dad had found a way to get me in, he'd find a way to get me out. "I need to find a place to live." Practicality asserted itself, because the Bay Area was a money suck. "And I can't afford to live down there. Besides, I'm signed up for classes up *here*, and so are you. So I need to go down and drop out and get the rest of my stuff. I'll… you know. Saturday. Saturday. And then I'll apartment-hunt on Sunday, and then I'll—"

"Rusty?"

"Yeah?"

Oliver reached behind the little gate, opened the latch, and took us through a fence made of jasmine into the backyard.

"First you're going to have Thanksgiving with us, okay? You've got a day and a half not to think about it. Please… just… just take that time, would you?"

I looked at him, still battling with my slippery white coat, and found I could manage a small smile. All I'd wanted for the last three months was to see Oliver. Well, I was going to see Oliver, and damn it, that would be time well spent.

"Yeah," I said, some of the tightness easing from my face and chest. "You betcha."

Oliver started to chuckle as we entered the house. "You betcha? What is this, 1959?"

I laughed a little and then let him open the side door to take me into his house.

Oliver told me once that he and his dad lived in a two-bedroom house. There was a den at the end of the hall, and they each had a bathroom, but basically, compared to my folks' house, it was tiny, with a low ceiling from the sixties, and even though the walls were a bright, sparkly white, all the light seemed yellow and dusty, because the shadows were there to eat it.

But that was okay, because really, there was no dust, not even on the dark wood floors, and the couches were done in a chocolate-brown corduroy—with the small dogs nestled in the pillows for color, I guess—and the floor rugs were navy blue.

It was pretty, in a boy way. Pretty and warm. I looked at the couch, and the four little dogs who eyed me from the throw pillows, and thought they had the right idea.

"I think you've scared them," Oliver said, surprised. "They're usually happier to—"

And brother, did *that* give them a hot wire up the ass. *Blam!* They were jumping up and down like suction-cup toys with springs. Oliver was suddenly besieged by tiny dogs—I thought a couple of them were Chihuahuas, but one of them was a Pomeranian, and I don't know *what* the tiny one with the ferocious underbite was. But boy, did they all love Oliver.

I laughed a little and dropped my bags behind the couch, because it was out of the way, and then came and took the oversized jacket out of his arms.

There was a peg next to the entryway, and I hung the jacket up there, then went to greet the dogs with Oliver. What can I say? I'd never had pets of any kind—I used to pet random dogs when I walked down the street, which had driven Estrella and my mother crazy.

I squatted down and joined in the insanity, petting little furry bodies when they'd let me. After a moment Oliver straightened up, and they all stayed within jumping distance. Oliver put his hand on my shoulder and bent down to murmur in my ear.

"Here, you distract them. I'll go talk to my dad. When they start to settle down, come into the kitchen. You can help with the tamales."

I nodded, but I didn't look up. These guys, they were happy to see me, and they held no complications. Not even Oliver could promise me that, and for a minute I needed them so badly, I sat down, right there in the entryway, and sucked up all the yapping, snuffly, licking, whining, toenail-clacking love they'd give me. I lost myself in it, and by the time Oliver's dad came out from around the corner, I was sitting cross-legged, my back to the wall, surrounded by sleeping furry bodies.

I almost closed my eyes and joined them.

"Rusty, he-ey!"

I widened my eyes and shook myself awake, then smiled at Mr. Campbell, who was smiling so much I knew Oliver had told him not to say anything. Oh God. This was going to be awkward.

"Hey, Mr. Campbell. Is it okay if I crash on your couch for the night?"

His smile relaxed a little, and I felt good. I'd given him a way to talk about it without saying too much. "Yeah, Rusty. Stay as long as you want." He held out a hand, and I moved some of the furry bodies (the black Pomeranian in particular didn't want to leave) so I could let him haul me to my feet.

"Thanks," I said, trying for a casual smile. "I'll get my stuff from the dorms over the weekend, and I should be out of your hair by next week."

I found myself engulfed in a tackle hug from the squat, fireplug-shaped man who looked like he could arm wrestle a bull and tap dance on its furious head.

"You will stay," he said quietly in my ear, "as long as you need." He pulled back and gave me a critical once-over. "And while you're here, you will eat. How can you work for me when you're so skinny? No. You have a week before my next job starts. We'll get you a place to stay, get you fattened up—you will work for me, and it will be good."

Oh God. My knees almost buckled. I had a *job*, and a place to stay, and someone besides Oliver and my sister and the dogs who was happy I was alive.

I managed a smile and tried not to cry anymore.

"Thank you," I said, and my throat was so swollen and raw the words hurt. "Thank you. I won't let you down, Mr. Campbell, I promise."

Oliver's dad waved his hand and made a dismissive noise. "Let me down, don't let me down. It doesn't matter. You try so hard, Rusty. You'll be fine. Now come on in, the tamales are almost out of the steamer, and we're wrapping them. Oliver was going to bring a batch to the homeless shelter later tonight, but there is *more* than enough for us to eat now."

So I went in and washed my hands and very carefully wrapped the tamales, which were already wrapped in corn husks and saturated in spicy tomato sauce, in tinfoil. Sometimes Estrella had brought homemade tamales and served them to Nicole and me when we were hungry after school. It was funny. Nicole and I were crazy about them, we *loved* them, talked sweet to her to get them, hell, even cleaned our rooms for them, but never, not once, had Estrella served them to my parents.

After spending an hour listening to Oliver and his dad lapse from English to Spanish and back to English again while I helped wrap tamales and pack them in a foil-lined box, I started to figure out why. Man, all I did was *wrap* them—I hadn't even prepared the cornmeal or the meat inside or wrapped all that in the cornmeal and corn husks—and it was more time than I'd spent on food in my life. You gave that sort of thing to friends or you served them to family or you offered them as a gift.

They were sort of a labor of love.

I got lost in the rhythm of the work, like a dance without music, and by the time we were done, I felt less hollow and achy. Then Oliver told me to wash up and set the table—for seven.

I was surprised, but I did it anyway—wasn't my house, right?

Just when I was done setting the table, the door opened, and I was under siege.

A Different Place to Swim

I WASN'T sure what to expect when Oliver's family walked in.

First there was Gloria, and when he'd talked about his Aunt Gloria, I'd always assumed she was one of those artsy people with the long tie-dyed skirts and the flowing coarse black hair. Maybe it was the health food thing, but whatever it was, I did *not* expect her to breeze in wearing a pair of tan slacks and a bright green Ann Taylor twinset, a lot like the one my mother was wearing when she kicked me out of the house. Even her hair was subdued, pulled back into a clip at the nape of her neck with a fringe of bangs across her forehead.

But unlike my mother in her tasteful pearls, Gloria was wearing big chunky gold jewelry with those bright black stones in it, which was good, because pearls were all about quiet, and quiet was *not* Oliver's Aunt Gloria.

Boy, was she a knockout. I mean, seriously, she might have been Oliver's aunt, but back in my girl days, I would have flirted with her for sport. She was pretty. She had Oliver's oval face and dark brown eyes and even the little inquisitive thing at the arch of his eyebrows, but mostly it was her smile.

"Rusty, I've heard so much about you!" Like Mr. Campbell, she had a little lilt in her voice, and it made it easier for me to smile shyly and try not to back into the corner of the kitchen, where I was finishing with the silverware on the table.

"All of it good," Oliver said quickly, and I shrugged.

"Then she couldn't have heard much. But it's good to meet you, Ms. Campbell—"

"Call me Gloria," she said with a warm smile, and I could feel my ears turning pink.

"Nice to meet you, Gloria." She was also wearing a long parka, and all the coat hooks were behind me, in the dark living room full of now-sleeping dogs. "Would you like me to take your coat?"

Her face lit up like a Christmas tree. "Oh my word!" She whirled and slid the coat off, and I dropped the spoons on the table and caught it.

"Oliver, look at him. Polite as anything. Why haven't you brought him by before?"

Oliver was standing in the glare of the kitchen lights, and his face was already flushed from cooking, but I could swear he turned a little pinker.

"His house is really nice, Aunt Gloria," he said, darting a quick glance at me. "Besides, he has a *pool*."

Suddenly I was back at this summer, where I invited Oliver over all the time, and he hadn't invited me over once. Had he been *embarrassed* of me? Well, why not? I mean, I'm the loser who couldn't hack it at Stanford, I'm the idiot who thought my friends were okay when they were really asswipes, and I was obviously defective in *some* way or my parents might have been able to take the gay thing in stride, right?

"Yeah," I said into the sudden silence. "Well, you shoulda known— dogs trump pool any day."

I turned then and moved into the living room to hang up Gloria's coat. I was so busy trying to swallow back my disappointment that I hardly heard Oliver excusing himself from the kitchen. I stood at the side entryway for a few minutes, wondering about that cab and that hotel room, when Oliver showed up at my side.

"I was embarrassed," he said quietly, and I couldn't meet his eyes. "About me?"

He snorted. "No! C'mon, Rusty—think! My house is small, my people are brown. You keep saying it, Rusty, but I'm not going to believe you're that dumb."

I looked at him, feeling naked. "You shoulda known," I muttered. I was thinking of the way looking at Oliver had become my whole world that summer. "You shoulda known that the dogs trumped the pool."

Oliver looked stricken and nodded, and I realized I wasn't being rational.

"I'm sorry. I'm... I'm sort of all over the place. You know, maybe I should, I don't know, take a cab, go hide out in your bedroom, something. I'm not going to be really, you know, stellar company tonight, righ—?"

I was interrupted as the side door by us flew open and three men, my height but broader, came barreling through.

Oliver rolled his eyes and laughed and backed up against me, mashing me against the wall. My brain shorted out, and all my insecurities died a quick and painless death.

He felt so good. It was like that touch, the rough feel of his slender body through his clothes, leaning against me through mine, was all I needed. I wanted to shiver, collapse around him, howl, and hold him to my body. *God*, did I need to have him in my arms. At the moment, though, the giant men were all yelling in Spanish and hollering at Oliver's dad, and it didn't seem to be the moment. I mean, I knew that, but I also knew that if I had much more time with Oliver in my arms like this, I might succeed in crawling through the back of the wall with my butt muscles alone in an effort to grab him and escape.

I gave Oliver a little shove, and suddenly he was being roughly embraced by the oldest of the men and shaken within an inch of his life.

"Hey, Ollie! You grew at least an inch, right? Yeah, you grew—"

"It's only been a month, Uncle Manny. Pretty sure I haven't grown in a month."

"Joey! Sal! Get over here! What do you think, you think Ollie's grown?"

Oliver grimaced up at the two other young men, both of whom looked only a little older than us.

"Hey, Joey. Hey, Sal. I haven't grown. Uncle Manny's a little high. You gotta watch and make sure he doesn't drink too much coffee on his way up the hill."

"It's only from Sacto, Oliver," Joey said, rolling his eyes. He was the tallest of the three men and the widest, with a wide-cheekboned, handsome face and a square hairline to match his square chin.

I don't know if Sal was younger, but he was certainly littler, and he was willing to buy into the lie. "Yeah, man, I swear it took Dad, like, sixty-four ounces of java to make it this time. He's got to lay off the late-night chat sessions if he wants to live to be old." Sal was shorter and skinnier, a lot like Oliver, and his narrow face was marred by acne scars, but he had the sort of smile that made you not think about that. Both boys had the big, brown eyes of Oliver's family, with the really thick lashes. I bet they got away with *murder* in school.

Manny turned to his sons and rolled his eyes. "Late-night chat sessions, right? I'm doing bills to keep you two in schoolbooks for the next three years. You'd think with twins, you'd want to study the same thing and save us some money, right?"

"Twins?" I squeaked, and Joey caught sight of me and shook his head sourly.

"Yeah. God was fuckin' laughing *that* day, wasn't he?"

"Joseph!" Manny snapped, and Joey grimaced.

"Sorry, Dad!" he sang as Manny moved to the kitchen. Then he rolled his eyes at Oliver and me and seemed to remember himself. He extended a hand. "Joey Campbell—we're Oliver's cousins."

I had to come out of the corner of the room to shake his hand and then Sal's after it. "Rusty Baker. A, er, friend of Oliver's—"

"My boyfriend," Oliver said smugly, and both boys widened their eyes and nodded appreciatively.

"Nice, Ollie," Sal chirped. "You finally snagged him! That's awesome."

I went to back up again, and Oliver reached behind his back and grabbed my hand. "He was ready to be snagged," Oliver conceded, "but he's shy. No freaking him out, okay?"

"Sorry," Sal said sincerely. "We just heard a lot about you this last year. We were sort of hoping you'd show up someday."

Joey eyed me up and down. "Yeah, but you're going to have to get over this whole shy thing," he said, apparently still sitting on the fence. "You won't last long here."

"Boys," Manny called from the kitchen, "take off your coats and come wash up!" And hallelujah, I was saved. They turned around toward the bathroom—which, by the way, I had never seen—and I went to follow them, only to be stopped by Oliver.

"You okay?"

I smiled brightly. "Never better. Let's eat."

He closed his eyes and shook his head and followed me into the kitchen. At least I wasn't trying to run anymore, right?

Dinner started with grace, which I was unused to, but it was nice, I guess. And then, after a brief no-nonsense sort of prayer from Oliver's dad, chaos erupted. Everybody was talking to everybody else, and tamales were being passed, and people were up in each other's business.

It was terrifying.

"So, Manny, where's Silvia tonight?" Gloria asked, and the two brothers groaned.

"No, no, no—don't summon her, she might appear."

Manny glared at his sons. "She flew down to San Diego to be with her family—"

"Yeah, she found out we were having dinner up here tomorrow and took off for the hills, man. Uptight, skinny bitch—"

"*Joey.*"

Joey glared at his father. "Dad, you're better than she is. Don't let her tell you different. Mom says so too. Says she's a money-grabbing—"

Mr. Campbell laughed. "Joey, you ever think maybe your mother's not the most... I don't know, *objective* person to talk about your father's love life?"

Sal interrupted earnestly. "Naw, Mom's totally happy with Jimmy the Lawyer. He's cool. His house has a pool, she doesn't have to work so much, gets to spend time with the new baby. It's okay. She's really trying to be a friend."

Manny looked uncomfortable. "Yeah, well, she's doing her best. But, well, yeah. I think Silvia and I, we're probably not really suited for each other."

"Yeah," Joey muttered. "For one thing, she voted Republican. I can't *stand* that shit."

"Hey hey hey!" Mr. Campbell put his foot down. "No politics at the table. That's the new rule I just made up right here."

Joey looked at his plate, embarrassed like a little kid. "Yeah, Uncle Arturo. That's fair."

"You dating anyone, Gloria?" Manny asked, and his son shot him a grateful look.

Gloria shrugged an elegant shoulder. "Men. They all want in your pants, but nobody wants to hold hands, you know?"

"Yeah," Joey said, nodding. "You hold out for someone nice, Aunt Glo. You're worth it."

"Sal, that girl you were seeing?" Gloria said, snagging some *sopas* and salsa from the lazy Susan in the center of the table. "She ever come home and meet your *papi*?"

Sal shook his head and looked embarrassed. "Nah, Aunt Gloria, she's not that sort of girl."

Manny grunted. "She's got money, and she's Jewish, and he's all up in his head. Sort of like Ollie was about this one, right?"

My face heated, and I glared at Oliver, who looked apologetically back. "You're sort of out of my league," he muttered to me, and I rolled my eyes.

"Yeah, if we're playing football," I said back, and Oliver laughed, holding his hand over his mouth because he wasn't quite done swallowing a bite of tamale, and looked at me with dancing eyes. He got a hold of himself, swallowed, and shook his head.

"Well, thank God we're not playing football, Rusty. I think we'll do okay without it."

And suddenly all the attention was on me, and I wanted to be one of the dogs. *They* got to sleep on the couch after being unconditionally loved. I was getting looked at by this totally nice family that didn't seem to have any problem prying into people's personal lives. I took a quick bite of tamale to make it clear I was done with *my* part of the conversation and waited for someone else to talk.

Oliver's Aunt Gloria took the gambit, and I sort of wished I'd said something instead. "That reminds me," Gloria said, smiling warmly. "It was nice of your family to let you come have dinner with us tonight. I'm sure they miss you after being away for so long."

Mr. Campbell, Oliver, and I all froze. I still had tamale in my mouth, and I tried helplessly to swallow it. Without a word Oliver passed me my glass of milk, and I was still washing stuff down when Mr. Campbell spoke up for me.

"Rusty is going to be staying here for a little while," he said quietly.

I wiped my mouth and said, "Only until I can find an apartment. I still have my savings from the summer. And a car. I need a car."

Mr. Campbell grimaced, and Manny said, "Hey, I can get you a car!" at about the time Gloria said, "I'll check my listings. I can find you a nice apartment, really close." And then both of them together, "Don't worry, Rusty. We'll set you up."

I smiled a little, completely in the dark, until Oliver laughed.

"You did things right, baby. Gloria's a real estate agent and Manny owns a car lot. If you were gonna get thrown out of the house, this was the place to have dinner."

I opened my mouth a little and shut it, and opened it and shut it, and turned about seven different colors. "Thank you," I squeaked at last. "That's nice of you. I'll take you up on that." I had no plans whatsoever of hitting up Oliver's relatives because they were being nice to me, and I hoped then that someone would move on, someone would save me from this conversation, keep it out of the places I least wanted it to go.

Joey (who seemed the type) just didn't want to drop it.

"Man, that's messed up. What'd you do to get kicked out? Flunk out of school?"

"No! I was passing," I said, because damn if I wasn't still proud of that.

"Then what? C'mon, bro, 'fess up. What sort of heinosity do you have to commit to get kicked out of the house the night before Thanksgiving?"

"I was kissing Oliver," I snapped back, annoyed. "It wasn't a hardship."

The entire table drew in the same gasp of air. I'm surprised they didn't keel over from oxygen deprivation. The silence was painful, and I chewed doggedly at my tamale and ignored Oliver, next to me, hiding his eyes behind his hand.

"Was it a good kiss?" Gloria surprised me by asking. I looked up and saw her again, just like she'd been when she walked in: beautiful, elegant, and kind.

I swallowed. "The best ever," I told her sincerely. "Totally worth it. Wouldn't change a thing."

"Good answer," Sal said, and I looked at him gratefully. He smiled encouragingly and poured me another glass of milk, because mine was apparently empty, and then he turned to his brother. "Heinosity? Hein*osity*? Who taught you English, time-traveling surfers from 1989?"

Joey shrugged, unimpressed. "Okay, brainiac, what word would *you* use?"

"Abomination," Sal said, looking smug. "But I wouldn't use it, because it was only a kiss."

Joey nodded, shoving another big bite of tamale in his mouth, which he talked through. "Yeah, man. That's messed up. There's nothing heinous about a kiss." He swallowed. "But abomination—man, *that* word has got to go. It makes me think of a big white hairy thing, and that thing is *not* sitting at our table."

Oliver looked at me and winked. "No, I'm pretty sure Rusty waxes."

His cousins busted up into laughter, and the adults all acted shocked, and I glared at him, not really mad, but really, really wanting to tell him that I didn't need to wax. My chest was pretty hairless on its own.

I remembered all the times he'd seen me half-naked by the swimming pool and realized that he'd liked what he'd seen. I relaxed then, laughing with the family and eating my dinner, and the conversation moved on to other things.

I helped with the dishes because Estrella had taught me right, and Oliver dished up pudding and whipped cream for dessert. The twins were in the living room, tearing it up with the dogs, and the adults were in the kitchen, talking. Oliver gave everyone their little bowl before grabbing my sleeve and dragging me around through the back way from the kitchen, down the hallway, and to his room.

"We'll see these jokers tomorrow," he said quietly, nodding to the ferocious amount of noise coming from the other room. "I thought you might want to come in here and decompress."

I nodded and followed him meekly, shoveling pudding in my mouth. He must have given me, like, three cups of it, and I didn't want to protest that pudding had never been my thing.

His bedroom was small and eclectic. He had a raw-sanded-wood twin-sized bed with a brightly woven wool blanket on top of a *Star Wars* comforter, and an IKEA desk made out of black metal and Formica. He had posters on his wall of *The Nightmare Before Christmas*, *Princess Mononoke*, and *Bleach*, and an art print by the guy without an ear that featured a vast starry sky, with stars bigger than the sun and darkness that didn't seem so dark.

He hopped down on his bed and sat cross-legged, then patted the space next to him for me to sit. I did, but I backed up against the wall, kicked off my shoes, and propped up one knee so I could lean my arm on it and eat.

His grin was quick and brilliant, and for a minute neither of us said anything. We just sat there and ate pudding.

"You should take them up on it," he said quietly, and I licked my spoon and felt some of the day plop on my shoulders like wet snow.

"Take who up on what?"

"Manny can get you a good car for cheap. Gloria can find you a decent apartment for cheap too. You should let them help you. They sort of keep an eye out for me and my dad since my mom died. It'll make them feel like they can help."

I nodded. "When'd your mom die?" I asked, thinking. I couldn't remember him ever talking about it before, but suddenly it seemed really important.

"When I was about eight. Cancer. My uncle Manny, he got his divorce about then. He kept telling *Papi* to date, but my dad never did." Oliver shrugged. "I'm not sure, you know? Is he waiting for me to move out, or waiting until it stops hurting?"

I thought about a world without Oliver and how I never would have gotten out of that bed. "Until it stops hurting," I said quietly. My pudding was about two-thirds done, and I had to take a break. I set it in my lap and then leaned my head against the back wall. "I hope it does soon. He's a good guy."

"He is. Did you mean it?"

I opened one eye and tried to think. "That your dad's a good guy? Of course."

"No, did you mean it when you said it was the best kiss ever, and it was worth it?"

I opened both eyes now and saw that he was worried. Well, he'd been worried I wouldn't like his house too.

"Totally," I said, trying to cover up the hurt and the sadness and the uncertainty. This was something I was certain of. I'd stand by that.

Oliver's lips quirked up at the corners. "Would you like to do it again?"

I smiled at him. "Well, yeah, but someone made us bring pudding, and I don't want to get it all over the bed."

Oliver rolled his eyes. "Ha-ha, very funny, smartass. Besides, you're half-asleep. I'm not going to try to woo you with my best kiss only to find you asleep at the end."

I shook myself and moved the pudding from my lap to the little IKEA computer desk and tried to look awake and alert. "Not asleep," I said seriously. "I defy sleep. I'll—"

Mr. Campbell's voice echoed down the hall. "Oliver, your cousins are ready to take stuff to the shelter."

My eyes must have widened or something, because Oliver laughed softly. "You're napping," he said quietly. "I'll wake you up when I get back."

"I'll come," I protested. "Seriously, I'll—" Yawn. "—come," I finished weakly. Well, shit. It had been something of a day.

He laughed and pushed me down, and I realized I'd be in here, in his room, in the quiet, and suddenly wanted nothing more out of my life. Oliver's stuff, Oliver's *smell*, Oliver's home, but I didn't have to talk to another person on the planet.

"You're a good person to offer." He pushed my head gently to the pillow and bent down to get the wool blanket folded at the bottom. He tucked me in like a baby bunny in one of those Peter Rabbit books and kissed my forehead. When he switched the light off, I spent all of a minute thinking that I wouldn't be able to sleep. I was out before I heard the voices fade from the living room.

SCHOOL

THE NEXT morning, I woke up to the sound of Oliver and his dad arguing over how long to cook a turkey.

"I'm saying it's too long!" Oliver snapped. "You don't understand how bad these things get!"

"And I'm saying give it time. Jesus, Oliver, you were always so patient as a kid, and you're going to blow it now?"

I rolled out of Oliver's bed partially clothed and yelled, "Fifteen minutes per pound!"

There was the pounding of feet down the hallway, and Oliver poked his head into the room. I was standing up, looking blearily around, wondering when I'd taken my jeans and sweater off in the night.

"What?" he said, eyes huge.

"That's how long you cook a turkey."

"Oookay." He looked *really* confused.

"Isn't that what you and your dad were arguing about?"

Oliver laughed a little. "Uhm, yeah. Sure. How about you come into the kitchen, and we'll give you some coffee, and we'll do the math."

I perked up a little. "You have coffee? Wait. Let me put on my pants."

Oliver snorted and went through his drawers. He came out with some sweats that looked way too big for him. "Here, they were my dad's. They'll be short, but they'll cover your ass."

I felt a little better after some coffee and oatmeal. It was the same kind in a package that I ate at home and in my dorm, and for some reason that was reassuring. As I was sitting there, polishing off my bowl, I took a deep breath and smelled not just turkey, but everything else. The kitchen had two stoves, and both of them were on, and there were pies on the counter. I squinted at the clock and saw that it was after ten and felt really bad.

"Jeez, guys. I'm so sorry. You've been up doing all this stuff, and I've been sleeping. Lemme take a shower, and I can help. Is there anything left to do?"

Oliver's dad laughed and then ruffled his son's hair. "And you were worried. I told you, Oliver, he was *tired*. What'd you say, five hours in the car? Give it a rest. He's not fragile."

Oliver nodded a little and glanced guiltily at me. "Yeah. You're right, *Papi*. He's stronger than he looks."

I sniffed. "I can still bench-press *you*," I told him, trying to hold on to my dignity. Oliver grinned, and I felt warm to my toes.

"Someday," he said mildly, "I'd like to see you try it."

"*Oliver!*" his father snapped, looking uncomfortable. "Even *I* know what you're trying to say there."

"He's saying that I need to work out," I said with another yawn. "Or at least get to work. When did you want me onsite?" I stopped for a moment and remembered my planning from the night before. "I'm going to need to go back to Stanford and get my stuff and check out of school this weekend—"

"Go to Stanford Monday. The traffic won't be quite so bad," said Mr. Campbell.

I nodded. "Yeah," I said, "but I need to go apartment hunting—"

"You can do that Tuesday or Wednesday," he said confidently. "Gloria told me she was setting some time up for you in the middle of the week."

I shifted uncomfortably. "You know, Mr. Campbell, I feel bad taking all your hospitality as it is. I don't want to put your family out or any—"

He smacked me upside the head. "Oliver's right. You *are* stubborn. Not stupid, but *Dios*, like talking to a wall. Take the help, Rusty. But first, go shower."

"Yeah," Oliver said, and he put my cell phone down on the table. I guess I'd left it in my jeans the night before. "I charged it," he said, "but it was going off a lot when I got back last night." He looked up and nodded at his father, who quietly left the room. "It's your sister. I checked. She's been texting me too."

I swallowed. "What'd she say?" I asked. Somehow it had been so peaceful here, unanticipated help or not, that I'd been willing to forget about the mess I'd left behind me.

"She was glad to know you're staying here." Oliver's voice dropped. "She says your parents put all your clothes and stuff from your room in boxes out on the porch. They're going to have someone haul it away tomorrow."

I swallowed. "That sucks." But it also made it easier. It was easier to walk away from my home if they'd already shoved me out the front door. That's what I told myself, anyway. I mean, I could remember Mom and Dad and being happy, right? Before I hit high school, we used to take trips together, without Estrella—educational, museums and stuff—but they'd loved me, right? They must have. There must have been hugging and kissing and....

I swallowed. I was stalling.

I checked my messages, all from Nic.

God, that was intense. Let me know if you have a place to stay tonight. I'm worried.

Oliver says you fell asleep in his room. Nice move! Are you going to let him tuck you in?

Mom and Dad are packing up your things and putting them out on the porch. We're eating dinner at three tomorrow. I think you should show up with a backhoe and some sort of forklift, and embarrass the shit out of them.

Dad's including the car keys in the boxes of stuff. Don't take it, Rusty, I think it's a trap.

They're on the phone to the lawyers now. They're both PISSED that they can't stop your access to your savings account. Good job, Rusty! You've got over 10K in there. You're not a poor orphan on the street after all.

Morning, big brother. Just text me back when you get my messages, okay? I'm the invisible woman here, and I can't believe how fucked-up our parents are. They keep thinking you're going to get all not gay. Don't they read?

I laughed at the last one.

If it's not the financial pages, I don't think so.

Her text was immediate and startled me so bad I dropped my phone.

Go get another phone. They're cutting off your data plan right now. And get your clothes before tomorrow.

Will do. Love you. Chat later.

<3<3<3

I turned off the phone and sighed. Would I have said anything like that a year ago? I thought of the boy I was, the one who sat at the lunch table and let Oliver take shit because I thought my friends were including him. No, that Rusty would not have told his sister that he loved her.

Well, that Rusty had never gotten a kiss that turned him on, and that Rusty had never almost passed Stanford.

Maybe home was no big loss if the guy who would say I love you was the one on the end of the phone now, right?

Yeah, I talked all bad in my head, but it was a whole other thing when I was sitting in Oliver's truck, looking at the neatly stacked cardboard boxes *literally* on the porch and the front lawn.

"I'm half-afraid it's a trap," I said glumly. "We're going to go out there and start moving shit, and they're going to call the police."

Oliver snickered. "I'd love to see that happen. They call the police, and I call the press."

"Great. Tell my sister that." It was Thanksgiving. Who was open to service your phone account on Thanksgiving?

"Yeah." Oliver put the truck in park and let it idle for a second before texting Nic. His text alarm sounded almost immediately. She must have been sitting on the phone.

"It's from your mom," he said grimly. "She says to come get whatever trash you want."

God. "They can*not* mean that!" For kissing a boy?

"They don't," Oliver said quietly, patting my knee. Suddenly I was aware of him, *really* aware of him, right next to me, both of us in the truck with our Starbucks (because they *were* open on Thanksgiving) and both of us... I don't know. Warm. Human. Male. I grabbed his hand, and he looked at me quickly and squeezed my hand back.

"They don't," he reassured. "They're hurt. You chose me instead of them, and they don't understand."

"That sounds real fuckin' wise," I muttered, but I didn't let go of his hand. He turned in the seat and I looked at him, and he grasped my chin and pulled me down for a kiss.

This one bloomed—a few quick kisses here, a slip of the tongue there. I took his face between my two hands and deepened it, opening his mouth and only pulling back when he let out a whimper of need and clutched at my chest.

"Rusty?"

"What?"

"Have you given any thought to which one of us is going to top?"

"I don't even know what you mean by that," I said, and he chuckled. "What?"

Oliver held out his forefinger. "Top." Then he made an O out of his other forefinger and his thumb. "Bottom." And then he inserted his pointy finger into the O and pulled it out and put it back in and pulled it out and… I had an immediate hard-on that could punch through the side of the truck.

"I have no idea." My mouth was so dry I almost couldn't say it.

His grin got bigger, and his finger kept fucking. "Well, think about that while we're moving boxes." And with that he hopped out of the truck, and I joined him, trying not to walk funny.

It took us about ten minutes to throw the remains of what I'd thought of as a happy childhood into the back of the damned truck, and the entire time I was thinking of the very grown-up things Oliver and I were going to do to each other when we got alone and naked.

There ought to be some sort of award for that, right?

When we were done, I turned back to look at the house, thinking my parents might want to at *least* come out to talk to me again. There was nobody there. I looked some more, and then looked toward Nicole's room, which was on the end. She had her window open and her face pressed up against the screen.

I walked up to the window and smiled. "Hey."

"Hey."

"Happy Thanksgiving."

"Estrella brought me tamales for lunch. That way I don't have to sit out in the front room for dinner that long."

"Anyone else coming for dinner?"

"Mom's douchebag brother and his perfect kids."

I winced. Uncle Richard and his wife, Debbie, were every mean stereotype about snobby white people, ever, but then, I guess so were my parents. My cousins were both girls who wore a size two, and the oldest had already had her first nose job. She was sixteen. "Excellent. Tell me what sort of lie mom cooks up about me, okay?"

Nicole's laugh was really sort of unpleasant. "She can't. Douchebag already called to tell me that they were going to be exactly on time, and I told him Mom couldn't come to the phone right now because she was moving your stuff out because you were gay."

I don't think my laugh was any better, but it sure did feel good. "You're really sort of awesome, did you know that?"

She stuck her nose in the air. "Of course!"

I forget how deep my voice is, and how much it carries. There was a noise from behind Nicole, and we both jerked and looked back. It was my dad.

"Rusty?"

"I'm sorry, Dad—I got all my stuff. I was telling Nicole happy Thanksgiving—"

"Rusty, you don't have to go. You can stay—"

"Just not with Oliver, right?" Because his voice had risen up, and I knew there was a big as-long-as attached to the end.

"Rusty, you know how we feel—"

"No," I said, feeling absurd about having this conversation through a window screen. "No, I don't. You never talked about it. Bigotry is rude at the dinner table, isn't it?"

Dad took a step back. "That's a really harsh word." He sounded almost hurt.

"And 'we'll kick you out' isn't?"

I saw something in his eyes then, in the way his jaw went slack, like he'd never thought of that before. A thing, a fragile wall made of translucent glass, broke behind my eyes. Moms and dads are supposed to know better, right?

"You didn't think about that, did you?" I said quietly, and then I remembered that Oliver's dad was waiting for us.

I reached into my pocket and pulled out my phone, and then wrangled the SIM card out of it. "I need that," I said needlessly. "You can wrestle me for it if you want, but it's got addresses and shit, and I don't think you own that, right?"

Dad opened his mouth and closed it, and I set my phone down on Nicole's ledge and turned around.

"Rusty?" Oliver said as I got near the truck, "We can stay longer if you want."

I shook my head. "I don't want to be here today," I told him. "I... I just don't." I didn't cry on the way to Oliver's house this time, but I didn't say anything either.

I HELPED with dinner again, and this time it was bigger, with more stuff and more of Oliver's family. There was one more uncle—Jorge—and he had a little wife with giant eyes in a pale face and three tiny girls who took one step inside and went apeshit over the dogs.

It was loud.

I had this sort of double vision. At my house there would be candles and a beautiful place setting right out of Martha Stewart, and tiny plates of gourmet turkey with some sort of spice that would make me gag or break out or something like it had last year. I could imagine my parents having stilted dinner conversation, and my Uncle Richard and Aunt Deb talking about all the trips they'd taken and how their bulimic daughters had been asked to model or excelled in the science fair or grade-bombed the AP exams or something. Nicole would be casting poisonous glances at the girls (who were actually so reserved I didn't know if they were nice people or not—they could have been sainted virgins, but you get stupid prejudices against stick-skinny women who don't talk), and my parents would be talking about how I just needed to get my focus, get my grades up, play football a little harder, something, and I would be that perfect son they'd always needed.

And then, on top of that vision, there was Oliver's house. The girls kept slipping away to pet the dogs, and Joey and Sal would *not* stop swearing, and Jorge and Maria-Athena were messing in *everyone's* business. I think being the one happily married couple of all the siblings gave them a license to pry. I could see that. Mr. Campbell might have been the older brother, but Jorge was second, I think, and all of them sort of looked out for Mr. Campbell, while he tried to mother all the rest of them. It was cute.

What was also cute was the way they didn't ask me a damned thing. They talked about everything from birth control to how much debt they were in (Aunt Gloria was super well-off, Mr. Campbell was in the black, Jorge was above water, and Manny was upside down in everything), but they didn't ask me why I was eating dinner here instead of at my parents'.

I leaned over to Oliver at one point, when it was Maria-Athena's turn to go chase one of the girls, and I meant to ask him if his dad had gone all phone tree on everybody so they wouldn't ask any awkward questions, and what I ended up asking was why all the little girls were named Maria-Something. There was Maria-Rosa, Maria-Cristina, and Maria-Felicia, and when I asked Oliver why they didn't just call them Rosa, Cristina, and Felicia, he said it was because Maria-Athena was

Mexican and very traditionally Catholic about all the girls being named after Mary and all the boys being named after Joseph. I was sort of glad I already knew Oliver's family was from Venezuela, so I didn't totally embarrass myself by saying something stupid like, "Aren't you guys *all* Mexican?" Oliver had sat down once with a globe and showed me that all of South America was fucking huge and that the countries were way different, like, even more than California was from Georgia or New York, so I sort of got that some traditions were stronger in one place than they might be in another.

What I was thinking instead was really a little more local and a lot more personal.

"What?" Oliver asked, because I guess my thinking face isn't subtle.

I shook my head. "I'll ask you later."

"No, seriously, what? You can't offend us, Rusty. You've *heard* our dinner conversation."

Yeah. It was true. Joey had just burst out with the fact that you had to remember to change the rubber in your wallet at least once a year because those things expired. Gloria had responded with, "Yeah, and if you use one with spermicide, make sure you change that up every three months, or it starts to *itch*," so I knew this family actually talked about stuff, which was great.

But nobody liked to talk about this.

"C'mon, we'll think you don't like us if you don't say something totally embarrassing!"

I smiled stupidly at him. He was the same guy I'd known in high school, but it was like that big white smile and those giant brown eyes had grown on me, until now they were the only things I could see.

"How come your family's so nice? My family's not even Catholic, and they won't let me in the house. Your family's all up in your grill about attending mass, but you and me, we sit here and they just…."

I trailed off, mostly because there was a lump in my throat I couldn't get past. God, it was so very after-school-special, wasn't it? Everyone was okay. The black kid, the Hispanic kid, the Jewish kid, the gay kid—they were all okay. All the other kids had to do was accept them. I'd seen six *thousand* movies that told me not to pick on someone who was different, and I couldn't figure out how *I* got what those movies were saying, but my parents, who should have known better, did not get it at *all*.

"I don't know," Oliver said, but like he was thinking about the question seriously. "It's a good question, Rusty." He looked at his family, who had all fallen completely silent, even Maria-Athena and the tiniest little Maria, who was all wobbly and sad because she'd had to abandon the Pomeranian who was now her total love slave.

Maria-Athena shrugged. "We love you," she said. "We ignore the preaching people on television who say it's not good, so we can love you."

I smiled at her. "*That*," I said sincerely, "is some thinking I can get behind."

The table laughed, and suddenly Mr. Campbell wanted to know why his brother hadn't gotten his little girls a dog, or a cat, or *something* with fur, because they *obviously* were hungering for that. Jorge was right back in his face with how come the great building contractor with a license in landscaping couldn't trim his own damned jasmine as it died around him, or rip out the morning glories before they came back and regrew over each other and made that mess along the fence deeper. Mr. Campbell responded by saying he was working against a deadline, and he'd be working his crew Friday, Saturday, *and* Sunday just to get done when he'd promised, because the rains had come in and kicked their deadline's ass.

Right there and then, I knew what I was going to do that weekend.

Since all the men had cooked, the two women stayed in the kitchen to do dishes and gossip, and suddenly the widescreen TV was on and everybody was on the couch watching a football game. The little girls were sort of disconsolate, but I'd set up my computer in Oliver's room, and I'd seen *Coco* peeking out of the youngest one's diaper bag.

When Oliver came in to find me, I was backed up in the corner of his bed with four sleeping dogs and three sleeping princesses draped around me and the credits of the movie rolling on my laptop.

He leaned against the doorframe, crossed his arms, and grinned. "Niiiiice!"

I felt my face heat. "Who won the game?"

Oliver shrugged. "I neither know nor care. It was enough that Sal's team beat Joey's, and we could watch Joey pay up."

I laughed. I'd heard some of that. It had sounded epic. Oliver came in then and ejected the movie from my computer and put it back in the case.

"You didn't have to play babysitter, you know."

I shrugged. "You guys were really nice to let me sneak away." Oliver smiled, but he wasn't really buying.

"It's because of my grandparents," he said suddenly, and my eyes got really big.

"The fact that you let me sneak away?"

"No, the fact that everyone's really all nice and accepting and the gay doesn't bother them, and Aunt Gloria's sex life doesn't bother them, and Manny didn't catch shit because of the divorce. It's because of them."

Okay. Family tradition. "Were they just super nice people?"

Oliver shook his head flatly. "No. Not really. Grandma was from a family with a lot of money, and she married a poor American, and from what I can gather? She was one pissed-off, bitter old lady. She was miserable to everybody. Gloria told me once she had to see a shrink for five years before she could lose enough weight to fit behind a steering wheel in a car. She showed me pictures. It was scary. She had to get her stomach stapled. And it was all Grandma, bitching in her ear about how she was so fat, and she needed to eat less, while all she did, day and night, was cook for the family."

I grimaced. I'd watched Nicole catch shit for her weight, and I'd watched how she ate to feel better about it. "That sucks."

Oliver nodded. "Yeah, and Grandpa was an asshole and talked down to women and shit. It was ugly. They both died early—car wreck—and the whole family, they weren't that broken up about it. My dad never talks about them, and Jorge, Manny, Gloria, they act like Dad raised them."

I smiled then. "Your dad is really nice."

Oliver nodded. "Yeah, he is. So anyway, my grandparents weren't, and my dad, he sort of... I don't know. Caught the niceness bug and decided to infect everyone else. And everyone else—they're just so grateful he's not Grandpa, they try to live as far away from all that as they can. Things like Manny's divorce and Gloria's sex life and Oliver is gay are things the family has decided not to pick on. I don't know if they had a sit-down and talked about it, or if they read each other's minds, or maybe they listen to my dad and spread the word—but I told my *papi* when I was twelve, and not a soul in this family has been shitty to me since."

He shrugged. "It's sort of the perfect story, you know? I mean, he was sad, and I think he cried and maybe went and talked to God in the church for a while, but I didn't see any of that. I just saw my *papi*."

I shrugged back, still piled with little girls and little dogs. "Since I'm sort of getting him by proxy, I'm not going to complain."

Oliver came to sit down. He had to pick up one cousin to lay her down at the foot of the bed with his blanket and shoo two dogs to the side, but eventually he managed to be sitting right next to me. I wrapped an arm around his shoulder, and we leaned back against the wall.

"I wonder," I said, feeling sort of empty and clean inside.

"Wonder what?"

"What it would have taken for me to know if I hadn't known you."

Oliver snuggled. "You would have known. One day you would have figured that you weren't watching porn for the girls, you know?"

I thought about it, thought about the last girl I'd been with—the one *before* "no dick before dinner." She'd been nice, with roundness in her arms and her shoulders and her breasts. Neither of us had been virgins, and we'd had a slow, easy time having sex in her room. But she'd moved to another school, and I'd been a little relieved. It was like I didn't have to perform an obligation anymore. What had it been that made that unpleasant? I tried to remember her hand on my skin, my arm, my stomach, my dick....

And felt nothing.

And then, so very clearly, I could picture Oliver's slender hand right on my—

I grunted and shifted on the bed, trying not to disturb dogs and cousins.

"You're right," I said tensely, his weight against my shoulder suddenly excruciating, too intense, painful with all the blood in my nerve endings there. I swallowed and let the wave of *must have now* wash over me, suddenly sweating with the will to *not* pop a boner, not here in this very inappropriate time and place. "I would have noticed."

Oliver looked at my face, frowned, and then looked down along my body.

And then he laughed, low and evil. "Oh thank God. I was starting to wonder if I still did that to you."

"Didn't go away." My voice was high and squeaky, and he chuckled again, patting my arm.

"Good," he said smugly. "Hold that thought." And then he looked around and grimaced. "But, uhm, you know. Maybe not literally."

I laughed in spite of myself. "That's *so* not funny."

"It is."

"No, no, it's really not."

"You're not looking at it from where I'm sitting."

"You're sitting a foot to the right of me. I'm pretty sure I am."

His look at my face was quick and furious, and I smirked back. Yeah, I wasn't smart, but that didn't mean I couldn't play with words too.

He pounded my arm with laughter, and the little girl nearest him woke up a little. (Maria-Cristina, I think, and she was wearing a red velveteen dress with black shoes and was disappointed that she didn't get to bring her stuffed bunny to Thanksgiving, but her parents were afraid she'd lose it. Oh yeah. I was paying attention.)

"Is the movie over?" she asked, and Oliver and I said yeah, and then her sisters started to move.

Oliver pulled up Netflix on *his* computer then, and we started *The Princess and the Frog*. By the time Gloria and Maria-Athena came in with pumpkin-cream cheese pie and whipped cream, we were all sucked into the movie—and Oliver was halfway in my lap, leaning with his head on my shoulder. He straightened up when they came in, but only to reach out and start helping them hand pie to the girls and push the dogs away when they got too interested in what we were eating. The Pomeranian had made himself my special friend. He sat there with his little snout on my leg and gazed at me adoringly while I ate, and I admit, I did let him lick some whipped cream off my fingers. Those eyes—who can resist?

Oliver's aunts hung out in the doorway for a few minutes after we'd all started chowing on pie, and they were looking into the room with that "Aw, isn't this sweet?" look women get when they see men taking care of children. My mother had never gotten that look—but then, my father had never taken care of us either—but I'd seen it in parks where kids were playing, and it made me blush.

They laughed and pattered to each other in Spanish, and then a brief flash of color washed over Oliver's face too.

"What?" I asked, and he shook his head.

"Nothing." He said something quick to them in Spanish, and when Gloria answered with an impertinent syllable, he sat there with his mouth gaping open in outrage, while the women laughed and walked down the hallway. I tried, but he wouldn't tell me what they'd said, and I dropped it. We were really having too nice a time to argue.

Eventually everyone left, disappearing to the other parts of the foothills and the valley they came from, and it was Oliver, his dad, and me in the same house. We went into the living room, and Oliver pulled up a movie, and once again, I fell asleep in front of the television.

Only this time I had Oliver in my arms.

And this time he was still there when I woke up in the morning.

"RUSTY?"

I woke up stretched across the couch with Oliver's back pressed up against my front. We were both covered by one of those colorful wool blankets, and Oliver was breathing softly and drooling on the couch in front of him.

It took me a few minutes of blinking before I realized Oliver's dad was talking quietly to me from the side door. "Mr. Campbell?"

"Rusty, my guys are working today while the weather holds. It's supposed to rain later this weekend. Tell Oliver you guys can have all the leftovers you want, and you guys can have the truck to go get a new phone when it gets dark, okay?"

I nodded, hoping I could remember that, and Mr. Campbell reached over from the head of the couch and ruffled my hair. "Don't worry too much, Rusty. Go back to sleep. You can wake up and plan, but don't forget, Gloria has Tuesday set aside for you, and Manny has some cars to look at that day too. You have a good day."

He left quietly, and I was stuck trying to decide whether to go back to sleep or to wake Oliver up or....

Hello.

I stretched my back and arched my hips forward and realized I was hard inside my jeans, and Oliver's backside was right *there* pressed up against me.

Yeah, we were both wearing jeans, but... I arched forward again, the stroking against my cock through our clothes both subtle and really super arousing.

In my arms Oliver made a happy little sigh, and for a minute I felt sort of bad, like I was taking advantage of him, but he snuggled backward and rippled his hips against the bulge in my pants.

I grunted, wanting more. He'd fallen asleep in a long-sleeved knit shirt, and my hand was right about at his waist.

The feel of his bare skin against my palm was magic. It was soft, and so satiny, and so warm. I spread my hand out and ran it up from the waist of his pants to his chest, feeling the skin skate by, until I got to the… oh, hello again!

I pinched my thumb and forefinger together around the different flesh, to make sure it was what I thought it was, and he groaned.

I went completely still.

"Stop and I'll kill you," he muttered, so I pinched his nipple again and breathed out when he rocked his hips back.

I buried my nose in the nape of his neck and smelled Oliver, plus all the food we'd cooked the day before, and sweetness, like pie, and some sweat and…. Oh wow! I breathed him in again, and he arched against my hand. Then he grabbed it and slid it back down his stomach and underneath the waistband of his jeans.

I reached down on my own and started kneading him gently under his clothes, and he unbuttoned his fly.

Oh God. Oh wow. I had my *hand* in Oliver's *pants*. I groaned again and kicked my hips forward and then found the outline of his cock through his underwear. It was growing harder with every stupid grope, and I suddenly longed to see it, smell it, *taste* it, but Oliver was hard in my hand, and I was hard in my pants, and I didn't feel like doing a complete body reorganization that would totally break the moment.

I settled for slipping my hand under the elastic of his briefs and straightening his cock so I could stroke it in my fist. It felt… well, wonderful and ordinary at the same time, but I knew what to do with one of these things—had, in fact, been using my own fairly frequently since middle school.

He moaned loudly and thrashed a little, so I wrapped the arm that was pillowing his head up over his shoulders, holding him still.

"Don't move," I ordered. "I want to touch you."

"Yeah, okay." He was panting, and he craned his head around. I didn't have to be a genius to know he wanted to kiss me.

I did, morning breath and all, and I didn't care. I just wanted our mouths together, wanted our skin together, wanted us close, closer, and the delicious hard pressure in my cock to be stroked, squeezed, massaged. Oliver arched up into my fist, and I stroked him a little harder and a little faster.

He made a sound then, in my mouth—I can't even describe it. It was like the word *passion*, which I sort of recognized in writing, but I couldn't put a feeling to—that sound was *passion* and I was starting to feel it, starting to *burn* with it, and I was sweating underneath the blanket even though I wasn't doing anything, and I could feel the smooth skin of Oliver's cock in my fist and the silky coarse hairs at his groin against my palm, the cap of the glans between the join of my thumb and forefinger, and all that feeling radiated out from my hand into my entire body.

I *hungered*. I wrapped my outside leg around Oliver's thighs and rutted against his backside. Oliver thrust into my fist so fast I clutched him tighter because I was afraid he was going to fall off the couch. He reached up and took the hand pressed against his chest and clapped it to his mouth, then sucked my thumb in, *hard*, and then released it, crying out from deep in his gut while his whole body bucked and arched and his cock spit wetness on my hand.

It was hot, hot and satiny, and all I had to do was think about tasting it on my hand and the growing pressure, glowing white light behind my eyes, exploded, and I was clutching him so hard he probably couldn't breathe, and I was spasming, coming, scalding and sticky in my underwear, when I hadn't even unbuttoned my fly.

I moaned a little into his ear, in the hollow of his neck, my hips still making those impotent thrusts, because even though I'd come, I still wanted more. Without hooking up his jeans or anything, Oliver rolled off the couch, taking the blanket with him.

"Don't go—"

His busy hands were working at my waist, and without warning or ceremony, he shoved my jeans and wet boxers down my thighs, and there was my erection, still mostly hard, dripping and wet. I didn't even get a good look at his face as he dropped to his knees and sucked it straight into his mouth.

I was suddenly harder than hard, and he was sucking me into the back of his throat. He made gagging noises, the kind that usually break you right out of a mood, but he pulled back and dropped his head down again, and there I was, right in the back of his throat, begging for mercy.

"Oh *God*! Fucking *Oliver*!"

He pulled back and paused long enough to grin at me, then slurped me right back down to the back of his throat. I ran my fingers through his messy, smooth dark hair, and he went down again and cupped my balls for good measure. My fingers tightened and it probably hurt, but he didn't stop. Just kept sucking and squeezing and licking and it was good, it was good, it was everything I wanted, God, his hot, shameless mouth sucking the come through my cock like a straw.

"*Oliver*!" and I tried to pull him away, to be polite, but he went down harder, and I came. This time it was longer, more drawn out, pleasure being dragged down a gravel road. He tried to swallow, but I'm sure the come in his mouth was a surprise to him (it would have been to me!), and I kept pumping come into his mouth while he held it, scalding, around my crown, which made me come harder.

Finally it was done, my balls were about drained, and he pulled back, keeping his lips pressed together. He held his hand in front of his mouth for a moment and then straightened and ran through the living room, the other hand hauling his pants up. I heard him spitting come out in the kitchen sink and grimaced.

"Sorry about that!" I called, straightening and pulling my pants around my waist. I padded into the kitchen, shamefaced, and he was drinking from a glass of water and spitting out. I got behind him and rested my chin on his shoulder, feeling that wonderful buzz you get from coming and a sort of embarrassment that he had to rinse my jizz out of his mouth. He wiped his mouth on the shoulder of his shirt, set his cup down, and turned, letting his pants drop to his ankles so he could hug me.

"No sorry," he said softly. His lips met mine and then parted for me. I swept my tongue in gently, relieved when he sucked on it a little before letting it go.

"No sorry?"

He smiled shyly into my eyes and then hid his head against my shoulder. "It was really sort of awesome."

"Yeah?" I felt like I'd won the lottery.

"Yeah." He pulled back again and kissed me, and this time I sucked on his tongue and let him pull back.

We smiled at each other for a while, and then he shivered, and we both sort of pulled ourselves together.

"Gotta shower," he said, and I figured we'd be doing that alone, because it took a while to get used to someone else in your space.

"Yeah."

"You go first; I'll make us breakfast. Then, I don't know, hang out until my dad gets back."

I grinned, thinking about all the trouble we could get into "hanging out," and then I remembered my thought from the night before. Well, I guess maybe we'd have to "hang out" another time.

"Hey, Oliver. Where does your dad keep his gardening equipment?"

I could tell by his expression he was taking that *all* wrong, and by the time I'd explained, he was looking at me like I was both a genius and I'd destroyed his last, best hope.

"YOU KNOW," Oliver said from his perch on the porch, "this is not what I had in mind when I talked about a day hanging out."

"I'm sorry." I was too. Both my hands were wrapped around the thick handles of a pair of pruning shears, and I kept thinking *Was Oliver's cock this thick? I think it was thicker. I think it was about this long. But I'd* really, really frickin' love *to see it this time, and taste it, and touch it some more and….*

Yeah. I meant well, but it's a good thing Oliver was out there to tell me what to cut and what not to cut, or I would have just razed all those damned fence flowers, thrown them away, and gone inside and used Mr. Campbell's son as my own personal playground. And I don't think Oliver would have minded one bit.

But no, we *could* have been doing that, but I was cleaning up Mr. Campbell's yard instead.

"Your dad's done me a solid," I said simply. "I'd really like to do something nice for him."

Oliver grimaced. "Rusty, he's my *dad*, that's what he—"

"Look," I said, feeling embarrassed at having to point this shit out, "I know *you* are used to your dad being a stand-up guy, but there's a reason I had to leave the damned house to come out to myself, okay? Your dad cried a little and went and had a sit-down with God. My dad boxed up my shit and cut off my phone service." Fuck. Rex. I hadn't called him before I'd given back my phone. I'd promised him I'd call him. He was probably frantic. "I know *you* take that shit for granted, but I'm not gonna, okay?"

Oliver sighed and stood up, dusting off his bottom, shivering as he did so because it was chill and gray and sitting on the concrete did *not* make it any warmer. There was only one pair of shears and one pair of gloves, so I'd been chopping everything down, since I had the height and (sort of) the muscle mass. Oliver had been using the gloves to haul the dead branches and stuff to the green waste can. I rode cleanup and raked the small stuff into a pile. It worked, actually. We each got to take little breaks, and it gave us a chance to talk, which was the best part.

But that's not why Oliver was standing up and coming toward me now. I wasn't done cutting down the last stand of dead flowers, so he wasn't ready to pick it up.

Instead he took the shears from me and set them down, and then took my face in his cold hands and pulled me in for a kiss.

It was the good kind, the kind that started off light and got deeper and heavier, until I grabbed his ass and hauled him closer. He chuckled and *gave* himself to me, with the same generosity as the rest of his family (although, you know, not quite giving the same thing). I drank it up, *ate* it up, and kissed him harder.

Wrenching back from his mouth was difficult, and we rested our foreheads against each other in the tarmac-colored chill.

"What was that for?" I asked, not minding.

"For thinking my dad walks on water."

"You are so weird."

He laughed, his breaths puffing between us. "Well, maybe I kissed you because you look sexy doing yard work?"

I thought of how many times I'd watched him squat down and pick up dead vegetation, his tight little bottom straining against the seat of his jeans. I'd been thinking a lot about the finger and the O, and I was definitely thinking I'd like to explore *that* part of Oliver too. "Hey," I said, thinking about it. "How come I didn't always want you like this?"

Oliver's grin was sly and sexy. "You did. You just didn't know it yet."

I laughed, but I thought there was more to it than that. I thought that maybe knowing who I was let me see better who Oliver was, and that's why I liked what I saw.

OLIVER'S DAD was surprised when he got home, and I looked at him, anxious. I'd followed Oliver's directions, and I'd been listening when Jorge had been complaining about what needed to be done, but I was still afraid I'd chopped down some vital flower or an heirloom morning glory or something that could never grow back.

He grinned, though, and clapped me on the back and hugged Oliver and thanked us both for the work, and a big fat weight dropped off my shoulders.

"Good, I'm glad I did that okay."

"You did great. Rusty, why don't you go wash up and then you can go get your phone, okay?"

I nodded. "Yeah, I *gotta* call Rex. I totally left him hanging yesterday."

I trotted off and left Oliver and his dad talking about me in Spanish. I *knew* it was about me, because it *was* in Spanish, and usually they talked English when I was in the room.

Later, when we were in the truck, I asked Oliver about it. "So, what'd your dad say about me?"

Oliver looked at me and grimaced. "He said we'd have to replant the morning glories in the spring, but that I should marry you if it meant I had to buy a dress and a veil."

I swallowed, and that didn't change the shape of what he just said, so I shook my head. "I got nothin'. None of that made any sense at all. Except for fucking up on the—"

"No, damn it!" Oliver glared at the road and wrestled with the wheel. The truck was too big for him. It had a bench seat, which meant we had to scoot it way up and my knees were around my chest, and when he had to use both hands to turn, it looked like he was dancing with a really large invisible woman. It meant he couldn't glare at me, and I was glad, because he looked *fierce* when he did that.

"Are you talking to me or the truck?"

"You! You didn't fuck up. He just thought what you did was really great, and he thinks you're a keeper."

I had a sudden, terrible thought. "Oliver?" My voice sounded small.

"What?"

"If you and I don't work, is your family going to stop talking to me?"

Oliver sucked in a breath, and his face scrunched up. "No," he said softly. "We still see Joey and Sal's mom for Christmas sometimes. Gloria's ex-boyfriends work for my dad all the time. Don't worry about it, okay? You won't get left again."

I wanted to take his hand then, but I wanted to live a little more, I guess. Still, hearing him say that? It took away a worry I hadn't known I had.

THE MINUTE my phone was reconnected, it made one, long, continuous chime. The AT&T store was still a little busy from Black Friday (and now I knew why they called it that, because traffic *sucked* and *all* the sales clerks were bitchier than my mom when she didn't get her fiber shake), so I waited until Oliver and I walked outside to call Rex without even checking my messages.

"Jesus, asshole, you couldn't write me an email?"

Doh! "Oh God. I'm sorry, Rex, I kept thinking that I couldn't use my phone—I totally… I'm sorry. I… man, the last couple of days have been sort of fucked—"

"Why are they coming for your clothes tomorrow?" he asked bluntly.

"Oh *fuck!*" Like six *zillion* people with kids turned around to glare at me when I yelled that under the overhang of the strip mall. I grimaced and tucked my voice a little closer to my chest.

"Rusty?" Rex sounded freaked out, and I felt like shit. I'd even set my laptop up in Oliver's room, but no, I'd used it to play DVDs on.

"My folks saw me kissing Oliver before I even got in the door," I said, the humiliation still fresh. "They kicked me out, took my car, left my shit on the front porch, and discontinued my phone. I just got to the store today to get a new one."

"No," Rex said, his voice low and soft and really shocked.

"No what?"

"No, nobody does that anymore, do they?" Oh no, he sounded really hurt.

"I guess my folks are sort of throwbacks," I said, feeling bad for him. I felt like I'd kicked his favorite puppy.

"God.… Rusty, just—what are you going to do?"

I brightened. I had a *plan*. "Well, Oliver's dad is letting me crash on his couch, and Oliver's aunt has a lead on a cheap apartment. Oliver's uncle is gonna set me up with a cheap used car, and I start working construction again next week." Rex grunted. I mean, it wasn't that far-fetched, right?

"So that's it? I was told your stuff was getting shipped out—I mean, is there anything you don't want them to have?"

I thought about it with a little bit of panic. I had my laptop and a phone that would play my music. What had I left back in my dorm?

"My books," I said, thinking about *Crime and Punishment* and *A Tale of Two Cities*. Both of them had sticky papers and highlights and notes scrawled in the margins about stuff Oliver had said. "My posters, the pictures. God, any clothes you can stuff in a box—"

"I'm burning that striped shirt you wore when you didn't get out of bed," Rex said, and I laughed a little.

"Yeah, you do that. Look—my personal shit first, my clothes second. Make sure you get that picture of you and me in the quad. It'll be like proof that I went there."

"Will do." There was a pause. "Rusty, this is so fucked-up. I can't believe… I mean, you *knew* this was going to happen, and the rest of us… we thought you were being afraid." Had I known? Yeah. Yeah, a part of me must have.

"Well, I guess I'm not surprised," I said thoughtfully. "Maybe I'm not that dumb after all."

"Shut up." Rex's voice was thick. "I'll box up and hide what I can. When're you coming down?"

"Monday. I'll text you. Let me know if it's safe to come in. I've got to go see if I can get an emergency drop form too, so it doesn't look like I flunked out."

Rex swore. "Fucked. Up. All right—I'll see you Monday."

And was it weird that I was looking forward to it? I looked at Oliver. "We're going together, right?" Oliver nodded, and I said into the phone, "Yeah, I'll bring Oliver. You'll get to meet him. It'll be good."

"Yeah. Awesome." But he still sounded disillusioned, and I felt bad. Rex was supposed to sound larger-than-life.

"I'm sorry I didn't call you on Thanksgiving—man, it must have been lonely."

"Not so much," Rex said. "Professor Pritchard took me out to Denny's. Said he was flying out to see his daughter over Christmas so he didn't have anywhere to go for Thanksgiving. It was okay. He brought his nephew—it was all good."

My brain was shorting out with the thought of hobnobbing with a professor like he was a real person. "His nephew?"

"Yeah, nice guy. Fucks like a god. Too bad he's in the closet."

And there was Rex back, all insecurities gone.

"I'll, uhm, take your word for it. I'll see you Monday."

"Yeah. Uhm, Rusty?"

"Yeah?"

"Man, you'll let me know where you land, right? I mean, I don't have a lot of *friend* friends. You're not just going to disappear?"

And wow. Just, well, wow. Rex who had it all together? Rex, who could pretty much fuck anything that moves? But then, it was hard to be a friend when you fucked first and asked first names maybe.

"I lost all my friends when I picked Oliver," I told him. "I would *love* to keep in touch."

"Awesome. I'll see you Monday." And we hung up.

I turned to Oliver, who was eyeing me suspiciously. "You're not just saying that because he's hot, right?"

I grinned. "*You're* hot," I told him. "He's a friend. He's saving my stuff so it doesn't get shipped to who-the-fuck-cares."

Oliver perked up, his blinding smile popping out. "I'm hot?"

The fluorescent lights backlit the halo of rain in his hair, and his lower lip was looking especially full. I reached for him and—ignoring the shoppers running around us all bitchy and frenzied and in dire need of one more fucking cup of coffee—I palmed the back of his head and brought him in for a kiss. He came, eager, pliant, and although at first I'd planned to plant a short one on him and then let go, his mouth opened, and he was so warm that I fell into the kiss, happy, breathless, and all of a sudden aroused.

"Jesus, faggots, get a room!"

The harsh mutter pulled me back, and I felt Oliver jerk in my arms. For a minute I thought of picking a fight, but I looked around and couldn't pinpoint the speaker. Any one of half-a-dozen men were walking around us, avoiding the spot where we were standing, so I figured I'd ignore the big scary word and take the advice. Necking in public had never been my thing anyway.

But then, Oliver was *definitely* my thing, so maybe that's why that one rule had changed.

"C'mon," Oliver said, not even bothering to look around. His mouth was swollen, and I could see a very faint darkening under his cheekbones where he was blushing, just for me.

"Where we going?"

"Home for leftovers and a movie. I worked today, damn it—I get my hanging out!"

We turned for the truck, and when Oliver's hand bumped mine, I tangled our fingers, and we kept walking into the chill, flat gray-black of the evening.

INVESTING IN A NEW TANK

I THINK Oliver was as overwhelmed with Rex as I'd been at first.

They got to spend lots and lots of time together as I was going around to my professors and the TAs, trying to get my add/drop form signed. The thing that sucked was that for most of them, I had to explain the reason.

My English 101 TA was almost as thrown as Rex.

"Seriously? I mean… seriously? That's why you're dropping out? Your parents pulled your dorm cash?"

I shrugged. "I guess it's better than losing my nut." Because, you know, that had been damned close to happening, we all knew it.

The TA shook her head, lots of straight, shiny brown hair falling around her shoulders. I liked her: she had apple cheeks and a big smile. In fact, she looked a lot like Jenny Brukholtz, and I guess if I'd had a type when I was dating girls, she'd be it. Maybe the fact that I hadn't had any fantasies about hitting that should have been a big clue that I was Oliver-sexual, right?

"I'll tell you what," she said thoughtfully. "I'll sign this, but you know the final is already online, right?"

I shook my head. "Yeah, but I haven't gotten to it—"

"No, see, that's the thing. Get it in before the deadline in two weeks, and you'll get your class grade. I mean, if you tank the final, there goes your… well, B-, but if you pass it, you've got three units from Stanford, how's that?"

I grinned. "That's awesome, Tracey. Thank you."

She shrugged. "Yeah, well, good luck—" She looked at my name on the top of the add/drop form. "—Russell Baker. Enjoy the holy hell out of your boyfriend for me, okay?"

Now Rex would have smiled and offered to do a threesome. Me? I blushed and said I'd try.

Professor Pritchard gave me the same deal, but that was because he had all his paper topics online already. People could have had their finals done from the second day of class if they could have figured it out without him. I was grateful. My trig professor couldn't do that, although he was nice about it and wished me luck as he signed my form. My chemistry teacher couldn't either, but my Early American Literature professor could.

So I was actually feeling sort of triumphant when I got back to the dorm and found that Oliver and Rex had taken care of stashing what was left of my stuff and were now toe-to-toe, arguing.

"I said that's not his."

"And I'm saying it is."

"I know what he brought. I helped him cram it in his car."

"Well, maybe I want him to have it. Did you ever think of that?"

"He's not sleeping with you under that thing!" Oliver snarled, and given that Rex could have snapped him in half like a Hershey bar, he must have *really* been feeling the jealousy thing.

Rex took a step back, hands out in front of him, clutching the quilt his moms had sent him before Thanksgiving. "Whoa! Stand down, little man. I've got no designs on his body, okay? I'm *trying* to give you a housewarming present. Is that okay with you?"

"Omigod!" I reached out and took the quilt from him without hesitation. "Seriously? You're *giving* this to us?"

I had *coveted* (good word) this quilt. I'd *hungered* for it. It had arrived three days before I'd left, and I'd tried to contain my envy. It was done in what I thought of as a tic-tac-toe pattern, in shades of blue and brown, and I remembered when Rex had opened up the box, he'd laughed.

Moms—it's like they love with handicraft, you know?

Did they make that for you?

Yeah—they have weekends, sometimes, where they've got nothing on the roster, and they get together and make them for charity or something. This one's a little more detailed—this one was meant for me special.

And that had been it. I'd *yearned* to be *loved with handicraft.* I remembered that day I'd crawled into my bed with the intention of never getting out, and thought about how much better that would have felt if I'd been covered by some sort of love.

"Rusty?" Oliver sounded hurt.

I hugged the blanket to my chest. "Isn't it beautiful?" I asked him. "It's warm too—see? All the stitching makes it extra heavy. And the back side is some sort of multicolored fabric—"

"Batik," Rex supplied helpfully, and I nodded, turning to Oliver with excitement.

"See? It's got a fancy name and everything. And…." I swallowed, suddenly seeing the tiny apartment I knew I was going to move into, the one that wouldn't have any furniture or any pictures on the walls or anyone else there who would care about me. "Wouldn't it be great on the wall? Or the couch? Wouldn't it be pretty? It would look…." I swallowed, suddenly filled with the terror of what I was about to do. "Wouldn't it look warm?"

The tenseness in Oliver's thin little face eased up, and his cheekbones stopped poking through his skin. His sigh sounded irritated, and he scowled/smiled at Rex, and when he spoke, each syllable came out very distinct. "Thank you," he said stiffly. "That is really thoughtful of you."

Rex pinched the bridge of his nose and squinched his eyes shut, like he was having trouble deciding which box Oliver belonged in. "You're welcome," he said, each syllable as mockingly separate as Oliver's. "Rusty is a friend, and I'd do anything for him."

Oliver relaxed a little more. "Yeah. Yeah. Okay. I guess that's true." He turned to me. "So, are you all done?"

I nodded and held up the paperwork copies I'd gotten from the registrar. "Yup. Officially dropped out of Stanford. Who wants to eat?"

Rex looked at the papers, stricken. "Wow. Wow. Okay. This is real." And I knew then that he would really miss me, and that he really liked me, and he would have liked me whether I was gay or straight or smart or stupid. It was good to remember that: there were good people out there. Oliver's family, Rex's family, Nicole. Even my professors and the TAs who'd helped me out; they were good people. Way more good than bad.

"You know," I said, suddenly eager, "there was this place that had sliders—you know, those little mini-hamburgers? They're supposed to be *really good.* Want to go there?"

Rex's face lit up. "*Yes!*" We all looked around the dorm room, and it looked really empty without my stuff, and without the quilt I was clutching against my chest.

"We can come back," I offered wildly. I didn't even know where I was going to live in a week, but I felt like I had to offer. "I'll only be up in the foothills. It's only a few hours away."

Rex looked so happy, and I realized then how important it was to have a friend who *wasn't* going to get in your pants.

"Yeah?"

"Yeah." I'd make it a priority. Get apartment, start living on my own, be with Oliver, visit Rex. "I promise."

LATER, AFTER sliders and dropping Rex back at the dorms, Oliver let me drive the truck back up the hill.

"Oliver?"

"Yeah?"

"Don't you have class today?"

"Yeah, it's okay. I emailed my professor."

"You've got friends at school, right?"

"Yeah."

"And at the library?"

"Yeeeaaah?" Like he may possibly know where this was going.

"Are any of them trying to get into your pants?"

"No," he muttered.

"Are you sure?"

His voice was getting lower and surlier with every answer.

"No."

"Do I need to be worried about them?"

Sigh. "No."

"Then I can keep Rex's blanket, right?"

Another sigh. "Fine."

"You won't hold it against me? Because it's a really nice blanket, and I sort of love it."

"Can we have sex under it?"

I had to breathe really deeply and concentrate on my steering.

"Can we have sex under another blanket and hang that one on the wall? I think those things are hard to clean."

He growled a little. "Okay. Fine. Can we have sex?"

Since Saturday, we hadn't really had any time alone in the house. "In the cab of the truck at a gas station?" I asked, puzzled, and he laughed like I'd forced him.

"No, damn it. I want to have sex with you in a bed. Or on a couch, at the very least. And I want it to be like last time, except I won't weenie out and run and spit if you come in my mouth."

I was getting hard. "Uhm… can we talk about this when I'm not driving?"

I didn't actually *see* the look Oliver shot me, but since he reached over into my lap and squeezed gently before putting his hands back at his sides, I'm going to assume he looked hella fucking evil.

"So, there's going to be sex?" he asked hopefully.

I tried not to groan. "God, yes."

"Exclusive sex. You and me, and nobody else, let-the-condoms-be-damned kind of sex."

"Oliver?"

"Yeah?"

"If I'm Oliver-sexual, then don't you think I'd have a hard time having sex with anyone else?"

Oliver laughed. "Okay. Well, consider me Rusty-sexual. I don't want to have sex with anyone else either."

"Rusty-sexual? That's my favorite kind of Oliver!" His laugh carried us all the way up the hill.

ON TUESDAY he had to go to work, but he dropped me off at his uncle Manny's car lot before he did. Manny didn't fuck around—he was a pro, and not the sleazy kind either.

First he sat me down and looked at my bankbook and helped me make a spreadsheet with what Gloria thought she could get me for rent, and a guess of utilities, tuition, and food, and then we subtracted that from what I'd made every month working for Oliver's dad.

The leftover amount was depressingly small.

Manny clapped me on the back. "No worries. Do you know anything about cars?"

And if it wasn't Oliver's uncle, I never would have said this, because most used-car guys made me think of piranhas. "No. Nothing."

Manny nodded, thinking. "Look, we have some cars we can sell you cheap. The thing is, they're older, they got some miles on them— they're gonna break down. It's why people go for the newer ones, because they're dependable. But we also have a service center here. So I'll make you a deal. We'll get you set up in an older model, something simple, so you can change the oil on it yourself. I'll have the boys show you; they've been doing it since they were in middle school. When it breaks down, you bring it here to the service center, and if you can help the guys out— stupid stuff, hauling tires, getting coffee—I'll give you a discount on parts and we'll call it even. It's not a new Toyota, but it's a start."

Well, given that otherwise I would have been combing newspapers for something with the main quality of "It Runs," I figured it was a pretty good one.

"That sounds like a plan," I said, all sorts of choked up, and he set me up with an older Toyota, a lot like the one I'd had but not a Prius, and maroon, and the paint on the top was flaking from too much time in the sun followed by too many times through the auto wash. The upholstery was faded too, but the engine? It was clean, and even *I* could hear that nothing was pinging or banging or anything. The tires were new, and the brakes were good, and for a hundred bucks a month, I couldn't ask for much more than that.

In fact, it was better than I'd dreamed of.

We made it through the paperwork and shook hands, and I felt really grown-up, until Manny asked me if he could buy me lunch.

And then I was a kid again, because (a) he took me to Red Robin, which is where I'd gone with my friends all the time in high school, and (b) he had the Talk with me, which was so damned embarrassing, I thought my balls might have crawled back up while it was going on.

"So, you two screwing around yet?" Manny asked over a Whiskey River BBQ cheeseburger. He asked the question and then took a big bite out of the burger, which was great because I could fix the short circuit in my brain before I answered.

"Define that, sir?" I said, not being facetious. "As far as I can see, Oliver and I have been pretty serious about everything we've done."

Manny rolled his eyes and then swallowed his cheeseburger. "Sex, *pendejo*. Have you two been practicing safe sex?"

Oh God. "Well," I said, eating fries out of sheer self-defense, "we've sort of been practicing until we get good enough to have sex at all, if you know what I mean."

"I don't have the slightest. Enlighten me." He took another bite of burger.

Kill me. Kill me now. "I, uhm, well, I haven't done anything that could get him pregnant?"

And he snerked—did that thing where you're trying not to laugh so you force food up your nose? I'd never seen an adult do that before.

There were a few anxious moments there, while he tried to swallow and cough and clean cheeseburger out of his nose all at the same time, and I kept plowing through my own burger (I got the teriyaki) because after going through that budget, I was starting to realize that meals like this were going to be few and far between.

"Oh my God!" Oliver's uncle Manny was laughing into his hand, and I was signaling the waitress for more fries. "You're freaking *precious*, Rusty. I don't know where Oliver found you, but he needs to keep you around."

"English," I said. "AP English. And I plan on being around for a long time." Manny nodded, and then I figured I'd answer his question in a way that didn't make him snerk cheeseburger. "And I don't think we need condoms. I haven't been with anyone in over a year, and I used condoms with her, and Oliver's still a virgin. I'm pretty sure we're really safe on the whole STD front."

Okay. He didn't snerk his cheeseburger. No. This time he sprayed soda all over the table, but about the time we got *that* cleaned up, the waitress came back with my bottomless fries and two more sodas, and it wasn't a total loss.

At the end of lunch, he was still chuckling, and after we'd walked out of the restaurant, he clapped his hand on my shoulder. "Rusty, my man, your parents may not believe this, but you are a serious catch. You keep on telling the truth and being good to Oliver, and this family—it's going to take good care of you, okay?"

I wanted to hug him, but I figured we'd had enough messes for the day.

AND FINALLY it was Wednesday, and Gloria was standing by me anxiously, and I was in that tiny apartment I'd known was coming.

It wasn't *great*. It had a bedroom, a bathroom, a living room, and a kitchen. The kitchen had one of those counters that adjoined the living room, so you could set food there and eat and didn't have to buy a tiny dinette table, which was good. It was right next to the front door, which was awkward, but the thought was nice. After the car, I could pay first and last month's rent on the apartment and maybe buy a futon and a desk. It's a good thing I already had a computer.

I looked around the four maybe-white walls and the thinning beige carpeting and remembered the *real* reason this apartment was good: it was about a half a mile from Oliver's place, and about two miles from the high school. They'd visit. I wouldn't be alone.

I smiled at Gloria and hid my reluctance. "Yeah," I said. "Sure. I'll take it."

She wasn't fooled. "I know it's not much to look at, Rusty, but it's in a decent neighborhood, and that's not bad. Once you've worked for my brother awhile, gotten on your feet, maybe we can have you rent a fixer-upper. Arturo says you're good with tools—you fix the place up, we'll give you a break on the rent, and if you like the place enough, maybe we can arrange to buy, you think?"

That was appealing, actually. My parents' house was custom-made—I remember my mom choosing the hardwood floors and both of them agreeing that a floor plan that would give them separate office space would be best. The arches were the coolest part, the ones on either side of the downstairs hallway. Could I learn how to build an archway? Lay flooring? Knock down some walls and build others? Yeah, like I said, I *liked* that idea. But looking around this little blank space, I knew that skill set—and the place to use them on—were a long ways away.

Gloria patted my arm. "Don't worry, Rusty. We'll help you make it a home, okay?"

I smiled at her weakly. She was wearing a multicolored twinset today in turquoise, maroon, and black, and her hair was drawn up in one of those smooth, elegant bun things. My mom would probably have her over for dinner, but Gloria was as different from my mom as two people could be.

"Yeah," I said, because going forward was better, especially when you couldn't go back. "Why not. When can I move in?"

DINNER AT Oliver's house that night felt sort of sad. It was stupid, right? Because I'd lived there, like, a week, but I was already into the routine. I helped feed the dogs, I took them out to run at night, and I washed the dishes. Oliver's dad was real nice about giving us time alone together, and he never tried to barge in if we were sitting in Oliver's room, basically hanging out. In return, I never tried to molest his baby boy while he was in the house. Of course, if he'd been *gone*, I probably would have been all over Oliver naked like a Rusty Baker shower, but a guy's got his limits.

Oliver was pushing mine.

I don't think he knew he was doing half the shit he was really doing.

He'd come out of the shower in his boxer shorts, stick his head in the living room, and say, "Rusty, you're up!" In his *boxer shorts*. And I'd see his little body, his little defined muscles taut under his still-wet brown skin, and yes, I'll admit it, I'd be *up*. He'd brush by me when I was doing dishes and put his hand on my hip, and suddenly I'd be shaking with the need to touch him and rut up against him.

When I got home with the car, I sat down at the table, and he leaned over my shoulder to check my and Manny's math. I could feel the heat of his hand through my shirt and hear his breath against my ear and my hand started sweating so hard, I couldn't hold the pencil. He took it from me and started redoing the figures on his own, and I didn't hear a *word* of what he was saying. Why? *Because all my blood was in my dick!*

Oh my *God*, I couldn't remember ever wanting anything or anybody as bad as I wanted Oliver when he was doing long division by hand.

After dinner that last night, when I was washing dishes, Mr. Campbell fell asleep in front of the television, which he did sometimes. I sort of loved it when he did that, because it was comfy and sort of vulnerable. I mean, I'd seen my parents' bedroom, and it was always immaculate, and the comforter always matched the seasons, and there were little back bolsters near the head and lamps on either side and a television mounted at the foot of the bed. Every night at eight o'clock my parents quietly retired, either to the den or the bedroom, where they would work or read or hang upside down like bats for all I ever knew about them.

But not Mr. Campbell. He fell asleep with his head on the back of the couch and his legs spread, slouching so his thick middle sort of came up to his chin. I watched as Oliver went and fetched one of those really colorful wool blankets from the closet and tucked it under his dad's chin.

All sorts of things went *throb* then; that thing in my shorts, the one in my chest, the pressure behind my eyes—I couldn't decide which thing to pay attention to the most.

Oliver walked into the kitchen and took the dish towel from my hands because, apparently, I couldn't think or move for myself. He tugged on my hand, and I followed him blindly down the little hall and into his room.

He shut the door and turned the knob behind him. It took a whole beat in my brain before I realized that he'd planned....

He was standing right in front of me, looking up into my eyes with those little apostrophes at the corners of his mouth, which meant he was holding back a smile.

He feathered a finger across my lips, and I stared at him, completely taken.

"Do you want me, Rusty?" he asked, his voice down at a gruff whisper.

Words have never been my strong point. I cupped the back of his head with one hand and the side of his throat with the other and claimed that wide, plump mouth with my own.

Ahhhh.... He tasted so good! We'd stolen a kiss here and one there. When I'd come home the night before in my car, with all my spreadsheets, he'd kissed my cheek. We'd cuddled on the couch, but I hadn't had this— open mouths, breaths mingling, tongues tangling, Oliver's pulse against the inside of my palm—in what felt like so, so long.

I wrapped my arms around his shoulders and crushed him against me, reassured when he grabbed my shoulders and wrapped one leg around my hips.

I was drowning, drowning, not able to breathe, but I didn't want air, I wanted more of Oliver, and he seemed to want more of me too. He dropped his leg and backed us up to the bed, and there was a moment's awkwardness, arm, arm, knees bent, and then I was on top of him, both of us in sweats and hoodies and all.

I ground between his legs and he shoved his hands up under my sweatshirt, and together we kissed and kissed and frotted, our breaths harsh and hushed in each other's ear.

Oh God. I needed him. That need tore through me... ripped away that layer of shiny I'd had since I'd crawled out of my dorm room bed, the one that made it look like Rusty was okay.

That quickly, tears were rushing my throat and my come was rushing my balls and I was weeping, coming, uncontrolled in his arms, between his thighs, spewing warm and sticky inside my underwear.

Oliver grunted, bit my shoulder, and arched frantically against me. He wasn't getting enough friction, I could tell, and I propped up on one knee so I could I reach between us. I slid my hand underneath his sweats, grasped him, and stroked. Once again, I could only feel him in my palm, but that was enough, because he bit my shoulder, made a sound like a mewling kitten, and came in my hand. I collapsed on top of him, burying my face in his shoulder and trying to hold on to myself since I suddenly felt so lost. The fronts of our sweats were gummy and kind of ick, but I couldn't make myself move. My shoulders trembled for a minute. I had to get up or I was going to lose it.

I rolled off him but only got to the side of the bed before he stopped me, threading his hand with mine and rolling into my chest.

"Rusty?"

"Yeah?" Please let my voice not break. Please. Oh God, please.

"It would be okay if you didn't move out, you know that, right?"

My breath felt like it had shattered my lungs. "I have to," I said, "I have to."

"Rusty, I mean, my dad wouldn't mind—"

"If I slept on your couch, Oliver?" I rolled away. "What kind of boyfriend would I be? What kind of grown-up would I be? We couldn't sleep in the same bed, because kids don't sleep in the same bed. We'd have to wait for your dad to fall asleep to get off, and that's like being at home and beating off in the dark. And… and *worse* than that—"

Oliver rolled over to his side, and I rolled back so we were looking at each other, our heads propped on our arms, our legs curled up so only our ankles and calves were dangling off the bed. It worked better for him than it did for me.

"What's worse than that?" he asked, and he put his hand up on my cheek and rubbed a thumb under my eyes. We both knew his thumb came away wet.

"I need to make a home," I said, not able to explain it. "I need a place. I can't be your person if I don't belong anywhere but your couch." I took one of those deep breaths that shuddered my whole body, and he scooted closer until his face was pressed up against my shoulder.

"What happened to me being your home?" he asked, and he was hurt, and I couldn't fix it.

"You are my home," I said, and it was true. "But I… I can't ever expect you to live with me and… and make a life together, if I don't have a place for us. I need to… how can you love me if I'm just some loser on your couch?"

And that last part broke me. I struggled to push myself up, but Oliver was tucking himself against me, scooting up so he could hold my head, folding me against his chest and kissing my temple while hot, angry, helpless tears trickled out because I refused to let them purge.

HE HAD to work the next day, but his dad let me use his truck so I could take all the shit my folks had thrown on the lawn to the apartment. I signed the lease, grabbed the key, and wrote a check from the checking account I'd opened the day before using my savings. Then I moved my boxes of clothes, my football trophies, my posters, the knickknacks from my dresser, and the small television and DVD player I'd gotten for my fourteenth birthday into the apartment, where they sat forlornly in the living room while I looked around.

I stood there, checking out the small space and the crappy light and thinking I should get some nails and put Rex's quilt on the wall, since it was on top of the boxes, when I received a text.

It was Nic. She had a minimum day at school and wanted to visit me.

I cheered, right there in my empty living room.

One more excuse not to be alone in this shitty apartment.

I went to pick her up in the truck, and, after texting Oliver's dad to make sure it was okay, we drove to West Sac and the IKEA store.

Given I had groceries, utility deposits, incidentals, and (oh, for fuck's sake, I didn't even want to think about it) Christmas, I figured I had about $500 to spend on furniture. One futon, some sheets, and a chest of drawers to set the television on in the living room *and* put the clothes in. Oh yeah, and coat hangers.

I could do this. I was prepared.

I was not prepared for how much fun she was in the passenger's seat. She asked for details about Rex, details about Oliver's aunts and uncles, details about the dogs, and details about the little girl cousins who ran around in velveteen dresses and fell asleep watching *Coco*.

"They're all named Maria?" she said, her eyes big, and I told her about how all women were Mary and all men were Joseph, and she nodded.

"Yeah, that makes sense," she said, and I figured to Nic, it did.

In return, she told me about how school hadn't changed one single bit from what I remembered, and how the algebra teacher was still a woman-hating dick, and how the sophomore English teachers were a toss-up between the hippie woman teacher who passed everyone and the hard-assed little black-haired guy who looked like he was wearing a sweater when he rolled up his sleeves.

I remembered these people, and I knew about the elevator in the two-story building where guys kept getting busted getting blowjobs, and how nobody sat down on the couch in the easy teacher's room because we all knew that thing would be seen from space if we ever put a black light on it.

Anyway, she was fun to talk to. As we turned off Highway 80, I actually took my balls in both hands and asked about our parents.

She sighed. "They… they don't talk about you, not in front of me. They sort of pretend you're still away at school, I think, and that their whole world is hunky-dory. It's weird."

Oh. Well, uhm. "Ouch."

I had to park the truck sort of far out, because apparently furniture is the premium Christmas gift, and it never failed to amaze me how packed this place was. Maybe it was the childcare facility and restaurant. Maybe shopping for furniture made a great date if there was free day care and a nice meal at the end. Either way, we got frickin' *lost* on our way through IKEA, and if Nic hadn't been able to read the damned map, we'd probably still be there. So, there we were. Futons, mattresses, dressers—I picked out stuff that looked like wood, but not mahogany or ebony because that shit didn't look warm. They had sheets and pillowcases, but Nic told me you could get that stuff cheaper at Target, and I needed to save my money.

God. Felt like it took for-fucking-*ever*, but Nic made it fun, talking about her and me and Oliver on the futon, watching my little television, and how she'd bring my stereo, which she'd appropriated during the big

Rusty purge, because she was pretty sure Mom and Dad had been going to give it to someone else.

As we were in the line, our big furniture pieces in boxes in the giant cart, I saw her texting furiously. Her shoulders drooped in relief, and I caught her eye. She shrugged.

"I convinced her I was shopping with friends. I told her they'd drop me off. She's irritated, but it's no big deal."

Yeah, no big deal now would be the third degree later. I could have gotten away with it. I was starting to see that now. I'd gone off with my friends for hours—no texting, no nothing. Mom and Dad had said, "We trust you." I was starting to wonder if that was actually code for "We're pretty sure we control you." Nic wasn't controllable, though. She had a mind of her own.

"I'm sorry," I said. "I don't want to get you in trouble."

Nicole's smile was almost frightening. "Don't worry about it, Rusty. If hanging out with you is the worst trouble I ever get into, they're getting off lucky."

I felt a sudden shaft of worry. "You won't, will you?" I was nearing the cash register, and I pulled out my wallet. God. I was going to be down to subsistence pretty soon, and I didn't have anything—not plates, not silverware, not even any food. That big yawning pit of the things I was giving up suddenly opened in front of my feet.

Then Nicole put her hand on my arm and smiled. "Get into trouble? No, Rusty. Don't worry. I'm not gonna start cutting and going all emo on you. It's much more fun to piss them off by doing things my teachers approve of." Like being friends with her gay brother, or getting a liberal arts degree, or being more interested in arts than business. I got it. Nicole was smart enough that just being herself was rebellion. She didn't need to go Danger Woman on me.

The pit closed up a little, got big enough to maybe jump over, or fill up with dirt, or swim across the muck in the bottom. I could do this.

I handed my card over and punched in my debit code and tried to still the shaking in my hands.

WE GOT to the apartment with barely enough time for me to unload my big furniture boxes and drop Nicole off twenty-five feet from my parents' driveway.

"Say hi to Estrella for me," I told her, and she kissed my cheek before scrambling out of the truck.

"I'll ask her to cook for you. She misses you."

I flushed. "Even with the gay and everything?"

Nicole shrugged. "Yeah, she talks about lighting candles for you until you find your way to God, but she told me this morning that she wanted to cook tamales for you if I could find a way to get them to you. I think she loves you anyway."

"Yeah?" Suddenly it was really important that someone else in that house did.

Nic paused at the door. "You know, when I'm grown up and I have kids of my own, they're not going to ever have to ask that question. I'll be by on Saturday. Mom thinks I'm going shopping with Jessica, but I'm totally bailing."

"Okay, how will you—"

"Bye!"

I figured if she needed a ride she'd text and waited until she got to the driveway before I pulled out. I didn't have nearly the hard time driving the truck that Oliver did, but for some reason it felt like the thing was fighting me the entire way back to the apartment. I had to park on the street in front of the building, because I'd forgotten that Oliver had my car (which looked strange—maroon, not my first choice of a color), and he'd parked in my spot.

I had a hard time opening the door to the apartment because my hands were shaking in relief. Oliver was there. I wouldn't have to be alone.

He was on the floor with the open futon box; he'd laid out all the pieces and was reading the diagram for how to put it together. He had his nose wrinkled, and I didn't blame him—those things never made any sense—but when I walked through the door and into the living room, he forgot about that shit and jumped up and ran into my arms.

I caught him and he hopped, wrapping his legs around my waist and pulling my head down for a kiss that I was happy to get lost in. After a few moments, though, I didn't want to kiss anymore—I just wanted to hold, and I did. His legs slid to the floor, and he let me bury my face in his neck.

"Rusty, you're shaking," he said, and I shook my head and managed a smile.

"Just glad to see you."

"Yeah, Aunt Gloria gave me her spare key. She told me to have you return it to the office because they need it."

He pulled it out of his pocket, and I took it and put it in my pocket.

Oliver grinned, the apostrophes at the corners of his mouth widening to parentheses. "Did you see?"

It seemed an obvious question, right? But when I said, "Yeah, how're you doing on that?" he lost his mind.

He gesticulated wildly at the futon parts on the floor, and the boxes with the dresser and the coffee table, and the mattress rolled up in plastic, and started swearing in Spanish. He was furious and irritated, and I'm sure he was very serious about wanting all the bastards dead or something, but he was just so damned cute—he even stamped his foot.

I took his pointed, dimpled little chin in my hands and kissed him midrant. When he had his composure again, I backed off and said, "See, you never look at those diagram things; you gotta hook that one part to the other part, like this, and then you get out the screwdriver—it's on the bag on the table—and if you do *this*—"

He nodded his head like he was following along, but I'm pretty sure he was as lost doing this as I was figuring out the SATs. That was okay; he held stuff when I told him and didn't ask too many questions that needed words to answer. We fell into a rhythm, and for a little while, I forgot why I hadn't wanted to come back.

We were halfway done, and I was thinking about taking a break and going to Target while it was still open so I could at least buy some fuzzy blankets and sheets, when there was a knock on the door.

The twins walked in with about a zillion plastic bags dangling from their hands. They both dropped the bags underneath the little kitchen counter-way thing, and Sal said, "Wait right here, we'll be back." and the two of them disappeared out the open door again, where the night was getting frosty cold. I grabbed all the bags and put them up on the kitchen counters, the better for Oliver and me to go through them.

One held an inflatable mattress, in the box but obviously not new, and another held sheets to fit it. A couple held staples—peanut butter, jelly, ramen noodles, bread, boxes of mac and cheese, a big plastic jar of applesauce, tortillas, a bag of shredded cheese, margarine in a big plastic tub, a zillion boxes of spaghetti, garlic salt, bottled sauce, bananas, apples, cereal, and a gallon of milk. And oh thank God, toilet paper.

And as we were clearing away the bags and looking at the groceries on the counter, the guys came back. Joey carried an old, faded box with a used set of cookware in it, and Sal carried a brand-new set of Corelle dishes, complete with a four-pack of glasses and a four-set of silverware.

"Mom and Maria-Athena say hi," Sal said, and I opened my mouth and closed it and made a whole other start before I could find a coherent thought.

"Your mother knows about me?"

Sal shrugged. "Yeah. Joey and I ate dinner there. Joey, like, spilled the whole story. He was pissed about you being out on your ear, because he knew she'd never do that to *us*, so she got the old cookware and the dishes for you to help you out."

I swallowed. I'd never even met this woman. "And Maria-Athena?"

It was Joey's turn to talk. "She likes to look in on us. Dad sucks at keeping the fridge stocked. We told her we were running stuff up to you, and she bought extras so you could eat."

"Yeah," I said, thinking it was late enough to break out the cookware. "I could definitely eat. What about the mattress?"

"Oh!" Sal was opening the box of cookware like he'd read my mind. He grabbed the pot and started filling it with water, and I guessed we were in for either spaghetti or mac and cheese. "That was Dad's, after he and Mom split up. His first apartment was a real shithole—he wasn't smart like you were; he didn't let Gloria help him. So Uncle Arturo ran that over on his first night, so he didn't have to sleep on the floor."

"Oh shit!" Joey sort of powered me aside and grabbed the spaghetti and the sauce and put them next to the stove, and I caught a clue and grabbed the milk, cheese, and margarine to put in the fridge.

"Oh shit what?" Oliver was sort of leaning against the wall, letting us clowns amble around the kitchen.

Sal turned the stove on and then reached around and smacked his brother on the back of the head. "Yeah, idiot—you don't just leave 'Oh shit!' hanging like a cat in a tree."

Joey glared at him. "Dumbest analogy ever. Anyway, we were supposed to bring *blankets*, dumbass, you remember that? Crap—and it's getting cold tonight."

Sal let out a whine. "But I was making us food. I'm starving, and I don't have any money for McD's."

"That's okay," I said, because I'd caught a glimpse at what was in some of those boxes as I'd unpacked. "I got blankets, at least for tonight. How about you guys cook and... kitchen, I guess, and Oliver and I will keep on—"

"Bad idea," Oliver said, looking at the futon parts with haunted eyes. "You assholes get out of the kitchen and let me do that. *You* get to go be all power jockeys who can build things."

It was agreed, and for a minute, between Oliver putting away pots and pans and dishes and me and the guys knocking stuff together with the hammer, wrench, and screwdriver I'd bought at IKEA, it got loud in there.

It settled down after a bit, and by the time we had the futon assembled in the corner of the living room, Oliver was dishing bowls of spaghetti. I gave Oliver and the twins the futon and ate sitting with my back propped against the kitchen counter.

"Is that thing holding your weight?" I asked, and Sal and Joey both wiggled their asses experimentally.

"Yeah, it's holding up okay," Sal said through a mouthful of spaghetti, cheese, and sauce. "What's our next project?"

By the time the guys left that night, I had a dresser, a coffee table, and a mattress that had been inflated by *all* of us because the little electric motor kept spazzing out. (One of us would get light-headed midblow and tap out.)

Sal set up the DVD player and small television on the dresser across from the futon, Oliver put the sheets on the bed, and I opened the boxes with my stuff in them.

I don't know what kind of sound I made when I got to the bottom of the last one, but suddenly everybody stopped what they were doing and looked at me.

"I, uhm, didn't know they'd kept these," I said, feeling stupid. I had reached into the box first to pull out the comforter I'd slept under before I left. It was the one I'd seen when I told Sal not to get blankets, a basic comforter in plain blue and brown. I liked the colors, but they were so... just... plain. Not the dancing little squares on Rex's quilt. Underneath that were the comforters I'd had as a little kid, the kind you get with cartoon characters on them. There was one with *Star Wars* and one with *Toy Story*, and the twin-sized sheets to match. I would have thought my mom would have given these away. And then I saw what was at the bottom of that and realized why she hadn't.

My baby books, photo albums, laid out like little grids with dates and doctor's printouts and percentile charts, and well, commentary written next to the dates, all in my mother's handwriting: Rusty's first steps—graphed at the 77th percentile. She'd written, "Promising in athletics." Rusty's measurements graphed on the curve—90th percentile height, 85th weight—and again, in Mom's handwriting: "Not intimidating, but powerful."

She'd had me tested when I was around three, and there was the psychological profile in my baby book, along with her notes for what it would mean for my future: "High interpersonal skills—will network well. Substandard symbolic logic skills—will need help in math. Average verbal skills—should be able to succeed in language with enough effort."

In the middle of one album were my first soccer pictures, a little white clone with a game smile and the trophy I was so proud of. I heard my father's voice in my head. *Oh, Rusty, everyone got one. It's not that special.* I swallowed, suddenly six again. The coach had said I was good at cheering people on.

I'd *felt* special. My sixth-place spelling bee trophy from middle school, and more of those damning photo albums with that cold-blooded commentary from my parents. After the baby albums, when I got to grade school, my father made notes too. "Rusty's friend Clayton has a father in business. A good contact for later. The football team is made up of parents from the Rotary. Better that than baseball." I'd liked baseball. I'd been better at it than football. I could vaguely remember my father saying something about not being ridiculous, one sport was as good as the other.

I swallowed. Then swallowed again. There was really only one reason my mom would have put all this stuff in the bottom of the box. All this stuff was grooming me to be a good little businessman, another cog in the family machine. I had obviously failed at that; there was no reason for them to keep all this data. I took a deep breath and remembered there were three other people in the room with me, trying to see what I'd do next.

I pasted a smile on my face and straightened with the blankets in my arms. "Well, good news is I won't freeze. Let's get the bed made. We can put the kid ones on the futon, they'll work."

"What about this stuff at the bottom?" Before I could stop him, Oliver bent over and started rummaging through the same things I'd just seen.

"No, you know, Oliver, that shit just needs to be shoved in a closet or burned or... It's stupid. It's... it's not necessary."

It's... it's...."

Oliver made the same hurt sound I had, and I dropped the blankets on the futon and took the stack of albums out of his arms.

"It's embarrassing," I said with dignity. "I'll put them in the closet in the bedroom. There's a shelf, they'll get dusty, maybe when I leave I'll forget they're even there—"

"Don't you dare," Oliver said, and his face was tight with anger. "I'll take them to my house. We'll salvage the good stuff." He wiped his eyes furiously. "The pictures are great. You were fucking adorable. The rest of this shit we can burn."

Sal and Joey looked at Oliver and me and then looked at each other. Sal said, "Okay, you know, that's our ticket to—"

And Joey stood up from putting the last screw in the coffee table and yanked the books out of Oliver's arms. He looked through the first one, the baby one, and grunted, and then turned a couple of pages and then grunted again.

"Yeah," he said roughly. "Oliver's right. The pictures are good. The rest of this shit we can burn." He shook his head. "Man, I used to have some cherished fantasies about growing up rich and white. Thanks for killing that shit dead. I ain't ever gonna dream that way again."

"I don't think it's all white people," I said, depressed. "My sister's okay."

"Your sister is awesome," Oliver said gently. Sal was looking over Joey's shoulder by this time, and I had to move.

"I'm going to make the air mattress," I announced to nobody. I had the sheets from my old bed in my hand. They would have fit, but I folded them up and grabbed the ones Manny had sent. They were bright red, but they felt cleaner than the ones in my hand. I mean, I *had* to sleep under that comforter, because it was all I had, but right now the more things that didn't remind me of home, the better.

A couple of minutes later the bed was made, the trophies were shoved in the back of the closet, and Oliver had set my clothes in the dresser and put the photo albums in one of the smaller boxes. The guys had broken down the bigger boxes, and they were all flat and ready to be taken to Manny's house—I guess he wanted them for a project or something—and basically, my apartment was almost my apartment.

The furniture popped up in the middle of the cold off-white rooms like mushrooms on the beige carpet, and the things that should have made it better, made it mine, the baby pictures and the soccer trophies, had been poisoned, turned to fungus with my parents' inhumane commentary on what should have been good memories.

I longed for Oliver's father's house, with the warmth and the coziness and the flowers in the garden.

Then Oliver said, "Wait—here. We've got a hammer, you bought some small nails—let's put Rex's quilt on the wall behind the futon." His pocket buzzed, and he grimaced. It was after eleven. He had school in the morning, and I was going to meet his dad so I could start on the next project. "It'll be the last thing before we leave."

Joey and Sal exchanged looks. "You guys can do that without us," Joey announced. "And you need to… uhm, snuggle or something."

Sal looked at him. "Subtle, Joey. Fuckin' subtle."

Joey grimaced. "Hey, I pound people on the head, you talk them out of suing."

I went for the handclasp-chest bump with Sal, thinking that would be the way to go, and I got hugged instead. And Joey too.

"Thanks, guys." Gratitude rushed like warm water in my throat. "Let me know if I can return the favor."

They said goodbye and grabbed the cardboard boxes and disappeared into the frosty night, and I turned to Oliver, who was suddenly in my personal space when I'd been so very careful to keep everyone outside it. The things in the bottom of that box had left me raw and uncomfortable, and I hadn't wanted anyone in my space, because it would be like rubbing an open wound with sandpaper.

"I'll walk you out. I, uhm—"

And Oliver put a hand on each cheek and pulled me into a kiss.

I needed that kiss. I needed that kiss so badly. I opened my mouth and let him inside, and he kissed me harder and deeper and harder until I shivered and wrapped myself around him and groaned.

Our bodies were so close, I could feel the insistent buzzing of his phone against my thigh. Pulling away felt like ripping my own chest hair out. (Hair. Singular. I didn't delude myself.)

I rested my forehead against his and caught my breath.

"You've got to go."

"I don't want to leave you here."

A sudden thought. "I don't have toothpaste. Or shampoo. You *definitely* don't want to be here in the morning."

"Rusty—"

I'd taken my shoes off, but I'd also unpacked my flip-flops, and I was still wearing my hooded sweatshirt. Everybody had been too nice to say so, but although the electricity was on, the heat didn't go on for another two days. Before the twins left, our fingers had grown stiff with the cold. I slid into my flip-flops, which were by the door, looking at my feet and nowhere else.

"I'll walk you to the truck," I told him.

He gestured helplessly to the wall. "We didn't even put your quilt up."

I laughed helplessly. "Oliver, I'm sleeping under the damned quilt. It can go on the wall after the heat goes on."

"But... but—"

His wore one of those big Army jackets, canvas and warm. It had a patch that said Campbell on it, and I wondered if his dad had been part of Desert Storm. I would put money on it, because his dad was just that kind of quiet guy who would do that and not brag about it, and I was grateful for the jacket now as I took it off the kitchen counter. It would keep him warm. I cut off his protests with a kiss and helped him into the sleeves, then buttoned it up under his chin.

I made sure the door was unlocked, so I could get back in, and then opened it and held out my hand.

"Come on, baby. We both have life in the morning, and this isn't the night I want you to stay."

His eyes were damned shiny and his frustration showed when he said, "I don't want to leave you here."

I smiled at him, and it felt genuine. "Hey, I've got food, I've got water, a bed, blankets—Rex even managed to save my pillows. Tomorrow I'll get shampoo and toothpaste, and we'll put stuff up on the walls. Don't worry. It'll be someplace you can come sleep over soon." But I didn't want him living there, I thought adamantly. He lived in a place with dogs and flowers. He couldn't live in this place, not with the blow-up bed and the cold and the walls that smelled like last year's paint.

Oliver shook his head, but he followed me outside, and I shut the door to keep in whatever heat there was.

I walked him across the lawn to his dad's truck and gave him the keys. He searched through his pockets, solemnly handed mine over, and then he grimaced.

"You could probably drive the truck to my house tomorrow. You know, I really like your car."

I grinned. "We'll trade off. I'll get there before you need to leave."

Oliver nodded and frowned a little. "Rusty, you don't have to do this alone."

I kissed him. "I didn't, right? I totally had company."

He got into the truck and drove away, and I hustled back to my cold apartment. I slept in sweats, under three comforters and a quilt, on top of a surprisingly comfortable air mattress, with my phone charging next to me as an alarm clock. As long as I stayed in my little blanket fort, curled up in the dark, I could pretend I was a kid, and the world outside made sense, and this was all for play, and someone would take care of me when I woke up.

It was how I got to sleep, and it was the lie I told myself every time I woke up because I could hear street noises from my apartment, and I missed the dogs sleeping on me on Mr. Campbell's couch.

I woke up in the morning groggy, cold, and hungry, but I was damned grateful for the milk in the fridge and the cereal in the cupboards. Oh, and for the toilet paper in the bathroom too.

The Key to Tank Decoration

I WASN'T expecting to work on Friday and Saturday, but Mr. Campbell needed me. On Saturday Oliver got the key from me in the morning and let Nicole into my apartment. Together the two of them put up all the posters and stuff I'd had in my dorm and my room at home. I only saw it for a minute, but I think they did a good job. I was so glad to be actually working for a wage at that point, contributing to the dwindling numbers in what was now my checking account, that I would have stayed there at the jobsite forever, pounding nails, cleaning tools, whatever Mr. Campbell needed me to do, so he'd know how thankful I was for the job.

But he didn't let me do that. He brought me over for dinner instead.

The first night, he said it was to celebrate my first day as his new employee…. Oliver had left a bag of toiletries—shampoo, toothpaste, a new toothbrush, body soap, face wash, a washcloth, two matching bath towels, and embarrassingly enough, a jumbo bottle of Astroglide—in the back of the Toyota when I took it home.

I was grateful, and I'm pretty sure everyone around me was grateful the next day too. The second night, Mr. Campbell told me to sleep over, and I was so tired from sleeping in the cold apartment—or not sleeping—and so happy for the warmth and the couch and the dogs, that I did.

Oliver curled up against me and slept too, and I didn't object to that either. I slept in, waking only to clutch Oliver a little tighter to my chest, and every time, he patted my hand.

The next morning, I woke up and I heard him in the shower. Mr. Campbell was sitting at the table in the kitchen, drinking coffee (which smelled heavenly) and eating granola. He looked content, I thought, wondering where that thought came from.

I realized I'd caught his eye as I was blinking awake.

"How you doing there, Rusty?"

"Omigod, izzat coffee?"

He laughed. "Yeah. Coffee. Did you miss it?"

"*So* much." There were little dogs all over me, and I was sitting up gingerly when Mr. Campbell walked to the side door, opened it, and gave a quick whistle. All of a sudden, there were no dogs, only a furry, yappy little tornado of animals out the door. I realized I didn't even know their names. They always were just treated like a pack.

"Thanks!" I yawned again. "If I could use your shower, I'll be out of your—"

"No, don't leave. We're going to get our Christmas tree today. Come with us!"

I thought of my apartment. On the one hand, I sort of wanted to spend time in it and see if maybe being there would make me hate it less.

On the other hand... well, it was *Christmas*, right? And my Thanksgiving had both really sucked and really rocked. There was still a little kid in me who believed in the pretty tree and presents and not being able to sleep at night because you didn't know what was going to show up with your name on it in the morning. Nicole had once crept into my room and talked all night about how she was going to get one of those life-sized kid dolls, the creepy ones with the hair you could style. She hadn't—she'd gotten a bicycle instead, and she'd liked it well enough.

The next year, Estrella took us to see Santa, and Nic told him that she wanted a goldfish. I gave Estrella my allowance that year, and Nicole had come into my room and talked about how she'd know Santa was *really* real, if only she ended up with a goldfish. She'd gone back to her room in the morning, and Estrella had set up a fish in a tank. It was a beta fish, because they crap less, but Nic hadn't cared. It had been a *fish*, and for another two years, Estrella and I had managed to keep her excited about Christmas.

The year before, Oliver had come to visit after the gifts in the morning. I'd known he was coming. He'd called me up the night before and told me he'd gotten a radio-controlled helicopter and asked if I'd like to help him fly it. I had like six of them (they'd shown up in my boxes of crap, actually), but I hadn't told Oliver that. My house was back from a hill. Across the street was undeveloped land that looked down over Blue Ridge, and Oliver and I had flown that helicopter through three sets of batteries. I remembered that, from the time he'd called me to the time he'd shown up and knocked on my door, his father's truck looming in the background, I'd felt that crystalline excitement in the pit of my stomach, the same feeling I'd gotten when I knew Nicole was going to get her fish.

Yeah. A part of me still believed in Christmas. And Oliver's dad had just asked me if that part could come out and play.

"Sure, Mr. Campbell. I can't think of anything better, actually."

He smiled, like my coming had been the most natural thing in the world, and asked me if I wanted a cup of coffee.

You know when people talk about a perfect day?

A perfect day for me will always start with tiny dogs and a warm house in the winter, and coffee, and people glad to see me when I wake up.

This perfect day moved on to a trip to Foresthill—no Christmas tree lot for Oliver's dad, no. We drove the two hours up to Foresthill and we picked out a tree, and I sawed it down, and Oliver and I carried it back. It wasn't a ten-footer—my folks always got ten to twelve feet—because something that big would be stupid in the Campbell's little house, but six feet wasn't bad.

They were selling wreaths too, with big fabric bows and ornaments already fixed into the boughs with wire. Oliver bought one of those with his own money, although Mr. Campbell's furious Spanish told me that was bad.

"He doesn't want the wreath?" I asked, blowing on my hands and shoving them in my pocket. I had that big winter coat, but I had left it at the apartment. I was wearing a plain old hoodie, no hat, no gloves, no scarf. All that stuff was back in my apartment, and I kept forgetting to put it on.

Oliver took my hands in his—he was wearing fleece gloves—and blew on my fingers. "No, he wants it, but I wanted to pay for it myself."

"Why?" I liked the wreath. It was Christmassy without being too big or overwhelming.

"Because it's for you," Oliver said against my fingers. "So when you wake up, you know Christmas is coming."

I should have protested, but his lips were touching my knuckles, and I'm not proud—I can admit it made me stupid. "Thank you," I murmured, and he smiled, that shy little smile that said he knew I was probably sporting wood. The Christmas tree place was hopping—lots of families, lots of people trekking into the six inches of snow and coming back after slaying a Christmas tree in the red dirt of the Sierras.

I didn't care. I suddenly loved him so hard, it was like my skin was bursting with it. I pulled his knuckles up to *my* lips and kissed them, and then I leaned forward and kissed *him*. His mouth was warm—he had a coat, a hat, and mittens—and I wanted to climb into that lovely, lovely heat. He opened his mouth and let me in, and my kiss kept going deeper, like if I pushed deep enough into his body, I'd find Christmas.

My erection actually made me stop, because I could hear kids shouting to each other, and parents shouting at their kids, and I didn't want to get freakin' arrested. Oliver and I had to rest our foreheads against each other to calm down, our breaths puffing white in the air that smelled like Christmas trees.

"You're welcome," he said softly. "I'll have to come over tonight and help you put it up."

I wrinkled my nose. "We're not going to be done decorating your tree until almost nine o'clock, Oliver. Maybe you should come see it tomorrow."

His eyes bulged and for a minute he looked furious, and then Mr. Campbell called to us both, and we went to help him tie the tree to the top of his big half-ton.

He stopped for dinner at the Ore Cart on the way back, and we got to eat these *gigantic* hamburgers that were actually grilled *in an ore cart*. One of the original ones, from the gold rush and everything. They had a history of the place on the menus. Apparently it was the oldest building in Foresthill because the roof was made of sod, and that meant that back during the gold rush it hadn't burned down like the rest of the town, which was made of timber and tents. There also used to be a bunch of tunnels underneath it. See, the place used to be a post office, and they weighed gold and handed out money, and people were afraid of getting robbed. So they built a tunnel going from the owner's house to the Ore Cart, so he wouldn't get robbed walking home, and one tunnel from the front door to the regular motel, and one tunnel to the hotel with the hookers.

That last part made me laugh pretty hard, and Oliver shook his head.

"What?" I asked through a mouthful of red meat and sourdough bread.

"Rusty, you would *never* take that tunnel," he said with conviction, and I shrugged.

"Well, I guess they would have had to have boys there as well as girls."

Oliver rolled eyes at his father. "Never," he muttered. "He would *never* take that tunnel."

Mr. Campbell laughed at his son like they were sharing a private joke. "Maybe he'd take that tunnel if the time was right," he said gently, and Oliver narrowed his eyes.

"The time is right," he said decisively. "You watch."

Mr. Campbell shook his head then, almost afraid. "No, no, no, no, no—Oliver, I'm a good *papi*, but not *that* good!"

Oliver gasped at him for a minute, and I kept plowing through my burger, not even trying to figure out what they were talking about. Food. What can I say? It's a weakness.

The tree looked great, though, when we were done with it. Mr. Campbell got out the box of Christmas ornaments from the garage, and there were a bunch of these icicle-shaped blown glass ones that looked like they were made of angel's wings, with a tint of gold in the glass. I was terrified to touch them. They would break, I was sure of it, with my slightest breath. Oliver took them from my fingers when he realized they were shaking.

"It's okay," he said quietly. "We break one or two every year. They were Mommy's—it's like she gives us a way to let her slip out of our minds."

Okay. Yeah. Frickin' great. I was glad Oliver was the one hanging those up. I got to hang up the other ones, the ones that they'd gotten from garage sales or discounted at Target, or that Oliver had made in grade school. The ones that were tempera paint and macaroni or wood. I loved those. Mr. Campbell made us hot chocolate and told us about each ornament Oliver had made, and Oliver didn't interrupt him, even though I could tell he was a little embarrassed. When we were done, and Mr. Campbell was going around to turn off all the lights before we turned on the ones on the tree, Oliver leaned over to me quietly.

"See, it's like he's giving his blessing. He's letting go of me as his little boy. It's good."

And before I could ask him what he meant by *that*, Mr. Campbell turned on the Christmas lights, and I almost cried.

It was so beautiful.

It wasn't perfect, or designed, or Martha Stewart, or even matching, but I knew about Mrs. Campbell's ornaments, and the ones Oliver had made in the third grade after she'd died, where he'd written "To Mommy" on the back of every one. I knew about the one that showed Oliver and his dad and said, *"Mi Familia,"* and the stocking they hung every year, where they put letters to Mrs. Campbell and told her about their year.

Just looking at the tree made me happy, made my stomach cold and excited, like Christmas was special, and I was going to be privileged to see it, and Santa was still there, and I'd get something even better than a fish.

I smiled at it and turned and smiled at Oliver, and he pulled me down and kissed me, so soft, so gentle, it wasn't hardly a kiss at all.

It was more like a prayer.

I had to leave—I did—but for a minute I almost wanted to cry with how bad I didn't want to go.

"Here," Oliver said when I pulled away. "I'd say get your coat on, but you didn't bring one because you should be smacked is why. I'll be right back."

I looked at Mr. Campbell and smiled, the shine in my eyes still making a halo around the Christmas lights. "It's a real nice tree," I told him, and the words were stupid and meaningless, but he smiled anyway.

"Thanks, Rusty. Don't forget your wreath."

I turned to the table. "Oh yeah! I forgot—that'd be a shame," and when I turned back, Oliver had a jacket and his school backpack, and another backpack. "What's all that for?" I asked.

He didn't answer. Instead, he kissed his dad on the cheek. "Can he take the truck tomorrow? I'll take his car. It steers better."

Mr. Campbell nodded. "Yeah, sure. In fact, Rusty and I can carpool if you get here early enough in the morning." He winked at me. "Rusty, I promise to have coffee, okay?"

I gaped at him. "Why's Oliver coming with—"

"Night, Dad! See you tomorrow," Oliver called and dragged me to my car.

"Oh *Christ*, it's cold out here!" I ran for the car and tried not to slip on the ice that lined the little cement walkway. I opened the door, threw the wreath in the back, and paused to say, "Oliver, get back in the hou—wait?"

Oliver was sitting in the passenger's seat, shivering. "Start the car, damn it! It's cold."

I did what I was told, because, hey, good at following orders, that was me, and then I turned to him in confusion.

"But why are you coming home with me?"

Oliver took a deep breath, and then another one. "Rusty?"

"Yeah?"

"You know I love you, yeah?"

I smiled. It was what had gotten me through the last couple of weeks. "Yeah, Oliver. I love you too."

"Good. So when I say this, I want you to take it in the best possible way, okay?"

"O—kay...."

"I have never, *ever* bought into the lie that you weren't smart. But I got to tell you right now, you are trying my patience as the stupidest *pendejo* who *ever* walked the earth."

"Oliver?"

"I. Want. Sex. Whole sex. With you. My *papi* knows it. My cousins know it. Manny, Gloria, hell, even Jorge and Maria-Athena—they *all* know it. But you? I have to sneak into your car. So drive to your little apartment, we'll hang up your wreath, and then you and I are going to have a long naked talk about how you can catch a clue, okay?"

My mouth dried out, my skin heated, and my cock stiffened at red-alert speed.

"Okay," I croaked, staring at him. He'd been gesturing with his quick little hands, and his lips were set mutinously, and his jaw jutted out all stubborn. This was not a fight I wanted to have. Ever. "Okay."

"Are you going to drive?" he asked, scowling so hard he had a little wrinkle between his eyebrows.

"In a second," I rasped. "When I won't wreck the car."

He nodded and folded his arms. "Take your time. It's only my virginity."

My mouth pulled up. "Yeah, Oliver. No big deal, right?"

His hand warmed my thigh through my jeans. "Right," he said softly. "Not if you mean it, and it's important. It's the most natural thing in the world."

I covered his hand for a moment, and when mine had stopped shaking, I took the car out of Park and drove home.

THE HEAT had kicked on, and I was damned grateful. We walked in, and I realized the one benefit of not having any stuff was that the place was tidy. There was a small pile of laundry next to the inflatable mattress, but not enough to make a load to take to the little apartment laundromat, and I'd washed the last dish in the sink before I'd left yesterday morning.

So the apartment was only a little chilly, and Oliver said, "You put the nail in the door. I'm going to go shower."

I did—the tools were still out on the kitchen counter from when we'd assembled the furniture, and there was a spare tack in the bottom of one of the drawers from the last people who'd lived here. By the time Oliver came out of the shower in a pair of sleep pants and a T-shirt, I'd done my Christmas decorating.

I smiled at it, looking sort of big and busy in my little plain space, and Oliver tilted his head critically. "We will get you more," he announced. "Your turn to shower."

I didn't argue. I hadn't showered since the day before, and we were going to be *naked* together. I pretty much wanted everything from balls to bunghole to be sparkly and clean. I hadn't brought any clothes with me into the bathroom, so when I got out, I was wrapped in one of my two towels and using the other one to dry my hair.

Oliver was practically *at* the door to the bathroom, and he grabbed the towel around my waist with insistent little hands.

"Wait, Oliv—"

And then I was naked, in the crappy apartment, with all the lights on. I resisted the urge to cover my crotch with my hands.

"It's, uhm, usually bigger than that," I mumbled.

Oliver stood on his tiptoes and kissed me senseless, kissed me until the shyness went away, kissed me until I clawed the back of his shirt up so I could touch his bare skin. There was no room for embarrassment in this kiss, no room for being afraid. There was just our mouths and our hands and the rasp of his clothes against my chest and my thighs and my groin.

His hands—quick hands, like darting fish—were all over me. My biceps, my shoulders, my waist, my hips. He had long thumbs, and they grazed that line between my thigh and my groin and I shook all over, washed hot and needy with that one touch. I pulled away, panting, and said, "Lights off."

He narrowed his eyes. "I'll turn *some* of them off. I'm not doing this in the dark."

I pulled back. "I'm not the boogeyman!"

He laughed and swatted my hip, and I really *did* cover up my crotch now.

"No, but you're beautiful and I want to see you. Jesus, Rusty—is it you or is it all white people?"

I blinked. My girlfriends had all done it in the dark too. "I don't know," I said, but then I remembered—*this* time, I'd get to see him too! "I'm getting under the covers. You do what you got to do."

You have to be careful getting on an air mattress, even one of the totally sturdy kinds that could survive a trip down the Amazon river, like this one. I slid in carefully, burrowing under the different comforters and the quilt, and shivered for a minute while Oliver turned off the living room light and the bathroom light and the overhead light in the bedroom. One of the things in my boxes had been my old lamp from when I was a kid. It was on the floor next to the bed, and Oliver had turned it on while I'd been in the shower.

He left it on now, as he stripped to naked in front of me, as quick as he could. He was in such a hurry, he almost fell over getting his pajama pants off, and since he was taking off his pants *and* his boxers, it was pretty funny to watch him struggle while his semi was flapping in the breeze. He smirked at me and then finally got his boxers off. I was still giggling when he glared at me and did something that shut me up right quick.

He touched himself.

Took that half-flapping wiener in hand, squeezed it until he gasped, and stroked it from the base to the tip, until it wasn't a wiener anymore, it was a fully erect cock.

It was still cold—Oliver's skin was a landscape of gooseflesh—but underneath the covers, I started to sweat.

I was stunningly, achingly hard.

He opened his eyes and shivered, then took off his shirt and rasped his short-cut, clean nails across his almost purple nipples.

"Nngh...."

"Where's the lube I gave you?" he demanded, his voice hoarse.

I fumbled under my pillow for it. I hadn't even had time to jerk off, but that didn't mean I hadn't wanted to.

He looked me square in the eye. "We're going to use that sometime tonight. You keep it ready and decide who you want to stretch me out, you or me."

My brain shorted out. I just lay there, sweating, cock aching, and watched him slide under the covers with me, wondering why he was the one getting done and I was gonna be the one doing him.

I opened my mouth to ask him, and he kissed me, and now we were both naked, and I was *shaking* with the need to touch all of him with my whole body.

Oh God. Everywhere. My hands smoothed over his arms, which were defined and not noodle-y but still slender. His ribs corrugated under my palms, and my hands were so big I dreamed about using them to hold him and keep him safe and warm, blanketing his body with my big hands.

He kissed me harder, and I rolled so he was under me, and then I just… mauled him, I guess. I kissed his neck, his jaw, the little dent between his collar bones. And Oliver? He moaned a lot and flapped his hands, and I think that was okay. I wouldn't have known what to do if he touched me. I needed him like crazy. I probably would have come with the first touch of his hand on my ass.

But he'd never done this before, and maybe that's why I was going to… oh God… the thought made my cock drool, and I was afraid I'd come if I even said the word.

"Oliver," I gasped, thinking we might have to wait for the part where we would need lube, or even need to worry about who was doing whom. "Here… I'm gonna suck on you—play with me back."

My head was at his stomach by this time, and I scooted around, ignoring the squeaks from the mattress, until he could grab me in his fist.

"Nngh… oh God… slower!" Because I needed time to look at him. He was average, I guess. I know I'm a little bigger than average, but he was perfect, circumcised and straight and veiny and just… perfect. I wanted to feel him in my mouth, and I shielded my teeth and pulled him in.

Oh wow. He was bigger in my mouth, against my palate, against my throat, and he made a noise, no words and no vowels, and his grip on my cock tightened and he stroked, clumsy but hard. I sucked harder. I had to, and he stroked again, faster. Oh man. Everything was tingling, and everything felt so good! I wanted it to last longer, but his cock in my mouth was starting to spurt, and I raised my head and lowered it, and took the bottom part in my fist, and he made that noise again and stroked me faster.

He spurted a little more, and I squeezed his base, and then he squirted a lot, and I was hungry for him, so hungry, that swallowing it down was easier than I thought it'd be, and he flailed around on my cock, and although it wasn't perfect, feeling him come down my throat, oh, damn, I was right… right….

"Mmmffff!" He spewed like his balls were made of jizz right when I shot off in his hand, against his shoulder, and both of us lay clenched around each other, shaking, spasming, until I was sure I could swallow it all.

I BARELY managed to pull myself up to put my head on the pillow next to Oliver. Oliver reached his arm out and pulled my head to his slender chest and I went, mashing my nose against his come-smeared pectoral in an effort to breathe him in and still my own shaking. God. Sex and love and touch and safe and… and *Oliver*.

The thought made me shake some more.

"Shhh…." he murmured, and I was consumed with panic that I hadn't done it right, that I'd done something wrong, that I wasn't worthy of him, because *Jesus*, look what we'd just done together.

"I'm sorry," I said through chattering teeth. "I didn't mean to. I mean, it was good, but you wanted me to… and I, just…. God, you tasted so good, and I wanted you so bad and…."

"Shhh…." he said again. "It was fine, Rusty. It was good. Best start ever, I swear."

But it wasn't good enough, wasn't *near* good enough, and I was horrified to find that my eyes were burning and my face was wet.

"I'll do better," I promised. "I swear. Next time will be better, and I'll take care of everything, just promise me…." My voice caught, and I was squeezing him so tight his ribs probably felt creaky.

"Promise what?" He sounded *really* confused.

"Promise you won't leave me alone," I said, my voice so clogged I almost couldn't get it out. "Promise you won't leave me in this shitty apartment, all by myself, when the only thing I want is you."

It was like he had eight arms and legs, and he was wrapping them around me.

"Never," he said next to my ear, and I closed my eyes and drank it in and believed it. It was all I had in the cocoon under the blankets: his body, warm and slender and sweet in my arms, and his voice, promising me things I had to believe or I wouldn't have been able to sleep, much less get up in the morning and move with faith through the world.

I FELL asleep a little after that, and I think he must have turned off the lamp, because when we woke up again, it was dark, and we were still naked.

His body was all smooth skin and a little bit of rough hair near his groin, and suddenly we were both made of hands. He didn't even start kissing me. One moment we were skin to skin, and the next his mouth was clamped over my nipple, and his hand... oh God. His hand was on my cock, and I was too out of it to even find his. I made this noise, it didn't even *sound* like a person, and behind my eyes the world was a kaleidoscope of white light. It was like the whole world was that feeling of his hand and what it was doing to my body, and I had no control, none, no way to think bigger or help him out or....

White light exploded outward, waxed red, gilt with black, then gold, and my entire body transformed, molecules, atoms, electrons, quarks, and when the cosmic light show faded, it was just me, in bed, Oliver on my chest, both of us breathing hard and covered in cum.

"God.... Oliver.... But I.... Don't you.... Can you...."

"I'm good, Rusty. Came in my fist."

"Washcloth," I mumbled, and he must have gotten one after I fell asleep the first time, because I remember the feeling of being cleaned off, my one washcloth warm and nubbly against my skin, and then I fell back asleep.

We woke up at six when my phone alarm went off, and I was so grateful he was still there I almost cried all over again. But looking around the apartment, with all the space, even with my posters up, I knew why I didn't want him to stay over again.

I shut off the alarm, and he pulled the covers over our head, but not so we could go back to sleep.

"Rusty?"

"Yeah?"

"When can I spend the night again?"

"God, Oliver—maybe wait until I have a real bed?"

"Fuck that. I'll be back this afternoon."

"Won't your father miss you?"

"Not tonight. Tonight he's going to some singles dinner with Manny. It's you and me."

I grunted, remembering something. "My sister's coming over after school. She told Mom she's going to a concert."

"Good. We'll play Scrabble and eat—"

"Top Ramen. It's all I have left for three."

"Screw that. I'll get her and go shopping."

"I'm going to have to be a grown-up sometime."

He kissed me, and my brain scrambled. He pulled back and said, "You're plenty grown-up. You just need another grown-up to help take care of you. That's my job. Shopping and sister this afternoon, sex tonight. Shower now. You first."

"We could shower together," I said hopefully. I wanted to see him some more.

"We'll end up having sex again. We don't have time for that."

Which reminded me. That bottle of lube was still under my pillow.

"Oliver, I'm sorry last night wasn't... you know... the whole big, uhm, lubricant sex thing you were—"

His hand fumbled in the dark under our blanket fort, and after smacking my temple and my nose, he found my mouth and pressed his fingers against it. "Rusty, you don't ever have to worry about that. You and me, together. It's all you have to worry about, okay? God." His voice shook. "Please, don't ever spend a night alone because you're afraid you're not enough, okay? I want all your nights with me, even if the heat goes off again."

I shrugged, not wanting to promise that, and kissed his hand. He cupped my cheek, and our mouths found each other. "Now go," he said gruffly. "We want to be able to trade cars so you ride with *Papi*."

We ate breakfast in a hurry—cold cereal—and I yearned for coffee. We made it to his house with five minutes to spare, and he kicked me out of the car because I guess he'd brought his books with him.

It wasn't until he drove away that I realized I'd be in the house alone with his dad when his dad probably knew what we'd been doing with our night.

I was standing in the yard, between the gate and the front door, when suddenly the dogs all flooded out, barking their heads off to see me. I bent down and petted them, shivering with how much comfort that was, and wondered again at their names. So far, I'd heard Little Dog, Stupid Dog, Papacito, and Peanut—but those names seemed to apply equally to all the dogs, so I wasn't sure if those were *really* names or just something you called a thing that didn't come anyway.

"Come in!" Mr. Campbell gestured from the doorway. "We'll make a thermos of coffee. Good, I see you found your gloves!"

He sort of had me at "coffee," and I followed him in. I guess it was good he wasn't the shotgun kind of father, because I really am that dumb.

He had a big mug poured for me, complete with milk and sugar, and I was trying not to gulp it boiling hot from pure craving.

"So," he said, setting the pot down and rooting through the cupboard over his sink, "Oliver, he's going to want to spend the night a lot."

I swallowed and spit at the same time, and it took a few minutes to clean that mess up. When we were done, and he'd finished dabbing at my shirt with a towel, he put the towel aside and patted my cheek like a grandmother.

"Rusty, I'm not a very modern man, not at heart. I admit, if Oliver was a girl, you wouldn't be welcome in my house this morning. But he's not a girl. He's a boy. Is that bad of me, that I worry less?"

I shrugged and thought of Nicole. "My sister's first boyfriend is gonna need an FBI background check," I confessed, and he laughed appreciatively.

"Jorge's girls—they are going to be virgins forever. It's not fair. I know it's not fair." He smiled a little, sadly. "Oliver's mother and I...." His brown eyes crinkled at the corners, slid sideways, and met my gaze slyly. "Well, let's just say her *papi* would not have been happy with me either. But she got married in the church in the white dress. Oliver was already a bump under the dress, you know?" He shrugged. "But she was such a good person—nobody was mean. Her parents, they were very old-fashioned, but we'd been planning to get married from the night we met. Her daddy, he told me, 'We half expected you to propose when you picked her up. We trust you with our little girl.'" He shrugged. "They live in Los Angeles. Oliver sees them sometimes over holidays and such. They're nice people, but when Teresa died, it broke their hearts. But they were kind to me, when I didn't know much about families who could be kind. I send them a letter every week."

I didn't know why he was telling me so much, except that it was about family, and now it seemed like I was part of that story too. "That's really nice of you," I said, feeling stupid.

He smiled a little. "When Oliver told me, '*Papi*, I like boys. To kiss. Not girls. I hope that's okay,' it took me a month to work up the courage to put that in a letter. I figured if they wanted to stop seeing him, I could pretend, right? Lie to him. Give him excuses. And I think it took them a while, because a week went by, and then two, and then I got a letter from Oliver's grandma. 'Arturo, that boy still looks like our little girl. Thank you for telling us. We won't tell our church, because he's still Teresa's son.'"

"That's really—" I breathed in hard. "I think that's good. That's nice. Your whole family, it's all about love."

Mr. Campbell clapped me on the shoulder, and he timed it when I'd set the coffee down. "Yeah, Rusty. Welcome to the family. You remember, you're always welcome for dinner. You ready to go now?"

I nodded, so relieved he wasn't mad about what Oliver and I had done last night that I thought the conversation was the best Christmas present ever.

On the way home from work that night, Mr. Campbell stopped at Target and ran inside. He came back twenty minutes later with a big shopping bag that he put in the front seat.

When we got to his house, Oliver was sitting in my car with Nicole, like they'd just pulled in. There was a bag of groceries in the back, and Mr. Campbell shoved the Target bag in there with it, not saying a word about it.

"You get meat?" he asked through the open window. Nicole hopped out of the car when she saw me and moved to the back seat, and I got in the front, figuring Oliver would drive.

"Yeah, *Papi*. Gonna make him enchiladas to last a while."

"Good. He's skinny. You're not a good husband if your mate is skinny, Oliver. He works hard. You make him fatter."

Oliver patted his hand as it rested on the car door. "Go change, old man, and put on some aftershave. You're going to scare the pretty women."

Mr. Campbell shrugged. "Not interested in the pretty women. Interested in the women who put out. I'm too old to screw around with girls and makeup. It's not right my son gets more action than me!"

Oliver made a face. "No more. Too much information, *Papi*. Go away! Go feed the dogs! We need to go so Nicole can eat!"

And Oliver's dad backed away laughing in the December darkness. It wasn't until we got to the apartment and unpacked that I realized what he'd bought at Target.

It was a bunch of place mats, decorated for Christmas, with matching napkins.

And a coffee maker. And coffee. And two mugs: one red, one green.

It was a blessing, I think, and Oliver told me quietly that he'd say thank you. "It's not a Christmas thing, Rusty. Don't worry. My family does Christmas right."

For a moment, though, setting the cheap coffee table with silverware while Oliver made chicken enchiladas, it sure felt like Christmas. Felt like the best holiday I'd ever had. Right up until the heater kicked in and the apartment smelled like burning dust, and the people upstairs started doing the cha-cha as we sat down.

God. The food wasn't quite as good then, was it?

But Oliver and Nicole seemed really happy, so I smiled for them.

Nicole was all full of excitement and chatting about school and the things the teachers were doing and the tree my parents had gotten. She reached into her backpack after we set the coffee table with our new place mats and before the enchiladas were done. What she pulled out surprised me.

"Hey, those're the ornaments we made."

She nodded. "Yeah. God, you were a sucky artist. Worst. Colors. Ever."

I looked at the little ceramic ornaments—an elf, a candy cane, a train, a teddy bear, a stocking. We'd been given acrylic paint and told to go to town, and I had. Mine were pastel pink, blue, yellow—all the colors of Easter, on the cherished symbols of Christmas.

"Well," I said sheepishly, "I was only nine."

Oliver came out of the kitchen, where stuff was cooking that smelled wonderful, and looked at the tiny figurines. "Yeah, but those are the colors of our people, Rusty. You ever think maybe you knew back then?"

I looked at him with a wrinkled nose. "Nicole's were all gray. No, not so much."

Nicole shrugged. "Yeah, I forget why. I think I was trying to make a political statement or something. I remember I resented the hell out of having to do art in our kitchen." Oliver laughed, took one step behind him from the living room to the kitchen, and opened the junk drawer for some pushpins. We hung the ornaments on the pins on either side of the counter so they framed the little eating space.

It looked kitschy and poor student—but bit by bit, the place was also looking like me. I had these moments of double vision, though. I'd stand back, and it would look charming and warm and real. And then I'd look again, and it would look small, and empty, and sad. Seeing the same thing in two different ways made me dizzy, and made me want Oliver home, with his dogs and his dad, even more.

We had enough time to eat and watch Nicole's favorite TV show before I had to bring her home. I told Oliver he could come with us, but he shook his head and said he'd do homework until I got back. I grabbed his shoulder as he sat on the futon, his books spread out on the coffee table, and kissed him. I had to. There was no confusion about kissing Oliver. He smiled up at me, those liquid brown eyes adoring the hell out of me, and I had a sudden shiver. This was who I was going to come home to.

Or it would be, if I had a real home.

It was so much easier to drop Nicole off this time, at the mouth of the driveway, and then watch as she made her way over the frost-crispy grass to the front porch. Our mother opened the door as she knocked, and that actually made me feel good. They were worrying about her. But I couldn't see how much, because by then I was backing up out of the driveway and hoping Mom couldn't make out my face in the dark.

The streets were icy as I made my way back to the apartment, and I forced myself to go slow. The first time the front wheel threatened to skew away from me, it hit me. I didn't have any health insurance, and this was my only car. Suddenly I knew, completely, how alone I would be if it wasn't for the little brown person sitting in my living room, doing his calculus.

When I got to the apartment and saw that light on, and him through the window, sitting there with his übercalculator and his notebook on his lap, I had a hard time breathing. I needed him. I needed him in a better place. But I needed him.

I kept it together, though. I had no place to go with this anxiousness, no magic to make this apartment any better. And I wouldn't send him home to an empty house because of my pride. Not yet.

I got out my computer and for the first time in two weeks tried to remember history and English and generally what I was doing with my brain.

And it was weird.

It was like having all this dire hand-to-mouth food/work/rent stuff on my mind made the other stuff so much less complex. I mean, I still had to use my brain, but it was like I had this understanding—this stuff was important, yes, but if I got it wrong in a paper on my computer? I could still feed myself in the morning. Oliver would still be here. His dad would still have us over for dinner. Nicole would still visit.

I could fuck this up, and it would suck, but it wasn't life threatening.

By the time Oliver was ready to go to bed, I actually had a rhythm going.

"Rusty, are you watching porn?" He stood to my side and was bending over my shoulder, trying to get a look at my computer.

I jerked my head up and frowned at him. "No, I'm trying to get those credits from Stanford, why?"

"'Cause you were smiling."

My grin stretched my cheeks as I realized I really was. And then Oliver's expression got all sober and serious, and he leaned his head over and kissed me.

I closed my eyes and the still-shitty apartment disappeared.

Oh wow. Carefully I closed my computer and set it aside. Then I stood up, kissing him the entire time.

This time when we got our clothes off and were naked, I had the teeniest little bit of room to think. And what I thought was that what we were doing, skin to skin, still felt too good to interrupt with things like lubricant and stretching and what goes where. I was still drunk on touching him, on the way his quick little hands stroked all over my body, and the way pulling apart from our kiss to breathe felt like drowning.

We made it to the bedroom, but we left little clothes puddles on our way. (The next morning I'd find one of my shoes in the kitchen.) And when we got there, it was urgent, but I made myself move slower, and I kissed places I might have missed. I fell slowly to my knees, kissing as I went down, remembering to pull on a nipple that tasted like plums in my mind, because that was its color.

His skin tasted so good, it was hard to stop kissing his stomach, his thighs, his hip, but there was that big thing in the middle that sort of called my name.

It went so smoothly into the back of my throat, I forgot there was a limit and sucked down harder, swallowing. He grunted and grabbed my hair, which was good. It was like the little prickles drove me on, made me hotter, made me wrap my arms around the back of his thighs and pull him tighter. I could do this forever, because he was inside me, and it was perfect, made me complete and whole in a way I'd never thought of before.

He was making urgent noises, half-framed words, almost moans, but his hands in my hair? They were telling the complete story. Hell, they were damned near making legal demands.

I pulled back and swirled my tongue around his crown, and he started shaking, so I did it again, holding him up. He grunted and let go of my hair, leaning on my shoulders instead, and suddenly I loved my big body, my height, my strength—I could hold him. I had something to give him, and I swirled my tongue some more and gave it to him again.

"Rusty," he managed, and I sucked him deeper. "*Rusty!*" I slid my hands between his thighs from behind, widening his stance, teasing the crease of his thigh, his balls, the cleft of his ass, with the sides of my hands. "*Ohmigod Rusty!*"

He came, and I could swallow this time, easier because I was upright, but then he spurted some more and I couldn't. He trembled and spasmed, bending at the waist and wrapping his arms around my head as I gently, gently helped him down to the mattress while I stayed on my knees.

Finally he was done, and I raised my head and grinned at him, my chin dripping with cum. He touched my cheek with a shaking hand. "Proud of yourself?" he asked, panting for breath.

I nodded and smiled, and he reached down his body and ruffled my hair.

"You're going to have to put the thing in the place sometime, you know that, right?"

I turned my head and wiped my mouth on the comforter under the quilt and said, "Scoot over! It's cold out here, and I want to snuggle."

"But you haven't—Rusty, you still got wood."

I snickered. "Got wood? Got milk? Got jizz?"

He giggled—not a snicker or a chortle but a giggle, right into my shoulder. And I wrapped my arms around him and laughed too. The laughter faded, and I was warm enough to run around the apartment and turn off lights and slide on my underwear (because sleeping naked sounds fun, but that thing starts to get in the way), and when I slid back into bed, he cuddled right up against me.

"You're afraid to, aren't you?" he said against my chest.

"Afraid to what?"

"Do the thing."

"We did the thing. It was great!"

"No. You're afraid to… I don't know. Take advantage. *Take* me."

I grunted. "It's supposed to hurt."

"It's also supposed to feel *great*!"

"Awesome. You do it to *me*."

"No."

I tried to look into his face, but he was almost under the blanket.

"You don't want to do it to me?"

"Eventually."

I brightened. "So, *eventually*, I'll do it to you."

"No."

"No?"

He sighed, and I guess he was tired of the game. He straightened up and propped himself on my chest. "You are more than a pretty face. You are more than a strong guy who has trouble with your papers. You're a protector. You protect people. You protected me through school, you take care of your little sister. You want to take care of me. Why don't you want to take care of me and do this?"

I flailed for words. "Nngh!"

And he waited, perched on my chest, his darting little hands smoothing along the definition of my pectorals and my ribs.

"I'm not very good at it," I said after the silence got too unnerving to actually let it go on.

He made a noise somewhere between a grunt and a *not good enough.*

I grunted back and then tried again. "The heat barely works, the television is tiny, and I don't even have a bed."

"I'd sleep with you on the street," he said unequivocally.

Now *my* noise was difficult to define. "I wouldn't let you."

He kissed me then, lingering just long enough to remind me that I *hadn't* finished. "Which is why I'd do it. When do I get to move in?"

"Nngh."

"No, seriously. I want to make a home with you."

"The dogs will die without you." I know *I* missed them.

"We'll feed the dogs every day. I'll see my dad *most* days. Hell, I think my Aunt Gloria is coming over here tomorrow to see how things are going. When do I get to move in with *you*? I thought you'd ask me, but you're being stubborn, so now I have to do the work. It's why I'm making you top first."

My brain shorted out, my words all flew south, and, of *all* things, my cock woke up in my undershorts. "Nngh!"

Oliver's hand found my weakness, and his hand was cool and firm as it slipped under the elastic to fondle that weakness back to hardness. "You keep trying to say that like it's a word. It doesn't *mean* anything."

He squeezed, and I said it again.

"See? It's why I need to ask you questions. You have to do your share of the work."

"Now you're just *playing* with me," I protested, and this time he squeezed *and* stroked, and I hardly heard him laugh, and I didn't know why he was laughing anyway.

"Yeah, Rusty," he said next to my ear. "I'm *playing* with you." He punctuated that with a strong stroke downward and a thumb-swipe across the head of my cock. I saw stars. "And I'll keep doing it until you give me an answer. When can I move in?" Now his speed increased, and I grunted, and the mattress creaked, and I had my answer.

"When I get a real bed," I told him, and his hand stopped moving altogether. "Don't stop!"

He pulled his hand out of my pants and folded his arms.

"Oliver!"

"Take it back!" he said, and I rolled away from him, onto my stomach, and started humping the bed.

"No," I moaned. It wasn't enough. I was aroused and trying to think and failing and the whole thing made me want him more.

"Roll over," he said shortly, and I kept humping the mattress.

"No. You're just going to stop again."

His lips, soft against my arm, made me still my stupid desperate humping. "I won't. I'm sorry. That was a shitty thing to do. Roll over, Rusty—let me love you."

It was the way he said it that kept me from grabbing myself and getting off. Pathetic and desperate—I know. But I wanted him to love me so badly. I rolled over and he was on me in a minute, kissing me and fondling me and stroking me. I groaned into his mouth and he moved his head down, pulling me out of my shorts and into his mouth almost at the same time.

I groaned again, too raw inside to hold anything back. It was good. So good. I wanted him so much and his mouth was just... ah.... God.... Down, up, down, up—sometimes the simple shit is all you need.

My climax blew through me all in a rush, seizing me by the throat and shaking me hard against the mattress and against Oliver. He held fast, though, wrapping his hand around me and milking me until my cock was tender and even the stuff that felt good hurt.

I made a pain sound then, and I felt him swallow twice, and then he wiped his mouth on the comforter under the quilt like I had. He pulled himself up to rest his head on my shoulder, and I wrapped an arm around him and lay there, panting for a minute.

"I want to move in with you," he said quietly.

"I want you to move into a better place," I told him. "How am I supposed to feel good about you living in this shitty apartment when you've got a real house—a real *good* house—right down the street? I don't even have a drawer for you to put your stuff in. I think we're pirating internet from the McDonald's behind the apartment building—"

"It's the Starbucks next door, and you're welcome."

I floundered for a minute. "Thank you. I didn't even think about internet. And *see*? What happens if we break up? I can't even provide basic shit for us, and you've got a family who loves you. What are you going to be able to tell people about your first boyfriend?"

The skin on my shoulder stung wetly. "I'd tell them that he was a really great guy, but that his parents really fucked him up, and that he never believed that I loved him no matter how hard I tried."

Oh fuck.

"A bed, Oliver," I begged. "That's all I'm asking for. A bed, a chest of drawers—but mostly a bed. *Our* bed. Can I at least give you that?" A bed, and some furniture, and an area rug and a heater that doesn't fizzle in and out and… oh Jesus, a bed!

Oliver's nod was mostly his cheek slipping around on his tears. "Yeah, Rusty. A bed. You're right. I waited this long. I can wait for a bed." He was totally lying. I so didn't know he was lying at the time, and it was the thing to say at the time.

"I love you," I told him, feeling helpless and stupid.

"I love you too. It's all we need, you know."

"Food is good. Heat's good too."

He sighed. "Yeah."

"We want to do this right, we need to remember that stuff."

"You keep saying you're stupid, but I don't believe it."

I sighed. I didn't want to tell him that the idea of Oliver on his hands and knees in front of me, his body spread and shiny and ready for me—*that* idea—had been following me around for two days. I *wanted* that idea. I *wanted* to be inside him. Yeah, part of it was that it was hella hot and it made me hard, but part of it was that it was *Oliver*, and he'd be *mine*. I could have had him like that tonight. I could have. I had been thinking tonight. I slowed things way down, and we could have *done* that.

But I didn't. Because I wanted a bed. I didn't want it quick and dirty and awkward because of the stupid mattress under our knees and elbows. I didn't want something sad and sort of silly because we were trying not to pop the thing we slept on. I wanted a *bed*.

"Believe it," I told Oliver right now. If I'd passed on that vision of him, brown skin shiny, cock in his own fist, then I really must be hella fucking dumb.

Old Fish, New Fish, and the Shiny Things That Catch Them

THE NEXT evening after work, I switched cars with Oliver at his dad's and stayed for an hour to play with the dogs.

Then I kissed him in front of his dad and told them both I needed to go home. He looked at me with wounded eyes, and I made a helpless motion.

"Your dad cannot *possibly* want me here for another night."

"No," Mr. Campbell said, "but only because I know that Gloria left a casserole at the apartment for both of you." The little Pomeranian was licking my fingers, and I found it hard to just pat him on the head and say goodbye. Man, that dog loved the hell out of me.

"Excellent," Oliver said, brushing by me. "I'll go get more clothes. Tomorrow I'll bring laundry over."

His voice was brittle, and I watched him go unhappily. I picked up the little dog and let him lick my chin.

"What are you fighting about?" Mr. Campbell asked me, and I grimaced.

"He wants to move in. I don't even have a drawer for him. I can't even keep a dog. What's this dog's name, anyway?"

"Peanut."

I flexed my fingers in the dog's silky fur. "Man, I really love this dog."

"I know you do, Rusty. But dogs need to be let out and let in, they need to be fed, and they need someone who knows better to do all that."

For a second I thought he was on my side, and I nodded, because he got it.

"Stubborn sons, on the other hand, they're perfectly good at doing all that for themselves."

"You think I don't want him in my place? Of course I do. But wouldn't you rather he stayed at home?"

Mr. Campbell shrugged. "Of course. But he can always come home."

Something inside me broke and bled. "Yeah. Well. I gotta go." I stood quickly and backed up. Oliver could go home, and I couldn't.

All I could go to was that shitty apartment, and now I was dragging Oliver there.

Oliver trotted out with his backpack over his shoulder, and I was still backing toward the gate. "I gotta go," I said again, looking at them both and feeling the totality of being an outsider just smack me in the head. "I.... Oliver, you stay here and pet the dogs... I gotta... you've got a home here. I... I gotta...."

I turned then and fled to my car and peeled out of there. I didn't look to see what Oliver was saying to his dad, and I told myself I didn't care.

Of course I cared. When I got to my apartment, Oliver's Aunt Gloria was there *and* my little sister. Gloria was setting a steaming casserole on the table, and she looked up and smiled at me.

"Hey, Rusty. Oliver called and said his dad's dropping him off in a minute, so you should be ready."

I looked around the apartment in sort of desperation. I wanted it to be *better*, and suddenly I realized—"Where'd the table come from?"

It was a little wooden breakfast table, with four scarred and sturdy chairs around it. There was a brand-new Christmas hot pad in the center, and four of my plates set around it on the place mats. There was a red poinsettia in the middle as a centerpiece.

Nicole was sitting at the table, doing her homework, and I looked at her a little desperately. "Why are you here?"

She looked at me and shrugged. "I took the bus. It's only a block away from where the bus stops. It's better here than at home."

"And the table?" Oh God. I was so confused.

"That's a gift from Manny," Gloria said. "He had it in his garage and pulled it out to use. It's okay?"

I looked at it and nodded, and for the first time since Stanford the tangle in my brain was too tightly wound for me to trace back any threads and find words. Oliver's family, my family, the things I needed, the things I wanted, what I wanted to *do* for Oliver, and what he wanted to be for me—it circled and muddled and I'd left him right there, in his driveway, because I didn't have any words.

"Is anything wrong?" Gloria asked. She sounded concerned, and I realized I'd been standing there, my mouth opening and closing in desperation, for a little while.

I shook my head. "I, uhm. I." Suddenly all those lessons from my parents, the ones about not offending people and not being rude when given a gift, kicked in. "It's great," my mouth said, while my brain scrabbled for something to hold on to. "It's really awesome. Thank you. The table, the food. My sister. It's great. I've got to go change. I'll be back in a sec, 'kay?"

Gloria smiled and looked relieved. "Okay. We can have dinner when Oliver gets here."

"At the new table," I told her numbly, hoping my smile didn't look too off. God. Oliver was going to hate me. I was so stupid. I swallowed, a little human emotion trickling in through all that politeness. "It's really awesome of you and Manny. Thank him for me, okay?"

She smiled "You can thank him. We're all doing midnight mass and Christmas dinner together. Everyone will see you then."

I nodded. Okay. Good. I could thank everyone when I went to midnight mass and sat down to Christmas dinner with this new family that was not going away. I swallowed again, and my eyes burned.

"Rusty, are you okay?" Nicole asked, and I nodded, which was a lie.

"I'll be back in a sec."

My construction clothes were jeans and work gloves and an old T-shirt with a hooded sweatshirt on top. I stripped out of those and put them in the pile, then found a decent pair of jeans and a clean T-shirt and sweater, wrapped myself in a towel, grabbed my clothes, and crept across the hall. Nobody noticed, and I dove for the shower, hoping I could pull myself together in there.

A home. *This* was my home. There were no grown-ups here and nowhere else to go. I had to make it the best I could.

It wasn't bad, really. The table was nice. I had some Christmas decorations up. I could do home things here, and I knew, during the weekend, I could hang out on the futon and do my homework and feel comfortable. I was happier when Oliver was here. That was not even a question. But this was my home now, and there was so much more I wanted it to be for Oliver. The hot water sluiced down my body and rinsed away some of the panic, and I tried to control the shudders and the stupid goddamned baby tears that wouldn't go away.

The bathroom door opened, and I stuck my head out of the shower to see Oliver, looking sober but not pissed, sitting on top of the toilet.

"Hi," I said. It was a word, right?

He nodded. "Hi."

"We're having a dinner party."

"I noticed."

"I'm freaking out in the shower."

"I noticed that too."

"I'm sorry I left you at your dad's."

Now his eyes narrowed, and I knew how pissed he'd been. "That was an interesting choice. Whyfor did you do that?"

I sighed and turned off the shower and waited for the water to stop dripping, then reached for one of my two bath towels.

After I'd toweled my hair and dried myself off, I wrapped the towel around my waist and stepped out of the tub. "I want to build you a house," I told him. "I want it to be maybe a little bigger than your dad's. But it's got to have a yard. We can garden and make flower beds and a lawn. It would have an open floor plan, you know? So we could talk while one of us was at the table and the other one was cooking or doing dishes, and you could listen to the TV while you were doing that. I like that. And the bedroom would have desks in it, so if one of us had to sit and work, the other one could sleep, and we'd know we were there. We wouldn't have separate offices. And the bathrooms would be bigger. And there would be a washer/dryer in the garage, or a mudroom or something like that. Probably a garage, because I like building stuff and I want my own tools. And we'd paint it exciting colors—like cinnamon and sky blue—you know, like that blanket you've got on your bed? And—"

I was standing in front of him at the toilet, and he stood up and held his finger against my lips. Suddenly just being near his body made me feel better. I needed to remember that—being near his body made me feel better.

"This is a good plan, Rusty. Why are you telling me this after leaving me on my father's lawn?"

I swallowed. Oh yeah. That. "Because this place, it's not like the one in my head. And you can always go home, but this is the only place I've got. And it's not that great."

He wrapped his arms around my waist, and I wrapped my arms around his shoulders and kissed the top of his head.

"I'm sorry I left you on your father's lawn."

"I'm sorry you're all lost inside."

My throat swelled, and for a minute I thought I'd have to get back into the shower again. "I don't think right when I'm not holding you," I apologized, and he hugged me tighter.

"Maybe you just need to be held some more," he said, and I nodded.

"Okay." He felt good against my body, and my next breath came easier.

"I'm up for the job," he said, and I smiled. The tightness eased up completely.

"I'm really glad about that." I meant that with everything in me.

"Good. Get dressed. I'll go talk to my Aunt Gloria."

I stopped him from pulling away and kissed his mouth, and he opened for me. It started out casual, and suddenly it got clingy and tight and when I pulled away, I realized we were a towel away from having sex in the bathroom with people outside. I swallowed and turned him around and pushed gently.

"Go."

He took a few deep breaths while I was getting my boxers on and finally went.

I came out and we had dinner and talked. Gloria liked my sister very much. By the end of dinner, they had plans to go shopping, and I wanted to bang my head against the table.

"Oh God. Christmas shopping. I'm so lost! What do I get everybody?"

I couldn't wrap my head around it. When it was my parents and Nicole, I'd spend *days* looking for something for Nicole. My parents got a gift certificate to the galleria. But now I had Oliver's whole *family*, and *no* money, and….

I looked at Oliver miserably. He was telling my sister about a new vintage clothing store, and how he was going to go look for some combat boots for cheap, and his face was lit up and his hair was framing his cheekbones and….

I wanted to give him the world. I wanted to give him the house I had in my head. I wanted to give and give and give until he had everything.

It's just… I had so very little to bring to the table.

"Don't worry about it," Nicole was saying while I lost my mind. "I'll bring Estrella here on Saturday. She'll teach you how to make cookies."

I felt a pang of guilt. "You can't do that to Estrella. Saturday's her day off."

Nicole wrinkled her nose. "Yeah, but she's worried about you. I told her I'd show her you were okay."

Okay. Okay. Well, I had to go shopping anyway, right?

"What should I buy?"

She gave me a list of stuff. I made her write it down, and Gloria added some suggestions. Okay. Great. I was getting a whole new skill set here. Balancing a budget, baking cookies, dealing with my emotions—it was like a crash course in being a human being. I could do this. I'd *been* doing this. It would be okay.

That night, after Gloria and my sister left, and the dishes were done and the leftovers put away (they'd be dinner for, like, three days), Oliver and I sat at our new table and did homework. We didn't say much.

I dozed off at my computer at one point, and when I woke up, Oliver was steering me through the darkened apartment. He helped me take off my pants and my sweater, but he left on my T-shirt and underwear. We both crawled under the covers on the creaky inflatable mattress that smelled like our sex from the night before, and he burrowed into my arms.

"No sex?" I yawned, trying to ramp myself up for it.

"No sex," he said, clinging a little tighter.

"Why not?"

"Because you just need to be held."

"God, you're smart," I murmured, and we fell asleep in a tangle.

THE NEXT day during lunch I texted Rex, because he seemed to know how to deal with people. He might be able to help me with this.

Rex, whatcha doin?

Studying. How are you?

Okay. Have a place. It only sucks a little.

Can I visit for Christmas?

Aren't you flying up to see the moms?

Before that. I'm done next Wednesday. I've got a week of downtime.

Yeah. Sure. I've got a futon.

Excellent. See you Friday.

I need to know what to get Oliver for Christmas.

Don't stress. I've got it covered.

Got what covered?

What you're going to get Oliver for Christmas. I'll bring it up.
Wouldn't that be a gift from you then?
Not if I give it to you and you give it to him.
I'm pretty sure I've got to pick it out.
Oh. Okay. Well, I'll give it to both of you. See you then!
Okay. Do you want my address?
Yeah. Email it. Later!

Yeah. See you then, Rex, and thanks for frickin' nothin'!

Well, that wasn't fair, and it would be nice to see him, even if the idea of the guy sleeping on my futon was sort of weird. But I still had no idea what to get Oliver, and it was starting to ride me hard. I couldn't give him the home I wanted, or a dog like the ones his dad had, or even a bed, because my budget was down to the bone at this point. It turns out that baking cookies wasn't cheap. He had brought me a family, and his family had brought me the beginnings of a life, and I had nothing to give. And I wanted to give him something. Something wonderful.

When I wasn't at work, where I needed my head with my hands or I'd hurt myself, it was all I could think about.

BY FRIDAY I'd turned in the papers for the professors who would let me, and I felt a sort of surge of triumph about that. Friday night the twins were the ones who brought Oliver from his dad's after work, and they stayed over just to hang. They brought a brand-new garland of tinsel that hadn't made it out of the box last Christmas. We strung it around the little space with the ornaments near the wreath, and I had to admit, the place was still a little bare, but it did look like Christmas. We watched TV and listened to them bitch about their love lives until one in the morning, and then they hauled my old sleeping bag out of my closet (it'd been in my boxes of stuff) and crashed on my futon, using their sweaters as pillows.

Oliver and I slept, curled tightly against each other, in the bedroom.

"Hey," I whispered, even though we were both falling asleep.

"Yeah?"

"Why do people keep coming over here?"

"Don't you like it?"

"It's awesome. Whyfor? Are you making them?"

Oliver grunted. "No. If I had anything to do with it, we'd be having sex right now."

My entire body blushed at the thought of sex with people in the next room. "Uhm. No."

"See? No. They like you. This is having friends, Rusty. I know you've done this before."

"I have," I said shortly. "This is different than friends. This is family."

"Derp!" he said shortly. "If I'm not getting any, it had better be for family."

"Derp?"

"It's a word."

"God, you're cranky."

"No. Sex. Go to sleep."

But he snuggled closer when he said it.

"Oliver?"

"Derp?"

"I love you."

"I love you too. More specifically, I'd love for you to suck—"

I kissed him, laughing. I mean, I'd specifically love to do that too. But there were people in the next room. Because even though I hated this apartment, apparently they liked me enough to stay. Blessings were always mixed—I hadn't known that as a kid. I was starting to know it now.

THE NEXT day, the twins got up and bought doughnuts, which we had with coffee from the new coffee maker. They were still there when Nicole arrived with Estrella.

"You couldn't have called?" I asked, gasping at my sister. "I mean, you never said a time—"

And that's about all I got out before Estrella rushed forward and engulfed me in a hug. She's round and soft and nice to hold. She used to hug me a lot when I was a kid, and I wondered when I'd grown out of hugs like that. How had I relegated Estrella to the same box as my parents, an adult to ignore, when she was the one here in my crappy apartment, hugging me like she missed me?

"Rusty!" Two squishy kisses, one on each cheek, and I didn't even feel the need to look around and see if Oliver, Sal, or Joey were laughing.

Smiling, maybe, but I was pretty sure they wouldn't laugh at someone who was there to be my friend.

"Hey, Estrella," I said, going in for another hug. "It's real nice of you to come by."

"Here," she said. "I've brought you something."

She reached into the big paper shopping bag hanging from her arm and pulled out something I hadn't thought of in years.

"Oh my God! *Santa!*"

It was the Santa cookie jar that Estrella used to pull out every Christmas. It was big and kitschy and gaudy—Santa's suit was too red and his cheeks were too round and his eyes were way too blue—but Nicole and I had loved it. It was the cookie jar Estrella had brought out when Christmas cookies became available. It meant something important.

"Here," she said, walking over to the refrigerator. I took it from her and put it on the top of the fridge and then wrapped my arm around her shoulders for a hug. Her dark hair was a messy halo and pulled back in a bun, and I kissed the top of her head.

"Thank you," I said quietly. "I love that here."

"Your sister and I miss you," she said.

I took a deep breath. "I miss you guys too, but I've got a place here." And people kept visiting. Maybe *crappy* was relative.

"Oliver will take care of you," she said, and she might have been lighting candles for me to save my soul, but she sounded happy to think we were together.

Sal and Joey stayed with us the whole day, and yes, we all made cookies. Estrella had also brought an old Mixmaster and the glass bowls—I remembered this one from our kitchen—and I was the guy in front of the mixer, scraping the sides. Nicole measured the stuff for me to put into the dough, and Oliver scooped it out of one of the big glass bowls and onto the cookie sheet when I was done. Sal and Joey manned the stove and the frosting station.

We were making a *fuckton* of cookies.

I kept saying, "Okay, guys, we were only supposed to *learn* how to make cookies, so I'd have something to give for Christmas."

"Rusty," Sal said, his voice serious, "you've only got, like, two weeks left. I say you just cook until the supplies run out."

"But they're all going to be gone before Christmas!" Was nobody seeing this? I took a giant bite of dough, because it was the sugar kind with the touch of lemon and I loved that.

"Then we'll make more, *Papi*," Oliver comforted. "I get paid Monday. I can buy some supplies."

The dough sat like a lead ball in the bottom of my stomach. "I don't get paid until the last day of December," I said, and I thought dismally of how much money I had left. "How am I going to get you a present?"

"You don't have to give me anything," Oliver said, whapping me on the back of the head. "My present will be the chance to move in."

"You practically live here anyway," I said sourly, because the whole *Rusty wants to wait for a bed thing* didn't seem to have stopped him from spending the night at all.

"Yes, but if you make it official, I'll be able to bring my furniture over, and your lamp won't have to sit on the floor."

"But if we don't have a bed, that would be a royal pain in the ass." Without looking I caught his hand when he tried to hit me again.

Oliver growled and said something awful about my private parts in Spanish, or at least I assume, because Estrella smacked his hand with a wooden spoon.

"Ouch!"

"That wasn't nice," she said. "If you're going to say things like that, say them in English."

Oliver glared at me, and I narrowed my eyes and glared back. "I said you were so stubborn, you'd let your balls drop off before you fucked your own fist."

I stopped glaring and thought about it. "Yeah, you could be right, but I think it might be in your best interest not to let that happen."

Nicole's laughter pealed across the kitchen, Sal and Joey both groaned and begged us to stop talking, and Estrella glared at us all until someone asked me why I hadn't taken Spanish.

"Because I'm stupid," I said seriously. "I was busy getting my Cs in French."

"That wasn't your fault," Estrella said, coming forward to show me how to clean off the beater before the dough threatened to clog it and stop the motor. "Your mother made you take French. *You* wanted to take Spanish because then you could talk to the gardener."

I blinked. "Wait—wasn't that, like, in fourth grade? I don't remember that."

Estrella rolled her eyes. "*I* do. That is why I was not so surprised when you started kissing this one. You sure did like Nando."

I felt my face heat. I'd forgotten all about the summer when I'd followed that man around like a puppy. "I, uhm, didn't realize… I mean. Uhm. I didn't even think about…."

Estrella wrapped her arm around my shoulders. "Your mother fired him, do you remember that?"

I looked at her, horrified. "No. I—"

"You cried. I remember. But later, when you were choosing classes for middle school, you said Spanish so you could talk to Nando if you met him again, and your mother said French."

"God." I turned off the mixer and started to clean the beaters. "That explains *so* much."

She laughed gently. "You have always been a good boy."

But not that bright. I didn't say it aloud, but I was thinking it. Oliver must have known that or read my mind or something, because he wrapped his arm around my waist and kissed my shoulder. "Nando can't have you," he said seriously. "I'll teach you Spanish. *Te amo, mi amante.* You remember that."

I mouthed the words. "What does that mean?"

"It means you should let me move in."

By the time Estrella and Nicole were ready to leave, we had piles and piles of iced cookies on the counter, and freezer boxes of more that were ready to be iced and decorated and put onto decorative paper plates, which I didn't have yet.

"Oh God," Nicole swore as she was putting on her jacket. "You guys have to eat most of those and give me something else. I'm fat enough already."

I was going to make her stop, but Joey did my work for me. "What in the hell is wrong with you two? Rusty keeps saying he's stupid, you're worried about fat—*Jesus*, Rusty's gonna be fine, and you've got boobs and a butt and I don't see why that's a bad thing."

Estrella spoke sharply to him in Spanish, even though she hadn't met him before that morning, and he looked at her mutinously. "No! No, I'm not going to apologize. She looks just fine. She's cute! Give her four years, I'll be grabbing her ass."

I turned around and was about to deck him, Oliver's cousin or no, but Nicole was smiling at him, a sort of luminous, transported look in her face. "Yeah?" she asked, and she sounded greedy for the answer. "You like my ass?"

And to my shock, Joey, who had seemed unshakable, blushed.

"You need to wait four years," he said with dignity, and then he opened the door.

My mother was standing there, her hand raised to knock.

Oliver and I had hung back in the kitchen so we could usher everyone out, and even though the oven and all the people had kept the place warm, I felt a sort of sleety sweat wash over my body, and only Oliver's hand in my own kept me grounded.

"Uhm, Mom?" I said, and she ignored me.

"Nicole, you haven't answered your texts for an hour."

She looked at me apologetically. "My phone lost charge." Then she turned to my mother. "We were coming home."

"I saw Estrella's car," Mom said, her voice sounding sort of lost. "I remembered today was her day off, and your coat was in the back. I could see Rusty in the kitchen window."

"Good," Nicole said with dignity. "Now you can take me home and Estrella doesn't have to."

Mom didn't move. She just stood at the door and looked around. I saw it through her eyes for a moment and wanted to run and hide. The kitschy decorations, the cheap IKEA futon, the Formica counters, and the new, badly installed tile. I wondered if she could see the inflatable bed from the hallway and hoped the floor would open up and swallow me.

"Rusty, you *live* here?" she asked after a moment, and I had a sudden moment of defensiveness.

"I've got a kitchen full of people who want to be here," I snapped. "Who's in *your* house right now?"

She gaped at me, and Nicole turned and gave me a thumbs-up. I smiled weakly and turned to Estrella. "You're not going to become like Nando, are you?" God. What if I cost Estrella her job?

"No," Estrella said loudly, looking my mother in the eye. "Today is my day off. I can do as I wish."

"Is that my Mixmaster?" Mom asked, her voice cracking, and Estrella looked proudly at her.

"No. That is the one you gave me five years ago. You gave me a new one last year, and this was mine to do with as I pleased."

Mom flinched, and I wondered what was happening between the two women that I didn't understand.

"Oh," she said after a few moments, and I stood there.

Then I remembered that Estrella had taken her day off to teach a bunch of stupid kids how to bake cookies for Christmas. I hugged her, realizing how short she was all over again. "Goodbye, Estrella. Should I make some cookies for you?"

She pulled back and smiled and kissed my cheek. "I would love some, Rusty. Nobody's ever offered before. I've always had to bake them."

I smiled at her, feeling goofy and pleased. I could give her something no one else had. She pulled away then and walked with dignity out of the apartment while my mother shifted aside. Sal and Joey didn't even look at her as they walked by, but I watched as Nicole hugged them both and said she couldn't wait to see them again.

Mom flinched at that and still kept staring at the inside of my apartment. Finally it was just her, standing there in her caramel-colored Nordstrom coat and leather gloves. "You don't even have a bed!" she snapped, her voice accusing, and I glared at her, suddenly angry.

"Shut the door. You're letting out the heat."

Oliver took that as his cue and ran forward, slamming the door in her face. We stood there, in our warm kitchen that smelled like cookies, and stared at each other for a second. I dragged my hand through my hair and realized that it was shaking.

I took two deep breaths and turned back to finish securing the cookies in a big freezer container Estrella had brought in her magic shopping bag, and Oliver waited until it was all done and the container was sealed.

"Rusty?"

"Yeah?" I said. I kept my attention on the counter in front of me, making sure it was as absolutely clean as it could possibly be.

"I don't even know what you're thinking right now."

I took a deep breath and let it out shaking. "I'm thinking I hope Estrella and Nicole don't get into trouble."

"Yeah? 'Cause you sound like you hurt more than that."

I closed my eyes hard and pretended they weren't burning, because he was right. "I'm sort of wishing that wasn't happening."

He was suddenly mashed up against my back and his hands were looped around my waist. "I'm here to make it better, Rusty. We don't need a bed to do that."

I wiped my hands off on a towel and turned in his arms then, holding him so tight my arms shook. "You make it better," I whispered, because it was true.

"You're making a home for me," he whispered back, and then, coupled with what Estrella had said about making her something that she'd always made for someone else, I got an idea about what to do for Oliver for Christmas.

THAT NIGHT we ate a small meal of spaghetti, because it was easy, and went to bed early. We started out kissing, slow and hard, and then faster and harder, and then like we'd drown if we didn't taste each other deep on the back of our tongues. His hands shoved at our underwear and our shirts and I shoved at them too, and when we were naked, he wrapped his legs around my waist and ground up, our groins matching and meshing, and both of us hard and scrabbling for friction.

He kept one arm wrapped around my shoulders then and fumbled with the other hand under the pillows, coming back up with the lube. I don't know how he did it one-handed but he did. He dumped lubricant all over his fingers and snicked the lid shut, then moved his fingers back behind him, and I felt a cold, bright excitement as I realized what he was doing.

"Are you stretching yourself out?" I asked, pressing my lips against the side of his neck.

"Yesssss...."

I shivered and bucked against him. His cock started to drool against my stomach, and I kneaded his backside with one hand while I steadied him with my other palm.

"Are you ready?" I put both hands on his bottom, feeling his hand moving between his cheeks. God—it was *erotic*, like nothing else I remembered ever being, and he pulled his hand away and wiped it on the sheets for a second before scooting up on his knees. I leaned back against the pillows and bent my own legs while he positioned himself, up, up... I felt his hand on my cock, placing it at the edge of something tight and rubbery and slick, and he started lowering his body on top of mine in the dark.

He stopped halfway down my crown, hissing and breathing hard. I stopped moving, looking up at his face in the darkness, as he closed his eyes and thought really hard about something. While he was thinking, he slid down, a little at a time, a little bit, a little bit, moaning softly until....

Oh my God!

"Ohhhh.... Oliver!"

He popped past the crown of my cock and let out a sigh of relief, then pulled up a little, and down a little, and up a little and down, going down farther each time, until he was... oh God. He was seated, all the way, with my....

I couldn't even think of what part of me was where. I was shaking too hard with need to even make the thought. "Oliver?" I squeaked, and he bounced up a little, and then down again, and now I moaned. "God, yeah, please. Keep going, baby. Keep going. Oh my God. It feels so good...."

It did. I'd never had such a slick, tight grip on my cock before, not in a hand or a mouth, and Oliver's breathy little gasps made it sexier, because I think it felt good for him too. I reached out and grasped his cock as it flopped between us, grabbing it and stroking it, and shivered when Oliver's moan came deep from the pit of his stomach.

"Rusty, don't stop!"

Both of us then, him bouncing up and down, me stroking him, and he found a rhythm as he clenched and rocked and gripped and stroked me with his body. The air mattress bucked and squeaked and trembled beneath us, but I didn't care, didn't care, because my vision was going black and my skin was washing cold and a surge of pressure shivered up my balls and rushed my groin and....

"God, yes!"

Above me Oliver started shaking, and his voice was broken as a sound from the center of him rumbled out and his cock spurted hot in my fist. Our movements became frenzied and spastic then, and for a moment all I could feel was the hot and the liquid and the hard grip around my erection. Then Oliver fell forward, panting in my ear and nuzzling the side of my neck.

"Was that so bad?" he panted, and I wrapped my arms around his shoulders and rocked him. Our bodies separated, and there was a gush of fluid, but I didn't care. Tomorrow we'd do laundry, but tonight....

"You're amazing," I mumbled, wanting to clutch him to my heart forever.

"It's okay, even without the bed?"

The mattress was only half-inflated, and we'd have to refill it tomorrow, but that's not what I was thinking right now.

"We don't need a bed to be in love," I told him, feeling weepy, and he kissed the corner of my eye where water was sliding out. I'd forget those words in the morning, hate myself for forgetting my objective, but right now I couldn't imagine giving up what we'd just done for something as stupid as a bed.

"No, we don't," he said softly, and then it was just us, cuddling until we ran to the bathroom to clean up and put on our underwear.

THE FLYING FISH

OLIVER SPENT the next night at his father's house. I managed to convince him that I needed the night to plan his gift, and since it was the truth, he bought it. (I'm pretty sure lying to Oliver was not something I could ever do. I had a hard enough time trying to get him to believe me when I was pretty sure I was right.)

I spent the night with some big pieces of paper, a new pencil, an eraser, and some Sharpies. And, of course, with all my hopes for us, my dreams for what we could be, for the things I wanted to do for him.

It was all I had, but he kept telling me that all I had was enough, so I was going to run with that. I was going to fly!

The next morning his father brought him to the apartment so he could take my car again, and he ran a bag of his clothes inside before his dad and I left in the truck.

On his way out, he glared at me. "Don't I even get a key?"

"Can't you even wait until I have a spare made?"

"Yeah, okay. I didn't see no present in there. What were you doing with your time?"

He was standing in front of me before I slid into the passenger seat of his dad's truck, and I cupped his chin and kissed him, our breath hot in the morning frost.

"I was making your present, and I hid it so I could have a chance to wrap it. I swear, Oliver, I think it's something you'll like."

He narrowed his eyes at me. "You say that. For all I know, you're making plans to crawl in bed again."

I kissed him again, this time in apology. "I swear, baby. I'll never scare you like that again."

He glared. "So, now you're calling me 'baby'?"

I smiled and kissed the tip of his cold, cold nose. "Only if you hate it. You can spend the night tonight, I swear."

"Do I get a key?"

"Do you want to make a copy? You'll be done before I will, and this way your dad can drop me off here."

He narrowed his eyes suspiciously. "Yeah, yeah, okay. I'll do that." He squinted at his dad. "You'll drop him off here at six?"

Mr. Campbell rolled his eyes. "Oliver, he's a good boy. I'm going to take care of him. Now go, or you'll be late for class!"

I went to hop in, and then I had a thought. "Hey, Oliver, did I tell you Rex was staying over Friday? We'll have to make some cookies for him too."

Oliver grunted. "Christmas trees and reindeer only. No sexy men. Pervert."

I laughed and got in the truck, and Mr. Campbell looked at me funny. "Did he just call you a pervert?"

I shook my head. "No. He called *Rex* a pervert. Are we really laying in the drywall today? I want to try that. It looked pretty cool."

Mr. Campbell laughed, and I started thinking about what we could get him that wasn't just cookies. As we rounded the corner toward the bare house we were working on, I thought maybe some flower seeds, because his yard wouldn't be the same without them.

It was right then when I realized—hey! I was finally not just thinking about living past Christmas.

I was finally thinking about spring.

BEFORE REX got there, we made a sort of lasagna that Oliver was really proud of. I was proud of the salad in a bag. It was an extravagance, because his check was so small, but I liked vegetables.

I picked Rex up at the bus station, a little awed because he'd *do* that, get on a bus with a thousand pieces of luggage and go to a place he'd never been before. I was going to drive him to the airport the next morning, and I'd been on a plane before. Those trips had been planned with my parents, though. It occurred to me, as I was driving into Sacramento, following the directions Oliver had written down for me the night before, that from now on all my trips would be planned by me and Oliver.

The thought was not as scary as it might have been.

Anyway, once I picked Rex up, he started talking a mile a minute about everything from banging the professor's nephew again (which, by my count, was the only person he'd been with twice), to how many times he'd gone pee in the tiny toilet on the bus, just to see if he could hit the center (and, for the record, I was pretty sure I would have missed the center. I was seriously impressed by his aim).

He didn't stop talking until I got him to our tiny apartment by El Dorado Hills and helped shoulder one of his three suitcases in the door.

"Just set that one down on the couch," he said, putting the two smaller ones in the corner. "That's the one with your gifts in it."

I looked at him uneasily. "Gifts?" We had a big plastic freezer box full of cookies for him, but that was all. As it was, I was fully aware we'd be eating at Oliver's dad's house a lot between now and New Year's Eve.

"Yeah. My moms sent you a fuckton of stuff when I told them to make my ticket from Sac."

"Your moms?" I said blankly and then called, "Hey, Oliver! Come say hi to Rex."

The bedroom door opened and he stumbled out, looking sort of yummy, warm, and sleepy. He'd been studying for *his* finals all week, and I wasn't surprised that he'd fallen asleep after we'd put the lasagna in.

Rex was on him in a second, giving him the same massive, body-cracking hug he'd given me, and Oliver's eyes swam a little as he regarded me over Rex's shoulder. "Hello, Rex," he muttered, and Rex hugged him some more.

He finally put Oliver down and beamed at him for a minute, and Oliver blinked up all mussy and flushed. It occurred to me that maybe being hugged up next to Rex all hard like that had turned Oliver on a little. If it had been anyone but Rex, I would have been jealous as hell, but it *was* Rex, and he was sort of larger-than-life. Larger than *our* lives, anyway, and you could be attracted to him like you'd be to a movie star, but it wasn't personal. Rex was just that hot, and it didn't mean Oliver didn't want me.

"Good to see you guys!" he crowed. "You're looking awesome! I love the place—the Christmas decorations are perfect!" He pulled out his phone and started taking pictures, walking into our bedroom without warning. He came back looking all smiling and touched. "And you guys are using the quilt. I'm so glad. I was afraid you'd hang it on the wall or something. The moms really like it if their stuff gets used."

"Well, we were going to do that," I confessed, "but I didn't have any heat for the first couple days, and it's still not great now."

"Well, good," Rex said, putting the camera in his pocket and then turning around to dig into the suitcase. "The moms made you something special and then sent a bunch of other shit too. Here!"

He threw a quilt at me that wasn't big enough for a bed but was perfectly big enough for a wall. It was a lot brighter than the bed quilt—was, in fact, a rotating rainbow of jewel tones on black squares, each set of colors bleeding into the other. It was a bright/dark rainbow and it had a pocket of material sewn across the top so you could put a pole in it and hang it up.

"Oh my God!" I gaped at it in my hands, thinking it was gorgeous and perfect and almost exactly what I needed to put up on the wall behind the couch.

"Yeah, put it down. I've got some more stuff for you."

He proceeded to pull out quilted place mat sets—*not* Christmassy but black and brown instead—and dish towels and another set of bath towels and bath mats (which we didn't have; we'd been stepping on the wet tile and trying not to slip), and new sheets—black rainbow-colored—and pillowcases, as well as (Oh my God, really? They'd *shipped* this?) a toaster.

I looked at the toaster blankly as Rex set it in my hands. "Wow. That's…." I was *not* going to cry in front of this guy again. I just wasn't. "Your moms did all this? For us? I don't understand."

Rex shrugged and smiled, looking like every other kid in the world who'd been embarrassed by his parents. "Well, you know. I told them you'd gotten kicked out, and… I mean, I guess there's a reason I don't have any grandparents. I think they wanted you to have an easier start than they did. Oh, wait!" He grinned and went back to his magic giant suitcase, which was now empty. "Here!"

What he pulled out of the suitcase sort of took my breath away.

It was a Christmas ornament, a silver and gold heart. Not kitschy and tinselly and everything—this one was *real* gold and silver, wound together, like holly but in the shape of a heart. It was big enough to sit at the top of a tree, but it hung from fishing line instead.

"That's gorgeous," I breathed, and turned it to Oliver, who had his hand over his mouth. "Oliver?"

Oliver looked sort of miserable for a minute, like he couldn't bear to be this grateful to Rex. Then he came to my side and looked at the thing, tracing the little flat spot on the top with his fingertip.

"Rusty & Oliver," he read, and I peered closer because I hadn't seen it. "First Christmas."

"We should put it up," I told him, excited, and he nodded, looking a little shell-shocked. Well, now he knew how *I* felt after his family sort of moved in and adopted me. I went to the kitchen and got a thumbtack and then went to the little window/counter thing where we'd put all the other decorations, snagging a kitchen chair as I went. I stood on the chair and put the thumbtack in the ceiling, then wrapped the fishing line around it, letting the decoration hang there, in the center of our little Christmas decoration corner, and grinned at it.

"Tomorrow I'll get a dowel to put in the quilt," I told him, feeling proud. "Look at the place, Oliver. I mean, it's not perfect, but it's not bad."

Oliver squinted up at me, and he looked like maybe he was trying to figure out how all this optimism fit into the dark place I'd been last week. "It's wonderful," he said, his sarcasm showing. "It's like it's not even quite the same room."

I grimaced and hopped down. "I… I don't know," I said, not sure I had words for this. "It's nice I've got some family to contribute."

Oliver's expression finally softened. "Yeah, yeah. It looks gorgeous. I especially like the toaster."

I grinned some more and actually moved in to hug Rex myself. "Jeez! Thank you! Thank the moms for us. I mean, we've got a big box of cookies for you. You can give some to them, right?"

Rex nodded. "And speaking of cookies, I smell something *really* good. What's for dinner?"

Dinner was good. I'd bought some soda earlier, because we weren't old enough to buy beer. Anyway, we sat and talked and ate. Rex helped me clean up, and Oliver set up an old DVD in the player for my tiny television, and we sat and watched the movie all together on the couch. I sat in the middle and cuddled Oliver, and Rex sort of cuddled both of us, and I was happy. I'd made a family too—and Rex was the big brother and Estrella was the aunt and my sister was, well, my sister. When they talk about a man having his pride, I think this is what they're talking about. I had pride that Oliver's family wasn't the only one picking up the slack.

I DROPPED Rex off at the airport the next day, and the rest of that week was a frickin' blur. We finished cookies for everyone, and we bought some seeds and starters for Oliver's dad, and me and Oliver picked out some T-shirts for my sister that would show her boobs a little and didn't hide her body. We bought some small stuff for Oliver's cousins, figuring the cookies would do most of our gift-giving for us, and then we wrapped everything and put it on that little counter, surrounded by Christmas stuff, and that was our tree. I took Oliver's present, rolled it up, and put it in one of those tubes you use to mail posters and stuff and *then* wrapped it. Of all things, I was not very nervous about this present. I thought he'd approve.

Or he would have, except, well, I kicked him out of the apartment.

When Rex had been there, I'd been fine. I had family, pride, I could live with the place, that was all great. But then the fucking mattress deflated, and three days before Christmas Eve, I realized I could make do all I wanted with everything else, but that for us to be together, we needed a bed.

He was still pretty pissed.

See, we were trying the sex again after Rex left, and the sex was good—I mean… well, *good*. Oliver was on his hands and knees this time, and he had his hand on himself, because he was only shy in front of me when I could see him, and I was… well, lost in the whole pounding inside of him thing. It didn't feel any worse than the first time, and, in fact, it was getting a whole lot better, when I thrust so hard Oliver went flat into the mattress and suddenly there was a *pfffffitt* sound and there we were, both facedown on the floor while my entire body spasmed in orgasm. Oliver was still thrashing around on my cock with his hand on his own body because he hadn't come yet.

I stayed still until he came, trying to support my weight a little, and as soon as I heard him grunt and felt him clench around me, my hands slipped, and I was *really* on top of him, and there was nothing under us but sheets and two thin layers of polyvinyl ex-bed.

We were still breathing hard, and I could hear Oliver's muffled voice. "Rusty, we broke the bed."

"Yeah," I mumbled. "I guess we finally get to sleep on the futon."

We cleaned up and moved, but you know what? I don't see how Rex and the twins did it, because that thing *sucked*. So the next morning I told Oliver he was sleeping in his own bed until I could reinflate the mattress.

The first night I used bicycle tire patches, and it worked until about 3:00 a.m., and then I was back out on the futon again.

The next day after work, two days before Christmas, I tried bicycle tire patches *and* duct tape, which Mr. Campbell let me take from the jobsite, probably to get Oliver out of his hair. I'd had dinner at their place the night before, sort of. I hadn't eaten much because Oliver was glaring at me the whole time, mad at me for deserting him, and it was hard to enjoy the food.

I knew he was mad, but I didn't know what else to tell him. I couldn't rob him of his home and his dad and his dogs if I didn't have something to give him. Even though the apartment would always be shitty, the bed, at least, was a *promise* that things would get better. I just couldn't do it. I couldn't claim I had a home for us if we didn't have a place to sleep.

So there I was, still in my construction clothes, patching my bed with rubber glue and duct tape, when there was a knock on the door and then it just *opened*, and Nicole and my mom walked in. I glared at them through the bedroom and into the living room.

"Seriously, Nic. You're just that comfortable?"

She looked sheepish and apologetic. "Sorry, Rusty. I was going to wait *since it's your freaking apartment*"—she glared at Mom—"but *somebody* thought we had the right to barge right on in."

I squinted at my mother. She was wearing a tasteful twinset in ecru under her camel-hair coat, and her ash-blonde hair was impeccable.

"Hi, Mom," I said, using my teeth to rip the duct tape for what I hoped was the last hole. Apparently when we'd exploded the thing with sex, we'd popped the seam in about six places. The whole apartment reeked of rubber and glue. "I don't have a Christmas present for you, but Nicole's is all wrapped and everything." I smiled at Nicole. "But I was going to give Nicole cookies to give to you and Estrella."

Mom frowned. If I didn't know better I'd say she looked hurt, but that was impossible, wasn't it? I mean, this was the woman who'd kicked me out of the house the day before Thanksgiving, right?

"Rusty, you're moving back home."

I looked from my dying air mattress to my mother again, fumbling through shock to find my feet. It occurred to me, in a blind, unfocused way, that I'd rather sleep on the floor, even with Oliver pissed at me, than go back home and pretend Oliver didn't exist.

The thing tumbling through my chest and out my mouth was anger, and it tore a bloody hole in my throat when I spoke. "Lady, that is not your call."

She jerked back, and I glared at her and placed the last piece of duct tape carefully before getting up.

"Rusty, you don't even have a bed—"

"I'll get one. My next check comes before New Year's. Oliver'll pitch in." If he was still speaking to me. Maybe if I started with "Move all your stuff in, and I'll have some faith," he would be.

"You're coming home for Christmas!" she snapped, except her chin was quivering and her lower lip was quivering, and I realized she was almost in tears.

"I *am* home," I told her. "Oliver and I are spending Christmas Eve together, and then we're going with his family to midnight mass." Because I was pretty sure that was still on. "We're going to his dad's for brunch, and we're giving cookies to frickin' everybody, and little toys to his little cousins and movie tickets to his big ones. And his family *asked* if we wanted to come, and they're *glad* that we're together. If you want to *ask* if we want to come over sometime, *maybe* we can pencil you in."

My mom pulled herself up like she was trying to be strong. "Rusty," she said, but her voice sounded off and broken, "be reasonable. Your father is so upset by this, and your family can give you so much more than these people—"

"These people?" And now *my* voice sounded off and broken. "You don't even know who *these* people are! *These* people gave me a table and chairs and a toaster and a mixer and a quilt. They brought me groceries and invited me to dinner and brought me a big fucking flower for my house! Nicole brought me decorations and Oliver.... Oliver brought me *home*. Jesus, Mom! I don't even know if you *miss* me. You didn't see me for *months* and then you kicked me out of the house. My family gave me *shit*, because as far as I can see, everything you gave me was to get something back. I got the clothes and the car as long as I toed the line. I wasn't *meant* to be this person you were trying to make me. But you know what? The person I am isn't bad."

"The person you are?" she asked bitterly. "The... the menial worker living in a tacky little apartment on an air mattress? What kind of life is this for you?"

Well, at least she cared. Sort of. "It's the kind where I'm loved," I said simply. Oh, *now* I figured that out. I missed Oliver sleeping next to me so damned bad. "Now if you were going to leave Nicole here, go ahead. I'll give her a ride home."

Her breath hitched, and her face blotched, because I think I pretty much told her to get out of my house.

"Nicole is to have nothing more to do—"

"I'll run away and sleep on his couch. Futon. Whatever." We both looked at Nicole in surprise, but she had her arms crossed and her lower lip out. "Seriously. I came over to visit my brother and my friend. They're working college students. If that doesn't make your cut for friend, Mom, I *do* know who all the pot smokers are. I can go be friends with *them!*"

"Don't you dare!" Mom and I both shouted in tandem, and Nicole raised her eyebrows in surprise.

"Now, see," she said, obviously enjoying her position, "from Rusty, I know where that's coming from. You? Mom, you're going to have to prove you're not just trying to look good in front of your book club or whoever the fuck you're trying to impress this week."

"*Nicole!*" Mom clapped her hand over her mouth, and this time I couldn't mistake the look. She was hurt.

"Nicole," I said softly, trying not to puncture the silence that shocked the room, "I think maybe you should say you're sorry."

Nicole's chin quivered, and I realized it looked just like Mom's. "No." She took a deep breath through her nose and let it out over a wobbly bottom lip. "You're the one person I know who loves me. I don't *have* Oliver's family. I just have you. You can't tell me I can't see you anymore. I'll never make it through school. I won't. You were lucky, Rusty. Everyone loved you through high school. I don't even have the dumb jock thing. It kept you safe!"

I thought of the oversized shirts and how happy she was to sit in my shitty apartment and do her homework. I couldn't help it: I held out my arms, and she ran inside, and I comforted her.

"You are always welcome here," I said, and I glared at Mom. "Right?"

Nicole had started to cry in earnest, and Mom's chin was quivering too. "Great," she snapped. "I'm the flaming bitch and you're Mother Teresa. Wonderful. Is it so wrong for me to want what's best for you?"

"No," I said, holding Nicole more and more securely. "As long as you don't confuse what's best for me with what's best for *you*. Now go away. We'll drop her off by ten."

Mom looked at us both and then clenched her jaw. "Fine."

We watched as she whirled around on her low-heeled boot and stomped outside.

Nicole finished crying on me before we moved, and I was sort of glad I hadn't changed out of my work shirt, because it was full of mascara and crap when she was done. Finally she pulled away and looked around.

"Nice quilt. Where's Oliver?"

I thought of the irritated, mutinous look on Oliver's face when I'd taken him to his dad's yesterday morning. I'd had Mr. Campbell drop me off back here at the apartment after work, and I'd just told Oliver that there was no use both of us suffering if I couldn't patch the air mattress.

"He's spending the night at his dad's until we can fix the bed," I told her, feeling disheartened. "He's pissed."

She quirked her mouth. "What are you going to do if you can't fix it?"

I looked behind me, wondering how long I had to wait before the rubber cement settled under the duct tape. "Shoot it, and then go to one of those rent-to-own places that charge your firstborn and get one there."

Nicole shrugged. "You don't have to tell them that two roosters will *never* make an egg."

Now *that* was funny, and I was still laughing when I tried to reinflate the mattress.

AN HOUR later, after a dinner of mac and cheese, I had to call Oliver and beg for forgiveness.

"Let me get this straight," he snapped. "I'm at home, where I'm supposed to be all cozy and shit, and you finally admit you need your own damned car back so we can drop your sister off?"

I *thunk*ed my head against the wall while holding the phone.

"Yeah. Sorry about that, baby. She had Mom bring her over, and there was a big ugly confrontation, and I told her we could give her a ride home. I hope that's—"

"Your *mother* came over? And I'm only hearing about this *now*?" Oh great. He sounded hurt. Christmas Eve was tomorrow, and *damned* if my Christmas gift to everybody I loved wasn't a big fat box of Kleenex.

"Nicole needed the quiet," I said, keeping my voice down, mostly because it was true. "Mom's not easy on her either."

Oliver swore in Spanish, and I was *really* going to have to learn that language so I could know when he was hoping my balls fell off and when he was hoping something bad happened to someone *else*. "I can't believe we made cookies for them."

I shrugged. "Nicole was going to bring them home with her," I said. I couldn't seem to explain to him why that hope wouldn't die. My parents didn't seem to be monsters. Not the warmest people, no—but I kept wondering if they realized what they'd done.

"Yeah, yeah. I know. Your heart is too big. It doesn't leave any room for being pissed off."

Grimace. "Yeah, well, I must have a little pissed-off in me, because I yelled at my mom."

"Really?" He sounded downright chipper about that. "Good. You should yell more. That's okay, then. I'll be over in twenty. Dad gave me money. He wants us to get Starbucks."

"Oh, hey, tell him he doesn't need to—" But Oliver hung up on me before I could tell him I didn't want to take advantage of his father.

So we stopped at Starbucks and got a big eggnog latte and then dropped Nicole off at home. This time we drove all the way to the front of the driveway, so she just had to run up to the porch. She stopped and waved when she got inside, and Oliver and I waved back.

"So, uhm," I said into the quiet left when she disappeared into the house. "Do you want to come back to my place?"

Oliver grunted and blew on his coffee. "Did you miss me?"

"Derp!"

"You don't even watch that show," he said. It was true—I never got *South Park*, but I *did* like the word.

I was driving, so I made sure the car was in Park. I turned to Oliver then and tapped his chin until he turned away from his coffee and into my kiss. He tasted like eggnog latte, all warm and sweet, and I smiled when our lips touched.

"I missed you," I said when I pulled back.

"Me too. I'll stay the night tonight, but tomorrow, we're gonna move all my shit into the apartment. No exile just because the bed dies. I *live* there. You can't get rid of me now."

"But your bed is so small...." I whined and he shrugged.

"It's better than the futon, and it's what we got."

I studied my coffee for a minute. "I wanted to make a better place for you," I confessed, thinking about the hopeful pictures I'd drawn the week before. "I want you to live in a real nice place."

His hand on my leg was warm, and I won't lie, it made my dick wake up and start sniffing for him, since he'd been gone and all.

"I'll live anywhere with you," he said, and there, in front of my parents' big two-story, with the manicured lawn, in front of everything I'd turned my back on, I had to kiss him again.

SO, WEIRDLY enough, we were moving his furniture into the apartment when the delivery van arrived.

I didn't work Christmas Eve, so early that morning Oliver and I took his dad's big truck and moved his dressers and his computer table and his books. We were going to go back for his bed, but while we were setting the other stuff up in the bedroom, his cousins showed up to help. And while they were poking around the gifts on the counter instead of helping, the movers arrived.

"Russell Baker?" The guy in the front looked bored, and I stared at the pen and the clipboard he shoved at me with stupid eyes.

"That's me. What's this?"

"How should I know... wait. Floyd! What are we bringing out?"

"A bed. What do the instructions say?"

"Oh—wait. Here."

The guy pulled a card out of his pocket, plain and white. Oliver had moved from the bedroom to peer over my shoulder as I read it, and I felt a sudden, warm loosening of my chest.

"What's it say?"

I swallowed. "It says, 'Merry Christmas, Rusty and Oliver. If you have time, we would like to see you on Christmas Day. Dinner is at 3:00 p.m., but anytime would be fine. P.S. Thank you for the cookies.'"

Oliver looked at me and then looked up at what the guys were schlepping in. The mattress and the box spring came first. The frame came next. It was nice—good quality, oak furniture, stained gold and solid as a rock. A queen-sized pedestal bed, the kind with the drawers in the bottom for extra space.

Oliver wrapped his arms around my waist and leaned his chin on my shoulder.

"Merry Christmas," he said quietly. "Should we go?"

I looked at him, those earnest brown eyes so intent on my face. I think I fell in love with him the minute I saw him. I wanted him, wanted him in my life from that first second, watching him sit in AP English and not take any shit. He was my family. He was my home. But you could never have too much family and never have too much home. It was good to live in a world where we were loved.

"Yeah," I said, kissing his forehead. "But for dessert. Your family gets us for dinner."

When he smiled so big his dimples flashed, the little grooves in his cheek framed his mouth like parentheses. I could watch him smile like that forever.

Maybe life would let me do that.

That night, when the bed was set up and made, Oliver lit candles for the kitchen table, and we ate homemade pizza and sparkling cider and exchanged gifts.

Oliver got me (with help from his family) a toolbox, with a beginner's set of construction tools in it—a hammer, a square, a level, a tape measure, and a screwdriver. It was big and sturdy, and I loved it. It sort of said I was a man who could make my own life, and that was a big thing to believe.

He'd also taken all my baby pictures and put them in a separate album. This one he'd written with captions of his own: *90th percentile height—he grew too tall, his short boyfriend has to look up…. Lost a tooth—it grew back, his smile is beautiful…. Played football in high school…. Will play softball with his boss's company in spring.*

I looked at the album and clutched it to my chest. It was a good childhood. It must have been. He was sitting in our apartment and we were grown-ups together. It worked that way.

And then Oliver opened my gift and clapped his hand over his mouth.

I'd made him plans. A house. I'd left room for him to change things—how high the ceiling would be, how big the yard, how many dogs, if we wanted cats. I'd drawn in flowers, because I wanted them, and a fence and wall colors, and a big kitchen, the kind with a block in the center. And a living room with a corner big enough for a Christmas tree. And a study with shelves for his books.

Everything I could think of that went into Oliver's home, *that's* what I drew in, and I'd used big and elaborate letters to label the bottom.

Rusty and Oliver's Home.

Because I didn't want to be alone in there, right? And he had to want me there too.

He cried a little, and I didn't give him crap about it. I think he wanted me there. I think it was okay.

Diary of a Flying Fish

Our first Christmas was good. I mean, not our best—the bed took some getting used to, and dessert with my parents? Oh my God! Were they stiff! In the middle of crème brûlée, Nicole said, "Hey, Mom! Boo!" and my mom barely blinked.

But they got used to us.

I don't know why they made the switch—sent the bed, made the peace offering. I think that, in the end, controlling me wasn't as important as knowing me. Now when I go over, Dad keeps trying to get me to invest in stock options for my business. I don't think it's that kind of business, and I keep telling him that. He gets a kind of baffled stare, but he did help me get benefits, and that's important. I think Mom likes us over because it means Nicole keeps talking to her. Maybe I had been the child who was all planned for, and Nicole was the child who was just supposed to be loved. I put a big crimp in those weird expectations parents have for their children. Maybe they were a little like me—turning your life around to let in the unexpected isn't easy. What matters, I think, is that they try. It's uncomfortable, but you know? We got a bed out of it, right?

I mean, my parents are never going to be like Oliver's family. In five years the Campbells have all but adopted me. Birthdays, holidays—there's the whole family for dinner.

We've watched Sal get his heart broken again and again, and Joey break hearts the same way.

And then we watched Nicole graduate from high school, still round in all the right places, and we watched Joey's heart break when she went away to college.

She texts him every day. I think they'll be all right.

Mr. Campbell turned Oliver's old room into a drafting room, and we went to classes together on drafting and architecture and design, so he could design houses he loved and get them approved to be built. It was while we were doing this—and I quickly realized that design was *not* my strong point—that I decided to start my own business. I was doing really good as Mr. Campbell's employee, but I had such an interest in how to do *everything*—plumbing, electrical, basic construction—all that stuff. Basically, once I knew a little about *everything*, I knew enough to *fix* things. I started out doing favors for Oliver's family. I helped Manny fix his roof and his ex-wife pull out some dead plants. And then they told their friends, and their friends hired me on a per-job basis for side work. And then that grew, and I couldn't work two jobs and go to school, so I went into business for myself. And then Joey, who hadn't been that excited about school even when he *could* get the classes he signed up for, became my first employee.

So there you go. Rusty Baker, handyman. That's me. Oliver is still attending school and studying library science, and he'll be great at it in a couple of years. But I support us both in the fixer-upper Gloria promised me. I've been fixing it up for two years—it's almost not an eyesore, and it's not nearly close to the dream house I promised Oliver on our first Christmas. But this fall I got around to planting bulbs. Maybe by spring we'll have the flowers I always wanted. And that's okay. We live there together, and we're happy, and maybe when you get older, your idea of what's perfect changes.

For example, during our first year together, I would've thought *this* place was perfect.

I was currently doing some plumbing work for Mrs. Jenny Halliday. Yup. It's true. Ms. Dick-Before-Dinner married the guy who hated my guts for liking Oliver best. They lived in a swank house that I happen to know his father paid for, because the market has been shit and Brian's about as bright as I am, which meant he wasn't the world's greatest stockbroker. But anyway, Jenny had hired me on recommendation, and it wasn't until I walked into the two-story house with the giant living room and the vaulted ceiling that either of us realized we'd once gotten *really* personal with each other.

But that was fine. She was actually a really nice girl, and since I didn't usually have to see Brian because he was at work, I came in and fixed her house, because whoever had built this swank place in the hills hadn't had half the work ethic Oliver's dad had driven into my own thick skull.

But it did make Jenny a real regular customer, and she was always very kind. She greeted me at the door and asked me about Oliver, and today, because it was Christmas Eve, she gave me a mug of hot chocolate.

"You're going to have to deal with Brian today," she apologized, grimacing. "He's sort of taken apart the whole thing and put it back together. He's furious that he can't figure out how to snake out the u-joint."

I laughed. Brian pretty much ignored the fact that we used to know each other in high school and treated me like the hired help, which I was. I didn't point out that I made more money than he did, and he *constantly* pointed out that I spent some of my days elbow-deep in shit.

On this day, all it took was a specialized tool, and with a little bit of jimmying, I'd earned my triple-time fee by producing a couple of sparkly things in a clot of hair.

"There you go, Brian," I said cheerfully, spreading the earrings out on my hand. I set them on the counter and went back to reinstalling the u-joint with a good bit of air in the trap so the hair wouldn't clot so badly. "I'm sure Jenny will be happy to get those back."

"Those aren't Jenny's," Brian said, and his voice rang hollow in the little wood-paneled bathroom. I scooted out from under the sink because he sounded so strange and saw the horrified look on Jenny's face. For a second I thought I'd caught Brian out being a douchebag, and then he looked at his wife in honest hurt.

"I thought you said that ended in college."

Jenny looked at me unhappily. "She… she came to visit. You were off on that golf thing with your dad. I'm sorry…. Brian, it… it just happened."

Oh.

Oh dang.

I cleaned up in record time, talking all the way.

"Well, okay, Jenny, I'll send you the bill. I gotta get going. This was sort of a special thing, right? And Rex is coming by with his boyfriend, and I gotta pick them up at the airport and…."

God himself couldn't have shut me up, and I think I was still babbling when Jenny showed me to the door.

A part of me, though—a part of me remembered that horrible semester at Stanford and how badly I'd needed a friend.

I turned to her right before I passed the threshold. "Jenny?" I said, and the face she turned to me was red and puffy and wet. "Jenny—look. If you ever need to call me, or Oliver, you know, just to talk? If you need a friend? You go ahead, okay? Oliver and me, we like company."

I was covered in drain yuck, and I smelled bad, but that pretty girl in her ivory twinset and slacks threw her arms around my neck and kissed my cheek.

"Thanks, Rusty. I might take you up on that."

And then I was in my used half-ton, the one with my logo and my number on the magnetic thing on the side, and I was heading home to shower. We really *did* have to pick up Rex and his boyfriend later that evening.

Oliver was waiting for me. He'd cleaned the house and walked Peanut, the Pomeranian who loved me best. As soon as we'd started renting the house, Oliver had asked his dad if we could keep that one. Mr. Campbell had brought him over with his very own dog bowl and food and everything, and at first I'd been worried. Peanut was used to having all his other dog buddies around. I didn't want him to get depressed. But one weekend I visited PetSmart to get him a new halter, so we could walk him around the neighborhood, and I came home with a gray-and-white kitten too. Peanut and Crackers got along really well. When we weren't in the house, they slept on each other. When we *were* in the house, they slept on us.

Oliver had cut his hair somewhere around his sophomore year in college. It was almost the bowl-cut he'd had in high school, but somehow the lady at Supercuts convinced him it was stylish and he kept it that way. I missed the sort of long, black waves by his face, but I didn't mind it short. It reminded me of the quirky, opinionated geek I'd fallen in love with.

"How was Dick-Before-Dinner?" he asked as I walked into the house. He'd gotten ready for company—vacuumed, swept, done dishes, sprayed air freshener so you couldn't smell the dog and the cat—generally made the place spiffy—and started dinner, which meant he liked Rex even more when he had a steady lay.

It was a small house, but still way bigger than our first apartment. We had a guest bedroom and a couch (we'd given the futon to Sal when he moved out with his girlfriend), and we'd even bought a television bigger than a schoolbook. We still slept in the bed my parents bought us, even though there was enough room for a king-sized in the bedroom. There was actually room for the Christmas tree in the corner of the living room. We had lights now, and we'd bought more ornaments in the years between, but we still hung that first one, the heart, above the tree like a star, and the ornaments Nicole had brought over were still on the tree with the new stuff. Estrella's cookie jar was still on the refrigerator this time of year, and last week we'd taken a day and gotten together with her and made cookies.

I looked at Oliver now, wearing a plain white chef's apron over clean jeans and a button-up shirt as he put the casserole in before dinner, and smiled. Yeah, he spiffed the place up for Rex, and he trusted me to go over to Jenny's house and play big dumb handyman, but Oliver was still jealous and snarky toward anyone who'd ever wanted to see me naked. I made very, very certain to never give him anything to be jealous about.

"Dick-Before-Dinner is now diving for clams," I said and watched his black eyes dart as he put that together. When they widened, grew enormous and limpid like an anime character's, I knew I'd made a good joke.

"No!" he said after he'd shut the oven door. He held his hand up to his mouth. "Really? Does Fuck-Face know?" Oliver was not a very forgiving person. Rex was lucky he was sort of Superman.

"Does now," I told him. "But she's sort of…." I bit my lower lip, thinking about the word. "Lost. Confused. You know. I told her that we'd be good to talk to. So. You know. If she calls. You can*not* be all jealous or anything."

Oliver stepped across the kitchen, and I shooed him out of my arms.

"You're all clean, and I'm all covered in crap! Let me shower and change, then you can—" But he wrapped his arms around my waist anyway.

"We have a washer and dryer now," he said against my chest. "I'll shower with you and change again. Rex's plane doesn't get in for two hours. I need to hug you now."

I hugged him back because I sort of liked that plan. "Why the need now?"

"You've got an amazing heart, baby," he said, snuggling. "I'm so very glad you share it with me."

I got all stupid teary-eyed. "I'm just lucky I'm Oliver-sexual," I said, and he smiled up at me, that thing in his eyes, the thing that said I was all that and perfect, even though we both knew I wasn't.

"You and me both. Now kiss me so we can have sex in the shower."

Yup.

The two of us had gotten really good at planning in the last five years—that one sounded like a winner.

AMY LANE is a mother of two grown kids, two half-grown kids, two small dogs, and half-a-clowder of cats. A compulsive knitter who writes because she can't silence the voices in her head, she adores fur-babies, knitting socks, and hawt menz, and she dislikes moths, cat boxes, and knuckleheaded macspazzmatrons. She is rarely found cooking, cleaning, or doing domestic chores, but she has been known to knit up an emergency hat/blanket/pair of socks for any occasion whatsoever or sometimes for no reason at all. Her award-winning writing has three flavors: twisty-purple alternative universe, angsty-orange contemporary, and sunshine-yellow happy. By necessity, she has learned to type like the wind. She's been married for twenty-five-plus years to her beloved Mate and still believes in Twu Wuv, with a capital Twu and a capital Wuv, and she doesn't see any reason at all for that to change.

Website: www.greenshill.com
Blog: www.writerslane.blogspot.com
Email: amylane@greenshill.com
Facebook: www.facebook.com/amy.lane.167
Twitter: @amymaclane

Choose your Lane to love!

Yellow

Amy Lane Lite
Light Contemporary Romance

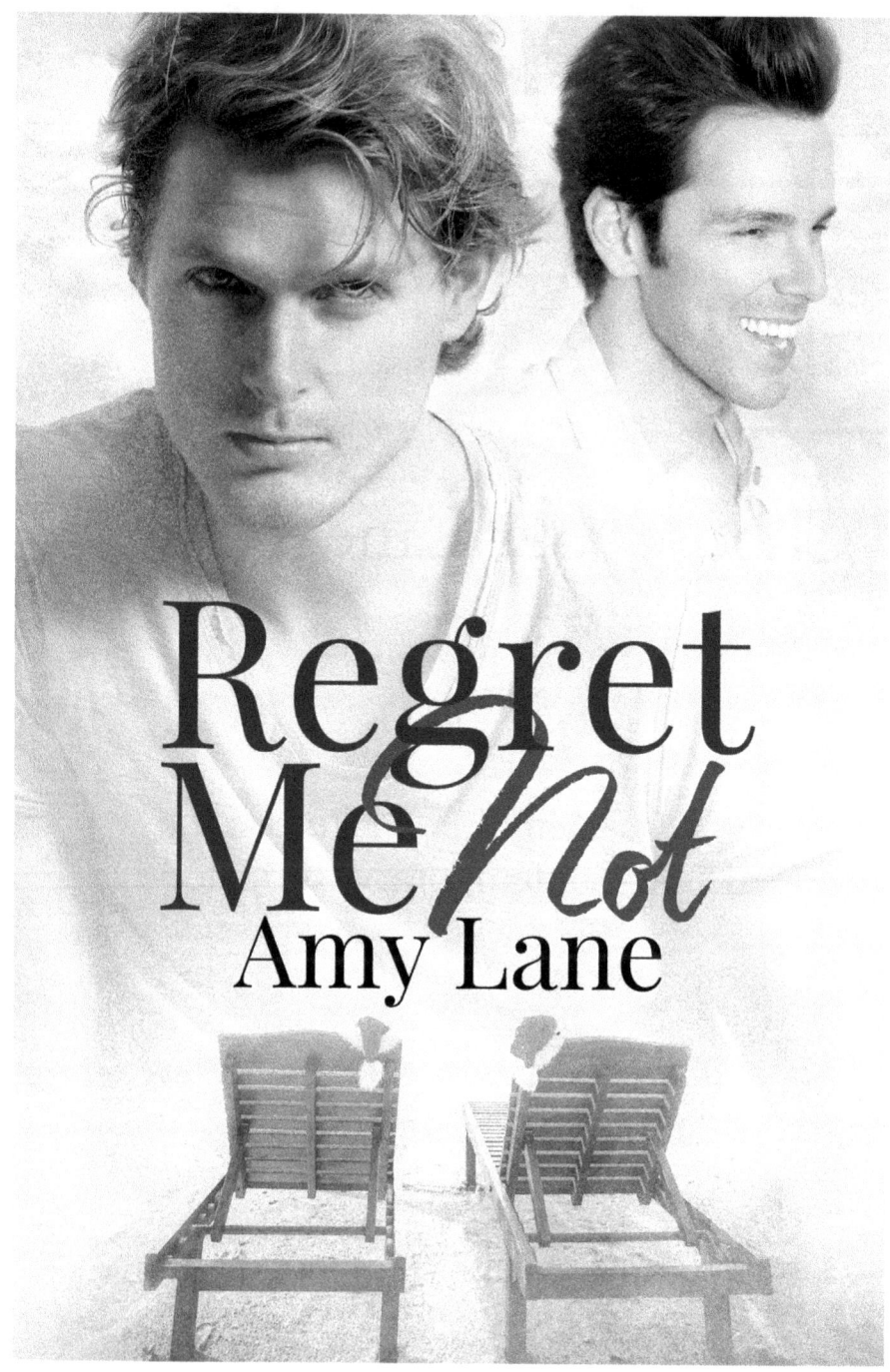

Regret Me Not

Amy Lane

Pierce Atwater used to think he was a knight in shining armor, but then his life fell to crap. Now he has no job, no wife, no life—and is so full of self-pity he can't even be decent to the one family member he's still speaking to. He heads for Florida, where he's got a month to pull his head out of his ass before he ruins his little sister's Christmas.

Harold Justice Lombard the Fifth is at his own crossroads—he can keep being Hal, massage therapist in training, flamboyant and irrepressible to the bones, or he can let his parents rule his life. Hal takes one look at Pierce and decides they're fellow unicorns out to make the world a better place. Pierce can't reject Hal's overtures of friendship, in spite of his misgivings about being too old and too pissed off to make a good friend.

As they experience everything from existential Looney Tunes to eternal trips to Target, Pierce becomes more dependent on Hal's optimism to get him through the day. When Hal starts getting him through the nights too, Pierce must look inside for the knight he used to be—before Christmas becomes a doomsday deadline of heartbreak instead of a celebration of love.

www.dreamspinnerpress.com

THE VIRGIN MANNY

Amy Lane

The Mannies

Growing up and
falling in love...

The Mannies

Growing up and falling in love…

Sometimes family is a blessing and a curse. When Tino Robbins is roped into helping his sister deliver premade dinners when he should be studying for finals, he's pretty sure it's the latter! But one delivery might change everything.

Channing Lowell's charmed life changes when his sister dies and leaves him her seven-year-old son. He's committed to doing what's best for Sammy… but he's going to need a lot of help. When Tino lands on his porch, Channing is determined to recruit him to Team Sammy.

Tino plans to make his education count—even if that means avoiding a relationship—but as he falls harder and harder for his boss, he starts to wonder: Does he have to leave his newly forged family behind in order to live his promising tomorrow?

www.dreamspinnerpress.com

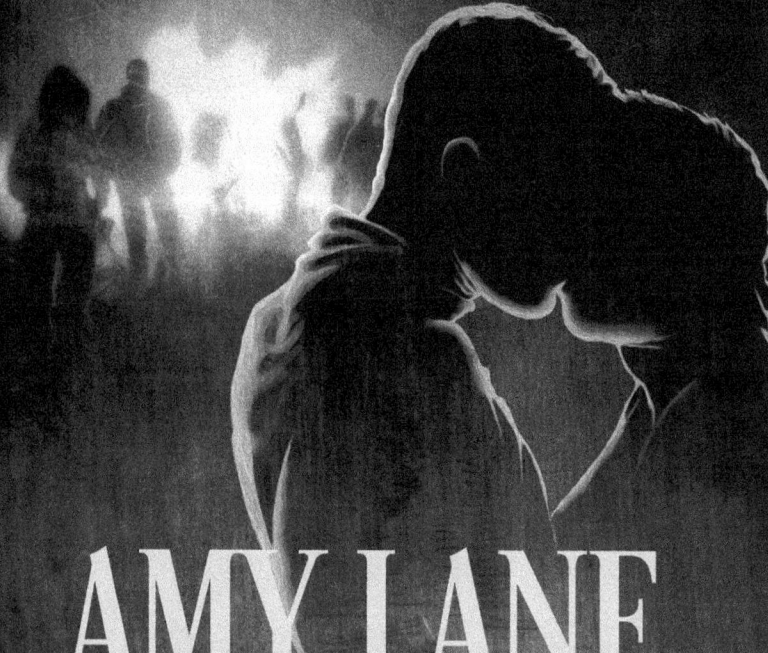

BONFIRES

AMY LANE

Bonfires: Book One

Ten years ago Sheriff's Deputy Aaron George lost his wife and moved to Colton, hoping growing up in a small town would be better for his children. He's gotten to know his community, including Mr. Larkin, the bouncy, funny science teacher. But when Larx is dragged unwillingly into administration, he stops coaching the track team and starts running alone. Aaron—who thought life began and ended with his kids—is distracted by a glistening chest and a principal running on a dangerous road.

Larx has been living for his kids too—and for his students at Colton High. He's not ready to be charmed by Aaron, but when they start running together, he comes to appreciate the deputy's steadiness, humor, and complete understanding of Larx's priorities. Children first, job second, his own interests a sad last.

It only takes one kiss for two men approaching fifty to start acting like teenagers in love, even amid all the responsibilities they shoulder. Then an act of violence puts their burgeoning relationship on hold. The adult responsibilities they've embraced are now instrumental in keeping their town from exploding. When things come to a head, they realize their newly forged family might be what keeps the world from spinning out of control.

www.dreamspinnerpress.com

CROCUS

AMY LANE

Bonfires: Book Two

Saying "I love you" doesn't guarantee peace or a happy ending.

High school principal "Larx" Larkin was pretty sure he'd hit the jackpot when Deputy Sheriff Aaron George moved in with him, merging their two families as seamlessly as the chaos around them could possibly allow.

But when Larx's pregnant daughter comes home unexpectedly and two of Larx's students are put in danger, their tentative beginning comes crashing down around their ears.

Larx thought he was okay with the dangers of Aaron's job, and Aaron thought he was okay with Larx's daughter—who is *not* okay—but when their worst fears are almost realized, it puts their hearts and their lives to the test. Larx and Aaron have never wanted anything as badly as they want a life together. Will they be able to make it work when the world is working hard to keep them apart?

www.dreamspinnerpress.com